STORIES FROM THE FALL OF THE EMPIRE

Harvey Havel

PublishAmerica
Baltimore

PublishAmerica has allowed this work to remain exactly as the author intended, verbatim, without editorial input.

Hardcover 978-1-4560-3751-2
Softcover 978-1-4560-3752-9
PUBLISHED BY PUBLISHAMERICA, LLLP
www.publishamerica.com
Baltimore

Printed in the United States of America

For Yahya and Sakina Bengali, with love.

TABLE OF CONTENTS

A BOY'S BALL OF YARN

The expanse of their front lawn beyond the window panes of the living room rolled to the edge of the road like a slick emerald slide, as their home was perched upon a slight hill that fed into a quiet, mostly dormant street. Geo gazed longingly at the line of trees across from his house, its foliage lush and dense as though it hid something deeper beyond its wall. But the road was mostly empty, and he often wondered when a car or some other sign of life would stir his interest or lead him to some great adventure. It was more often the case that nothing pushed time forward except a few choice Woody Woodpecker cartoons or Looney Tunes reruns that he had nearly memorized by heart, save for the line of credits at the beginnings of them.

Geo sat in the living room of his family's drafty colonial home that stood along a quiet street. He had had enough sitting in his high-chair and being fed the usual oatmeal porridge his mother warmed in break-proof bowls and served strictly at mealtimes. She sweetened it with sugar, and the sugary porridge served as a kind of salvation from the sins of boredom and, on occasion, paling around with friends from Local School No. 43 about a half mile away. After learning how to tie his shoelaces and coloring on blank sheets of construction paper in kindergarten, he knew his life had much more in store, now that he was entering first grade at the local school. His old friends made the move with him into first grade, and the few math and word problems his teacher had given him were right on target with his abilities. But when he came home after an abbreviated play-group on most afternoons, he would only watch a few cartoons, ask his mother for some cookies and milk, and then get on his mother's nerves. He constantly asked his mother if he could go out and play with the other boys, but as was often the case, she ordered him to do his homework before any horsing around with his friends could be done.

On that particular afternoon, however, as he sat on the floor restless before his father came home, he sensed that his mother in the adjacent room deserved to be bothered again. When he fell into moods such as this—of wanting to bother his mother for no good reason at all other than to be paid attention to—he would tiptoe into the room where she could be found knitting a blue sweater. Once safely inside, he would yell at the top of his lungs. She would then jump out of her seat and chase him through the house, where he would hide in the same closet he had always hidden in. She usually discovered him buried beneath a pile of his father's old clothes, tickling him and then leaving him panting from an extreme laughter that left him exhausted and a little sleepy before dinner.

On the afternoon in question, he prepared to scare his mother again. Carefully he moved quickly along the furry carpet and hid behind the big brown sofa where he saw his mother working on another grand project. His objective was to surprise her as he had never surprised her before, as he thought himself to be at the pinnacle of manhood that was the first grade. So this, he thought, would be the scare that topped all scares, as he was a man that topped all men. It would make his mother jump as she never jumped before, and he wouldn't hide in the same-old musty closet anymore. Why, he'd actually use the stairs and hide in the basement, or perhaps run up to the bedroom and mess up the loveliness of his parents' neatly-made bed—comforter, sheets, and all.

But there would be no surprises that afternoon. When Geo sneaked into the room and winced at how the floorboards creaked and snapped much too loudly for him to get away with his most elaborate secret plan, his mother simply turned around and stared at him face-to-face as though she were ready and waiting for him all along. This had happened only a few times before, and it spoiled whatever fun he expected out of the encounter. She didn't seem to be too interested in chasing him around the house that afternoon either. A pile of blue yarn, all balled-up like round scoops of blueberry ice-cream, sat on the thick oak table beside her. She held knitting needles that came attached to what promised to be the lower-half of her new sweater. She looked a bit tired, and her watery blue eyes gazed beyond him into some vague memory that Geo didn't have access to. She wasn't crying exactly, but she seemed preoccupied by an idea that didn't necessarily involve him, and this was a cause of concern to him who assumed that his mother paid all of her thoughts and attentions to him and no one else.

She did smile at him, however, as though there were some glint of wisdom he had yet to learn from her. He had had enough of learning at the school, and now his own mother had something to teach him? The audacity of it all! 'Forget it,' he thought. He headed back towards the living room with a definite plan to surprise her tomorrow, but before he could leave, his mother grabbed hold of his pudgy arm and selected one of the attractive balls of blue yarn from the pile next to her. The color of the yarn was more azure than dark blue and had been rolled up into tightly round beautiful ball.

"If you're bored, I want you to play with this until Daddy gets home," she said.

She placed the blue ball of yarn in his hands as though it were a treasured gift she parted with, and the gesture was so mysterious and extraordinary that Geo didn't know how to respond. First of all, he didn't know what to do with the ball of yarn, and secondly, he didn't see it as such a great gift at first.

"Now go and play with it," she said. "You're getting older now, and Mommy doesn't like being scared when she's working anymore."

Stunned by this near-fatal blow, he could do nothing but utter a weak and polite 'thank you' and wander dizzily back to the living room with his new ball of blue yarn that offered very little in terms of the adventurous excitement he craved. He returned to the television and plunked himself back down on the carpet, the blue ball of yarn in his hands.

He thought the idea of playing with the ball of yarn a little foolish. There wasn't much one could do with a ball of yarn except hold it, or use his small fingers to rotate it in his palm, or perhaps throw it at Daffy Duck who kept trying in vain to get Bugs Bunny in trouble. Daffy always lost for some reason, and there was nothing he could do about it, which was another source of frustration. He threw the ball at the television screen several times, but the yarn just rolled back to him. It didn't even bounce very well, and so the boy had a tough time wondering how he would make a plaything out of it. He was, however, fascinated by its color and how each thick strand overlapped the other thick strands so tightly that the ball refused to lose its shape. He rolled it on the carpet and threw it at the television a few more times until he realized that the ball of yarn was useless when it came to providing the entertainment needed to fill time until dinner. His father would be home by then, and perhaps he could throw the ball of yarn at his head while he ate.

When the pink sun set behind the tree-line across the road, however, a rosy hue flooded the living room, and the yarn turned a brilliant color, as the blue of the thread had more luster and depth to it. Geo suddenly stopped rolling it on the carpet and gazed at it for a while. For the first time in his life, he came into contact with what might have been a true work of art. The ball withstood his squeezing, rolling, and throwing it around so well, that there must have been something special about it, some kind of resilience that this ball claimed, and it stunned him how it still managed to retain its shape and beauty through the harrowing tests he put it through. When bathed in the pinkish light of the setting sun, the ball became something to be preserved and not to be toyed with as he did with his collection of Matchbox cars and plastic infantry men. The ball of yarn was different all of a sudden, because it seemed the definition of true beauty. It was perfectly round and uniform, its thread a vast network of lines that hid a hardened core underneath it, as though it contained a mystery or a puzzle that couldn't be solved so easily. His new perspective made a marvel out of the simple ball of yarn, and it wasn't long before he fell in love with it. He promised not to disturb it any longer and decided to preserve it on his shelf or at least tuck it away in his chest of toys for safe-keeping.

But as he held the ball of yarn up to his nose and inspected the tight, intersecting lines of thread, Geo noticed an imperfection that put his initial excitement to rest. While playing with it, one of the threads had frayed from the compact whole and stood a inch high off of what could have been a perfectly-rounded surface. The ball of yarn had suddenly lost most of its beauty right then and there.

He could only blame himself for such an abnormality, and he wanted to tell his mother about this aberration but knew he shouldn't disturb her. At the dinner table, though, he discussed the ball of yarn and the strange dilemma of the loose thread. He secretly wanted to run up stairs and view the ball of yarn again to find out why it had unraveled a little. His parents just looked at each other a little amused by their child's fascination with it. Yet before he went to sleep that night, he knew he had to do something, as he yearned for that initial feeling of beholding a truly beautiful treasure for the very first time, and with that single, confounded thread sticking up from the surface, much like a single strand of hair that stands upright from an otherwise shiny and slickly-combed scalp, the ball of yarn suddenly needed fixing—only he didn't know how to go about fixing it.

It wasn't like he could pat it down or smooth it over or mold it back into shape like a ball of overly-kneaded play-dough. Similarly, if he tugged at the thread, the yarn might unravel just a little bit more, and wouldn't it look tremendously odd that a perfectly round ball would suddenly have a wavy strand dangling from it like a misplaced noodle? How disappointing! He needed to repair it, certainly, but he didn't know how, and he soon concocted a plan to smuggle the ball of yarn into the school the next morning and have his friends take a look at it to see what they could do. He needed to find a way to tame the anarchy it represented, and perhaps his friends had a solution to the mayhem occurring on the ball's blue surface. He needed a second opinion, and he barely made it through a rambunctious night dreaming how perfect it could be. He hoped that the problem of the loose thread could be solved quietly, quickly, and painlessly.

The trick was to smuggle the ball out of the house without his mother catching him. And Geo used all of his gifted faculties available and a few cleverly orchestrated moves to carry out the mission. It amounted to sneaking the ball of yarn into his Batman-themed lunch box as his mother's back was turned.

At breakfast, she allowed him to sit at the table that morning instead of the high-chair, and as her back turned to squeeze oranges, he quietly hid the ball of yarn underneath a Zip-Lock bag of chocolate chip cookies and closed his lunch box just a second before his mother turned around.

"What did you just do there?" she asked while abandoning the oranges and spooning another helping of oatmeal mush into his bowl.

"Nothing, Mom," he said innocently enough.

His mother didn't push the issue any farther, although she looked at him suspiciously for a moment or two. It would be the first of many fibs he would use to elude the interrogations and the suspicions of his mother for years to come. Geo's plan had worked well, and he boarded the yellow school bus and kept quiet about the yarn in his lunch pail until his friends could help him with the problem.

The courtyard of Local School No. 43 had to be managed properly if he were to sneak passed the girls playing patty-cake and showing off the latest accoutrements to their Barbie and Ken collections. It required a speed and a skill that he thought he wasn't capable of, but luckily, at this stage of his first-grade development, the boys disliked the girls, and the girls disliked the boys. The rare bird that traveled between the two camps was often ostracized for it. And like most of his pals, he gave the girls an angry look as he walked passed them. This kept the girls at bay until he finally landed in the company of his three friends who ran in circles around him trying to tag each other out.

"Stop this childishness," commanded Geo. "We have more important matters to contend with."

The boys stopped in their tracks and looked at him as though they had seen a reincarnation of some of the world leaders they read about in their history textbooks. The three boys panted in exhaustion before Geo pulled them to a quiet corner of the courtyard away from the dreaded door to the schoolhouse where their teachers had the most annoying habit of calling them into their classes. They huddled over Geo's lunch box, and he even made them utter a small prayer before opening the lid and revealing the sky-blue ball of yarn that sat within.

The other boys gasped at its beauty as he brought it out for all of them to see.

"My God," said Dickie, the oldest boy of the four, "where did you get it?"

"It's not a good idea to bring something like this here," said Carlo, the shorter resident mystic of the group.

The third friend, an African-American named Colin, smiled knowingly, as though he had predicted that such a treasure would finally manifest itself in the courtyard, but he said nothing and only smiled.

Geo also smiled triumphantly, as he knew then and there that he had owned and possessed a special work of art that none of his friends could ever possess.

"I know what it is," said Dickie, using his wisdom and experience as the eldest boy in the group. "See, what we could do is roll the ball into the circles of those we don't like, especially the girls, and then from out of the ball will emerge these robot, machine-like claws, like the ones on my Tonka truck, and these claws will poke through the ball of yarn, and what will happen next is that these claws will turn into a giant robot and grab all of the women playing pattie-cake and hold them in its grip, so that, finally, we don't have to hear them playing that stupid game anymore."

But then Carlo announced his idea.

"No, no," he said, "this ball can be so much more, because whoever holds it will be able to harness a power that this earth has never known. Because the person who holds it high above his head will hypnotize everyone around it, hypnotize them enough for them to worship it. Out of the ball will come these flashing lights, like an electrical storm, and from out of the center of it these laser beams will fire right into the eyes of everyone who looks at it, and soon the entire school will be hypnotized by the ball, and we can do whatever we tell them to do, even our teachers. And people will come to worship the ball from all around the neighborhood, and if people think they can break its spell—think again. The laser beams will keep on hitting their eyes, hypnotizing them all over again."

Colin was a bit skeptical by their ideas, and offered only this:

"It's a beautiful ball indeed, but we have to be careful with it. We need a plan to get rid of it if it starts to get too unmanageable—especially if it starts to take over. The ball can be many things, and I was thinking that it could be used as a ball in a game of catch—something simple, direct, and short-lived. Because if we let it get the better of us, we'll have one big mess on our hands. I think we should keep it the way it is—it's perfect, blue self, and that we use it wisely."

"C'mon, Colin," Dickie and Carlo seemed to say at the same time.

"This ball has amazing potential," said Dickie, explaining his reaction. "We can't just let it be a simple ball. We can't just let it be what it is. The potential is enormous."

"I'm saying we use it," said Colin, "but we use it wisely and carefully is all I'm saying."

"You're so boring," countered Dickie. "My idea is that we should use it to start rounding up people right away."

"That's stupid," said Carlo. "Why round them up when we can have them do anything we want them to do?"

They continued to argue over the blue ball of yarn while slapping each other's back in excitement at the same time.

"Wait a minute," said Colin. "What's that there?"

"What?" said Geo.

"There," pointed Colin at the hanging thread that seemed to have grown since its lunch box confinement.

"Oh, that? That's nothing," said Geo.

All of a sudden, the smiles on his friend's faces turned thin and ponderous. They stood over the ball in silence, their disappointment palpable.

"Okay," said Geo, "so there's obviously a problem."

"Damn right there's a problem," said Dickie. "Look at that thing. It's disgusting."

"This must mean something," said Carlo. "It must mean something indeed."

"We must fix it all costs," said Colin. "Otherwise, this thing's worthless."

And for a while more, as the rest of the children yelled, screamed, and ran about in the courtyard, his friends openly expressed their confusion and disappointment that such a ball of yarn could be so beautiful and yet so flawed at the same time. In their deliberations, the first friend started ranting and raving at it.

"It's the yarn-maker's fault," cried Dickie. "You have to go to those corporate-types and demand that they fix it. They can't get a away with this. They just can't. I know the owner too—a real blowhard if I ever saw one. They're all part of this secret society, the commies that are taking over. It's all about who owns the wool, y'know—who owns it and how they make us decent children pay for it."

The other two friends chimed in with similar rants against the atrocities of the yarn-makers, until there came a point when all four of the boys openly and unabashedly yelled at the ball of yarn and criticized the corporate sector that sold its imperfect thread.

Just then one of the teachers swung open the door to the interior of the school, and the boys quieted down and feigned happy smiles as she passed. They made sure not to let on about the blue ball of yarn which had catastrophically lost its beauty. And at a free period in the school day the four of them met in private in the boy's bathroom.

During this most secret of meetings, they recognized how their throats had become too hoarse to yell at it anymore, and if they tried to, they'd be caught and punished by their teacher.

"I have another idea," said Carlo, as they huddled over the ball once more, the thread a bit longer than before and a puddle of water wetting it a bit.

"Yelling at the thing won't work," he said, his eyebrows mysteriously raised.

"But what about the yarn-makers?" said Dickie. "They have to pay for all those years of treachery."

"I have a better idea."

Soon thereafter, the four of them sat crossed-legged on the damp tile of the bathroom floor, their bottoms wet with sink water. They sat in a circle and put the ball of yarn in the center of the circle.

"We have to look at it differently," said Carlo.

He told the group to stare at the ball as though it were a fixed point on a wall. The plan required time and silence, and his idea was that the ball would mysteriously roll itself up into perfection once again but only if they contemplated its repair with an intensity that outdid their angry yelling and criticism. So they sat in silence for several minutes, their stares fixed and intense as though nothing could distract or divert their attentions from the yarn. But after several minutes of staring, their nerves on edge for fear of getting caught by their teacher, Colin broke the watery silence with what may have been a more reasonable approach.

"The damn thing just won't repair itself," he said.

"Let's give it more time," insisted Carlo.

"We don't have time," he countered. "It's almost time for lunch, and we haven't even done our alphabets yet. We have to try something else."

"What should we do?" asked Geo pleadingly, his eyes welling up with tears.

"This is no time to cry," said Dickie. "I think you should march down to those scummy yarn-makers downtown and make a stink about it."

"Just wait a minute," said Colin. "I think we should compromise with it. I think we should shoot straight through the middle of it. We obviously can't yell at it, and staring at it only makes unravel more. We have to blend the two extremes and take the middle path to show that we are undivided and unified in our efforts to have the sucker fix itself."

The two friends who had already had their turn grunted skeptically at Colin's new idea, as they both thought that with a little more time and coaxing, their methods would work. But they soon relinquished their powers to the more sensible boy who seemed the most reasonable.

They all joined hands and stood over the blue ball of yarn, and to implement the fusion of the first two methods, they stared at the ball and tried to appease it with soothing and healing words, thereby trying to get the dangling thread to reattach itself to the greater whole. Each boy took a turn appeasing it and praising it, but again time was running out and so was their patience.

"Damn," said Colin. "I was sure this would work. I guess all that's left is to confront the yarn-makers and tell them to repair it."

"I don't think we were at a hightened level of consciousness and awareness to stare at it and hope it would fix itself," said Carlo. "Only the masters can do that."

"Be strong and firm when you take it there," said Dickie. "They can't get away with this. I would go down there with you, but I can't be late for dinner."

"Yeah. I guess I'll have to go to the yarn-makers myself," said Geo resignedly. "I can't believe this is happening to me. It's just one darn thread, but how horrible!"

His three friends consoled him for a little while, and they gave him the confidence to carry on. They left the bathroom as quietly as they sneaked into it and joined the rest of their classmates a bit saddened and depressed that their efforts had come up empty.

Yet this sadness that Geo held deep inside of him slowly transmogrified into anger towards those who had manufactured the yarn. Dickie even passed him secret notes in code and provided him with the intelligence needed to thwart the yarn-makers. Dickie was very straightforward about what he must do, and he wished he were going along with him, but Geo knew better that some tasks ought to be handled alone. By the time their teacher opened the door to the courtyard and let the students race in glee towards the line of yellow school buses parked along the street, Geo's anger had reached its boiling point, mostly due to how Dickie listed all of the atrocities committed by the yarn-makers through the ages, and this, it turned out, motivated Geo to meet with the public.

Geo was neither polite nor delicate about refusing a bus ride home. Straight out of the gate like an Arabian steed, he marched from the school's courtyard to the thick of the larger suburb where squat, concrete office buildings blanched against the small shrubs and fallen trees that served as attempts to beautify what little of the city's natural environment remained. He must have marched for a good twenty minutes or so— his legs quickening, his heart beating out of his chest, and all the while he held the intense anger of someone who had experienced the worst kind of injustice.

Before he left the school, he had removed the yarn from his lunch box and had thrown it in the garbage. He saved the ball, however, as it now bulged out of his pants pocket like an awkward tumor. It caused passersby to gawk and stare at the little boy's deformity as he marched down the avenue. He promised to take no prisoners, and the madness would only end when justice was rightfully served.

Geo entered a glass building that had been tinted to block out the sun. It was cool inside as a blast of conditioned air swept over his red hot face. In front of an office door sat a female receptionist. She was a senior citizen and had the look of a demure librarian. Her hair was curly-gray, and she wore spectacles that had slipped down the bridge of her nose. She smiled sweetly and asked what he wanted while also offering him a Tootsie Roll.

"I don't want any candy," said Geo, trying to contain his anger. "I want to see the manager."

"Why on earth do you want to see the manager? And what do you have there in your pocket?"

"I'd rather explain that to the manager myself."

"Don't you want a Tootsie Roll?"

"No!"

The receptionist sighed at the sight of him, as she must have found him quite adorable. She thought he was sent for a school project or a research paper, and she sympathized with his wanting to get it in on time.

"My God," she said, "it's amazing how hard they make it for handsome little boys these days. I tell you what, dear, you just wait right there, and I'll get the manager for you. You're really a special little boy to be doing your project about our fine selection of yarn—straight off the sheep's back, as we say."

She couldn't see it, but the top of the boy's head might as well have been fuming. He hated being treated like a little boy when so much was at stake.

When the receptionist returned, he was told to enter the office behind her, which he did. But when he went inside, the office was blanketed in shadow. The dark outline of a larger figure sat at a desk with his hands clasped in front of him. Behind the solemn figure, several rectangles of sunlight escaped through closed blinds. The boy could barely see the man, but there was enough light available to notice that he wore a black suit and that his face was as cold and bloodless as a stone. The boys anger drifted off somewhere, and a chilling fear crept up his arms and legs. Apparently, the nice old receptionist was merely a front for the sinister darkness of this inner sanctum.

"Well, well, well," said the manager, his voice deep and commanding. "They send me a small boy to do a man's work."

The boy's fear had elevated to such a degree that he wanted to bolt from the room, but he had heard his teacher say that many great men often faced their fears instead of cowering before them. And with whatever courage he had, he pulled the blue ball of yarn out his pocket and placed it where one of the rectangles of sunlight exposed the hardness of the manager's desk.

"This needs to be fixed," Geo stammered. "And from what I know, you are the one responsible for it. I need this fixed right away."

The manager's face cut into the light, and the boy's heart jumped at the sight of him. His coal black eyes looked directly into his, and his mouth wore a frown so grave, that he might as well have been staring into the Grim Reaper himself.

"Oh, how cute," scowled the manager. "One of our balls of yarn."

The manager inspected it for a moment and said,

"I see nothing wrong with it."

He then threw it back at him. The ball hit Geo's forehead and fell to the floor, but he courageously retrieved it and shoved it into the light once more.

"You see this?" stammered the boy. "This thread is loose, and your yarn is unraveling. It's a defective product, and you are responsible."

"What was that, boy? Come again?"

"You heard me. You need to fix it."

The manager leaned back in his chair, his stone-cold face receding into the darkness of the room.

"I guess we have a problem, then, don't we. Do you know how many times some sorry sucker like yourself comes into this office begging on their hands and knees for us to repair their stupid ball of yarn? It happens over and over again—a flood of little pricks like you every eight years—and do you know what I tell them each and every time? I'll say the same thing to you, and you better listen good.

"You wanna take a piece of this company? You wanna piece of me?" he started yelling, "well, put your money where your mouth is! We hire the fiercest and the most bug-up-your-ass corporate lawyers in the world. We get 'em all from the cream of the crop—Harvard Law, Yale Law, Columbia Law—and we train them from birth to go after little shitheads like you, and when they do get a hold of you, they'll not only shake you down but your entire family as well. They'll take your house, your tricycle, and the shirt off your skinny back. You'll be left with nothing, nothing you hear me! Nada. You'll have to pick up coal off the street just to get by, and guess what? Even Santa Claus won't save you, because there is no Santa Claus, and there never was one. You won't have a pot to piss in after we're through—so go ahead—call your friendly lawyers and slap us with a lawsuit if you want your tiny little balls to take a pounding, because we eat people like you up for breakfast, lunch, and dinner!"

Geo was so shocked that he wet himself on the spot. His grabbed his ball of yarn off the desk and fled the manager's office, running from the receptionist who merely hummed a tune and filed her nails as he fled. He ran out into the hot sunshine, the dangling thread starting to coil. It had grown longer, and the clamminess of his hands only dampened and flattened it even more.

Geo ran for several blocks, weaving in and out of pedestrian legs, hoping to find a space of sidewalk where he could finally stop and breathe. But as his sprint out of the office mellowed into an aimless stroll, his fear slowly subsided, and a new reasoning told him that he shouldn't be afraid of the yarn-makers and their psychological, warfaring tactics. In fact, he should fight back. The manager, in other words, hadn't intimidated him enough to abandon his mission just yet. Certainly the meeting broke his resolve, but damn it, they just couldn't keep a good boy down. There was still a little fight in him and a chance to bring down the yarn-makers. And coincidentally, like a gift from Santa himself even though it was autumn, he saw another corporate building further down the avenue, this one made of brick in the hazy distance. A large, august sign swayed over the front door and advertised a law firm. With his strength recovered and his determination returned, Geo marched quickly towards the law offices while patting down his hair and brushing himself off before going inside. The ball of yarn, suddenly damp, oval, and dirty, continued to unravel in his hands.

The lawyer who met with him sure was a sexy woman alright, and she must have been married or at least engaged, judging by the glittering diamond rock that took up most of the space on her hand. Her lawyerly dress made her seem as though she had been at a desk or in a conference room all of her life, as though her upward climb had been preordained. Her skin was smooth alabaster, and behind her an assortment of degrees from this school and that covered the wall. Photographs taken with important men, mostly politicians and other well-known tycoons that Geo had sometimes seen on television, also hung on the wall below her fancy degrees. The boy knew right away that this woman would serve as a real threat to the yarn-makers, and when he introduced himself and she showed him to his seat, Geo told her all of what the manager had said. But for some reason unbeknownst to him, the lawyer was not phased by the manager's comments in the least.

"That's quite a story," she said matter-of-factly.

"Yes, it is," said Geo, "and I was treated very badly. He yelled at me and said that he would bankrupt my family."

"Okay. So what do you plan to do about it?"

"That's why I'm here. I need your help."

"I think there's something you don't understand about the real world," she said more sternly.

Geo sat there speechless.

"You see, we are a very reputable law firm here, and while I can understand your trouble, we don't usually help those who can't afford our retainer, whether you've been treated badly or not. Our retainer may be a little too 'far out,' shall we say, of your price range. I'm assuming you have a cute little piggy bank under your bed and maybe an allowance to buy gum or candy or whatever it is children buy these days."

"But I've been treated badly," said Geo, on the verge of tears.

"Life's unfair," said the woman. "I suggest you get used to it."

"But look at this ball of yarn," he said, holding it up for her to see. "It was once so beautiful and clean, honestly I tell you."

"Things change. You're just going to have to get used to that fact."

Yet in the pit of his uncertainty and despair, he had to make a decision quickly in order for the mission to continue. He didn't like the idea of lying. His first grade teacher had instructed their class that honesty was usually the best policy and that he should always tell the truth. But being forthright and truthful failed him at this point. The ball of yarn reminded him of how beautiful and fascinating life once was, and he'd do anything to restore it to its tightly rounded shape. He'd even tell a lie, because that was the only way he could save it from ugliness.

"My family has lots of money," said Geo finally.

The woman's coldness towards him mysteriously vanished at this admission.

"Your family?" she asked, her ears perked up like two antennae.

"Yes," said Geo. "My family has lots and lots of money."

"Well, how much money exactly?"

"We can pay you one trillion dollars," he blurted out.

The woman lawyer stood from her desk and circled around it to where the boy stood. She knelt beside him and suddenly took him into her arms. She pressed the boy's head to her bosom and wept without shedding any tears.

"Oh, my poor baby," she said, "my poor, poor little man. What they've done to you is terrible, unforgivable! and I know you've been hurt by society. They've victimized you, these cursed yarn-makers, and I'm here to make things right. You'll no longer have to suffer, because we're putting together the best legal team in the country, and we'll get those son-of-a-bitches to repair the yarn, this I pledge with my whole heart and spirit. They're cruel and mean, and I will make them pay. You've come to mamma, my dear, sweet little man. I'll be your mamma, and together we'll remake the ball of yarn, and soon enough it will be complete and whole and beautiful again. Don't worry, because mamma's finally here, little darling, and she won't give up. It may take some time, but I'm now on the case, so don't you worry..."

Geo couldn't help but sob along with her, his face pressed to her bosom. He cried in relief now that the ball of yarn had a fighting chance. The woman-lawyer gave him a box of chocolates on his way out to cement her commitment to his case. He never felt better and more confident than he did when he left her offices, and he ran home happy and satisfied as the ball of yarn bulged from his pants pocket as though glad to have met with the beautiful lawyerly woman who would make those yarn-makers pay once and for all.

But when he arrived home, his mother and father waiting for him at the dinner table, he remembered how the woman-lawyer told him that his case would take time, and Geo wondered how long it would take. The ball of yarn was still unraveling by the minute, and somehow he needed to try other avenues just in case the lawsuit against the yarn-makers didn't work. He sat at the dinner table within the curious gaze of his parents. When they asked how his day was with all of the suspicion and subtle knowing that parents often have, he said that it was a usual, regular, and uneventful day.

"Yes, but what did you do today," asked his father more sternly.

"Oh, nothing," said Geo. "Just another day at school, that's all."

And they quietly went back to eating their dinner and surrendered to the clinking and clanking of their silverware on crockery, as it was their only conversation for the rest of the evening.

For the few days that followed, however, Geo did not hear from the lawyer, and in the meantime he kept the ball of yarn carefully hidden in his chest of toys upstairs. At least it remained safe there, and no one would touch it. By putting it away he at least delayed the inevitable somewhat, assuming he could fight the temptation to take it out and gaze upon it every now and then. But even at school his three chums who had once assisted in its upkeep continued to bother him about the yarn, as they had further developed their own strategies about how to fix its unruliness. Geo advised them to trust the new lawyer he had hired, but his friends' never-ending concerns were relentless, and they added to his general impatience and hyperactivity.

On some afternoons Geo sat by the phone and simply stared at it, hoping the lawyer would call. But she never did. He had forgotten to take her business card and so relied upon her to call him with any news of the trial. Slowly, though, he lost his patience. It just so happened that he had been inspecting the ball of yarn every few days, and each time he handled it, the threads unraveled just a little bit more. This was not only perplexing but downright disagreeable to him. And due to the disagreeable and uncomfortable state of mind he found himself in, he started to eat chocolate chip cookies, of all things, to slow his anxieties and fill time until the woman-lawyer called.

His eating started slowly. While pacing in his room in anguish over whether or not to look into the health and well-being of the ball, Geo would run downstairs several times a night, open the bottom drawer in the kitchen, and quickly gobble up a few chocolate chip cookies to help him pass the time. He realized that the cookies helped him feel less anxious and impatient, and what's more, the cookies fed him strange and revolutionary ideas on how to return the yarn to its previous shape and beauty without having to wait for the lawyer to call him.

Each time he munched on a cookie he had grand visions on how to restore the yarn, and within a few days, he munched on the cookies round-the-clock. The intense visions he had of the ball's former beauty filled him with the kind of empty-headed bliss and pleasure that slowly interrupted his need to check up on it every day. But strangely enough, Geo lost his sense of judgment and soon began eating the cookies wildly while still checking up on the yarn in his chest of toys. After a week or two of wildly devouring cookies and staring at the ball of yarn, he had gained several pounds and now wobbled to school. His grades slipped, and he found himself failing all of his lessons. He ate so many cookies that he soon became sick to his stomach and had to vomit them up in the bathroom every few days. Nevertheless, the ideas that he had about restoring the ball of yarn really flowed, and one of them involved taking the ball of yarn out into the sunlight and re-capturing its virginal brilliance by having the sunlight heal it. But the question was how to return the ball to the same time zone.

Out of all of the ideas that came to him, returning the ball to same environmental conditions just after his mother first gave it to him seemed like the best of all ideas.

So after school one day, his grades plummeting and his teachers complaining off and on to his parents about his lackluster performance and erratic behaviors, Geo turned up the volume of the television in the hopes of muffling the sounds of his escape. He grabbed a full bag of cookies and the ball of yarn and wobbled his now-pudgy body to the roadside. The sunlight, he figured, had to hit the ball of yarn at the precise angle for the plan to work, and so he raised the ball high into the autumnal air to greet the rapidly-pinkening sun, the bag of cookies torn open in his other hand.

As he wobbled down the road, crumbs and whole chunks of cookie fell all over his shirt. He then raised the ball of yarn high into the air, hoping to capture the correct angle of the waning sun. But suddenly he vomited on the road in nauseous self-delusion. And just as the pink orb of the sun hovered closely above the tree line and grazed the surface of the ball of yarn, he heard the loud blip of a police cruiser coming towards him. Suddenly he was trapped in the high-beam of an officer's flashlight. The officers had responded to complaints that a young boy was roaming around the neighborhood in a most disruptive and disorderly fashion.

The officer's flashlight ruined whatever perfect light the sun gave, and as the bag of cookies tumbled to the ground and two brawny police officers made their way towards him, he knew that he was in trouble and quickly thrust the ball of yarn into the pants' pocket, lest the officers discover it. Unfortunately, the bulge at his side became the first thing they noticed.

"Hands up," barked one of the officers sliding towards him. And then he said, "empty your pockets slowly and put whatever you have in there on the ground."

Geo complied, and soon the police officers confiscated the ball of yarn at his feet. They gave him a few field tests as well, such as walking in a straight line, which he couldn't do, because he wobbled with excess weight, and they also made him recite the alphabet, which he couldn't do yet, because he failed all of the tests in school. He flunked these field tests on the spot. They then handcuffed him and shoved him into the squad car behind a metal cage that divided him from the front. Before he knew it, Geo was in a small jail cell downtown, the officers sitting across from him at dented aluminum desks doing paperwork.

Depressed and saddened, Geo kept asking for his ball of yarn, but the officer who kept it on his desk refused his request. Geo, however, grew so naggingly insistent, that the officer told him to quiet down, or else he would throw the ball of yarn in the trash. Still Geo insisted that they give it back. It was then that the two officers took matters into their own hands.

"You mean this ball of yarn?" asked one of the officers, holding it up.

"Give it back," demanded Geo.

"Oh, you mean this ball of yarn?"

"Give it back to me!"

The first officer said, "catch," and threw it to the second officer.

"Don't do that!" he yelled from his cell.

The officers, however, pleasured by this impromptu game of catch, played amongst themselves, and while doing so, the ball of yarn unraveled even more, the blue yarn spinning and coiling out of control and in midair as they thew it between themselves laughing the entire time, its shape warping and flattening until he could hardly recognize it. He could do nothing but watch as the tragedy of the scene unfolded.

The officers played with it until they were satisfied that he would keep quiet. Geo grew so frustrated and angry by their cavalier actions, that his small body and mind simply shut down in exhaustion and worry. He fainted on the bench of the jail cell and was knocked out for what must have been several hours.

The jangling of keys at the cell door startled him awake. Beyond the cage, his tall father stood before him too angry to speak. He paid the bail money, and the officers handed the ball of yarn over to him. But the car ride home was certainly not one of the most pleasant occasions he had spent with his father.

"What the hell has gotten into you?" demanded his father, once they were in the car. "A cookie monster, for Chrissakes?! Is that what you've turned into? Is that what we're raising you for—to be a cookie addict? You think you're so mighty and grown up to be devouring a whole bag of cookies, is that it? What shame you have brought upon this family. I mean, what am I supposed to tell all of our friends? That you have a cookie problem, and you're only in the first grade?

"Well, let me tell you something, mister, you are not to eat another cookie ever again, you hear? From this moment on we're leaving no more cookies in the house for you to sink your teeth into. I mean, the lunacy of it! And by the way, you're grounded for three full years. The only place you're allowed to go is to school and back, and you're lucky that the school has an after-school cookie rehab program, or I would have left your addicted ass in jail..."

Without comment or complaint, Geo went up to his room after they returned home. Luckily his father didn't spank him or anything, and at least he would be allowed outside for school, but other than that he was out of luck. He dropped the ball of yarn into his chest of toys and avoided it for a few days. And although he was still obsessed with making the ball round again, he knew his schemes had been getting him into the worst kinds of trouble. After all, he figured, he was only a boy, and why should a boy be given such a difficult and adult problem to solve? It just didn't seem very fair that the fates had somehow chosen him to repair the ball of yarn.

In the school courtyard the next day, his friends smiled sadly to him, as they had heard about his arrest and how his father had grounded him for three years. Geo was also depressed, now that he no longer worked on the ball. He hated cookie rehab, but he went every day as the town court had ordered. It wasn't until he came home after one of his many cookie-rehab meetings that something strange took a hold of him.

Geo wasn't allowed to watch cartoons anymore, and he wasn't allowed to go outside either. Quite naturally, under the restrictions of house arrest, his conscious state of mind returned him to the time when he first devoured those cookies. The crazy and half-witted ideas on how to restore the yarn returned to him as well, and once again he was pacing his room frantically as a dry cookie addict. He again started to have visions of how to repair the ball all over again. He even walked in circles in his room, as his addiction and the bliss of that addiction had again taken over. And within a cookie-related flashback, he envisioned building a time machine that would transport him and the ball of yarn back to that specific place in time when his mother had first given it to him. Out of all of his crackpot schemes, he knew that this one particular idea had to be tested.

Like a monk who searches for the meaning of life, Geo began to skip cookie rehab meetings and instead closed himself off in the basement of the school's library. There he devoured the most complicated scientific textbooks that would hopefully lead to his building of his first fully-functional time machine. He learned calculus along with vague and esoteric mathematical theories, and he even brought these books home and studied them in his room in the middle of the night. He read Plato and Aristotle, Einstein's theories on time relativity, and even the theories of the randomness of the universe, especially Planck's explanations of quantum mechanics. And while he secretly constructed the time transportation capsule from the maze of blueprints that he hid under his bed, he knew that he had to tell his friends about it just in case he never made it back to their time zone. He even thought about growing a beard to fit his newfound role as a mad scientist, but he could only muster up a peach-fuzzy upper lip to complement the inwardly-obsessed hermit he became.

After slipping the last few books he needed from the library into his rucksack, Geo finally decided to confront his friends from whom he had been estranged for several months.

"I've been hiding the time machine in my closet," he said to his friends in the courtyard as they kicked around a few stones. "I don't know if I'll ever return."

His friends embraced him warmly after he revealed his new plan, and they basically told him that he would be a national hero for sacrificing his own life for the sake of repairing the ball of yarn, as the world had been spinning out of control ever since the yarn began to unravel.

"Please tell my parents that they can have whatever's in my room in case I don't make it back."

They agreed to his last request, and with a somber nod of farewell, Geo lugged the last of the books home.

He put a few finishing touches on the time transportation capsule in his closet. The capsule itself was basically a large wooden box that plugged into the wall socket. There was just enough room for him to squeeze himself and the now-fully-untangled ball of yarn into the box. He also stitched a space suit that resembled the old radioactive gear that nuclear scientists had worn in those old science fiction movies he had occasionally seen on television. With his mother working on her knitting project downstairs, he fit himself comfortably into the wooden box and set the time and location coordinates to that exact time and place where his mother first handed him the ball of yarn. After closing himself in, buckling his belt, and checking the coordinates one last time, he finally donned the gas mask of his nuclear suit. He then threw the switch…

Geo found himself in complete darkness when he awoke. He turned on the lights in the wooden box and found that he had luckily arrived at the specified time and place. The ball of yarn, however, still remained untangled in his hand, the thread so long now that it piled near his feet. With a swift kick he broke down the door of his time machine. He emerged at the same date, day, and time when his mother first gave him the ball. In front of him he saw his mother next to those blue scoops of yarn as she knitted the lower half of the sweater. As he walked out of the box, much like an astronaut who steps on the moon for the first time, he witnessed the horrid and terrified expression his mother wore, as she was shocked beyond belief at the sight of a small dwarf in a radioactive suit emerging from his spacecraft.

She screamed at the top of her lungs, and Geo was so frightened by her uncontrollable screaming and cries for help that he quickly returned to the box with the untangled ball of yarn, closed himself within, and quickly fired up the machine to return to where he was before.

In the darkness of the box, he was knocked out again, and when he had revived, he pushed open the box slowly to find himself in the comforts of his bedroom all over again. He doffed his makeshift time-travel suit and then inspected the blue ball of yarn, which he thought would reconstitute itself through the time-travel process. To his genuine sadness and disappointment, however, all that remained of the ball of yarn was a single thread of dirt-caked blue wool that sat in a pile at his feet. Truly, this was the worst punishment of all.

Yet just as he returned from his long trip through the outer dimensions, his father came bursting into his room with a haggard and angry expression on his face. He looked tired and weak, as though something had sucked the life out of him. His father had also grown thin and scraggly. Geo suddenly heard the din and the chanting of a large crowd outside of the house. He wondered what had happened since his departure through time.

"You see what you've done?! You little worm, you see what a mess you've made?!"

His father then grabbed him by the ear, the single thread of yarn now trailing behind him as they marched downstairs. There, in the living room, sat his mother in a wheelchair as well as several police officers from the local precinct and a few men in lab coats scratching their hoary beards.

"A time machine?!" yelled his father. "Have you gone out of your freakin' mind?! And look at this—a lawyer's bill for one trillion dollars?! Have you totally lost your mind? And look at your sick mother. She says she's been hallucinating ever since you paid her a visit in the past. And these scientists—they all want to split you open and dissect every last part of you to see how you did it. And the D.A.'s office? They want to give you the electric chair. You've ruined us, you hear me little boy? You've ruined our lives!"

His father broke down on his knees and sobbed into his son's shirt.

"You're no son of ours," he said. "I hope you fry. You deserve to die for what you did."

From what Geo had gathered by this display in his living room, his own friends must have told on him and revealed to the town that he had built a time machine. And what had followed was the kind of small-town mayhem and lawlessness that put his family into the worst kind of trouble. And still he heard the great roar of the crowd outside on his front lawn. From what he could see behind the men who had assembled in his living room, several childhood pictures of him had been flashing on the television screen as a national anchorman had delivered his lead story about a child who suddenly discovers time-travel. That child was he. Geo then knew that this was the kind of trouble he wouldn't be able to wiggle out of.

Outside of his house, hoards of people rushed forward and chanted for his execution. They carried signs and threw rolls of toiled paper at the house. Riot police had assembled to protect the property and the people in it. The same officers who had arrested him the first time for chocolate chip cookie addiction forced his small arms and legs into a straight-jacket and wrapped heavy chains around him. They locked these chains and buckled his shins together. The boy still had the nerve, though, to carry the long string of untangled yarn in his teeth. He could think of no other way. The front door of the home suddenly swung open, and the crowd on the lawn swayed in the mosh-pit of its own frenzy. The cops then stood him up in front of the vortex of people. The din was so loud that he might as well have been deaf.

As the crowd continued its yelling and screaming, as they cursed, spit at him, ground their teeth, clenched their fists, and pulled out their hair, a dark cloud gathered above them, and soon it started to rain. Even under the auspices of the loud, ominous darkness, the crowd refused to stop chanting and calling for his execution. The photographers in a large pit at the edges of the house snapped pictures of him that blinded his sight. Geo tried to speak, but he knew that if he opened his mouth even slightly, the long thread would drop from his mouth and be gone forever.

A judge in a white frock, long black robe, and a grey colonial wig met him on the front steps. The judge held his hand in the air to calm the crowd. Miraculously, the crowd quieted to hear what verdict the judge would order.

"Have you anything to say for yourself, George?" announced the judge in front of rolling film cameras that captured the final moments of this young boy's life as he knew it, his straight-jacketed image sent through television screens all across the globe.

Geo didn't respond, simply because he couldn't let go of the thread in his mouth. He could neither hear nor see the judge either, as the roar of the crowd had deafened him and the flashes of light from the photographers' pit at the well of the porch had blinded his sight.

"Well, since you have nothing left to say for the high crime of throwing this world into darkness, chaos, and peril," said the judge, "I have no choice but to sentence you right here and now. Of course, since you are a small boy, I can't really sentence you to the electric chair. The straps won't fit anyway..."

At this the crowd surged in anger. The riot police in helmets and batons were poised to fire tear gas into the center of the crowd to contain them. The judge again raised his hands, and again the crowd quieted.

"But just because you are a young boy doesn't mean that we won't punish you for your blatant misuse and disregard for the good character our good Lord has bestowed on this town. So instead of the electric chair, this town, nay, this country—hell, even this entire world—sentences you to life in our maximum security asylum for the criminally insane. Take this rotten scoundrel from my sight!"

The police officers pushed Geo back into the house where he hopped along in his straight-jacket towards the back entrance of the house. Once in the back yard, a white ambulance with red crosses in its back windows, along with a line of armed guards, waited to take him away. They strapped his shivering body to a hospital gurney and rolled him inside the ambulance. Geo could see his father shaking his fists at him and his mother nearly comatose in her wheelchair as she extended a middle finger in his direction. Geo was certainly at a loss, because he didn't know exactly what he did that was so wrong, and in the deepest chambers of his own heart he knew he had gone to any length possible to repair and restore the blue ball of yarn which was then ripped from the clench of his teeth by the attendants in the ambulance.

As the ambulance drove down the road, the protesters carrying signs on either side called him terrible names, dismissed him as an evil demon, and threw their last rolls of toilet paper at the ambulance as it sped past them. Never before had Geo felt such fear at what the fates had in store for him next. He tried to imagine what the asylum for the criminally insane would be like, but he couldn't imagine it anymore than what a good chocolate chip cookie tasted like or the slaps of his friend's hands on his back when they had cheered him on, or his body being swallowed up by a wormhole as he cascaded through an outer dimension that had landed him in a different time and place altogether. He couldn't imagine these wondrous things anymore but only recognized the ongoing currents of fear and desperation that had now accompanied him in the ambulance. And now the yarn had been lost—a beautiful work of art and a bountiful treasure that was surely lost forever.

The ambulance soon stopped after a few minutes, and a gang of hospital attendants in white uniform swung open its back doors and wheeled him out. The clouds pelted him with razor-sharp rain as he was brought to a tall iron gate that seemed like the entrance to a fortress of some kind. He could not see above the high iron walls that surrounded the asylum. He dreaded the thought of spending the rest of his life in exile and in madness. The white uniformed men unstrapped him and stood him up in front of the gate, heavy and wet as it was. They then blindfolded him, even though he was already blind.

When they made sure that he had truly been reduced to being a deaf, dumb, and blind mute, the shoved him towards the foreboding iron gate. He hopped towards it in his straight-jacket.

Geo was then certain that this was the end, and even though he cried out a few times, the attendants in uniform still pushed him along when he grew tired of hopping. He could feel the drizzle of prickly rainwater hammering on his head and wan cheeks. He even cried out for heavenly help, but in his new state of muted consciousness, he couldn't hear the internal cries of his own screams. And when he arrived at the gate, it slowly swung open to greet him. He hopped inside not knowing what all of this finally led to.

The farther he hopped along, however, the farther the usual sounds of threatening screams and cries in his own head had become. Instead, once well-inside the gate, he heard—cheering? Wait, they were actually cheering for him?

Nimble hands untied the blindfold that restricted his sight. A blinding light hit him, and for a moment or two he couldn't see anything. Slowly enough, though, he could finally make out the same exact crowd that had called for his execution earlier, and the same exact judge who had sentenced him, and the same exact police officers who had incarcerated him—all of their faces shining happily and beaming brightly. They were happy, and they cheered just for him as though he were the hero of the day who had finally made it to a new and bountiful land beyond the walls of the asylum. A flock of white doves flew above him with olive branches in their beaks, and his friends in the distance kicked around a soccer ball and called for him to come near. A pair of beautiful blonde nurses unchained him from his straight-jacket, and once again he could walk, talk, hear, and see like any young boy his age could. The judge who had once worn a long wig, white frock, and black robe now wore a clown's suit. The judge smiled grandly and winked at him. His mother and father, both restored to full health, appeared before his very eyes.

"Welcome to the other side, kid," said the judge, his hand on his shoulder.

Without a moment's thought, Geo ran into his parents' arms where they showered him with hugs and kisses. The bright brilliant sunshine revealed a verdant field where chocolate waterfalls and candy-caned rivers flowed into infinity. The new world was at play all at once, and what had once been his own fear and dread at being sentenced to life in an asylum had been replaced and exchanged for feelings of wonder, beauty, serenity, and happiness.

And on the field there were jolly adults and children of all kinds singing and running about as the crowd cheered for him and danced to a musical jug band in celebration of his arrival. They ate birthday cake and gave him a slice as they welcomed him into their fold. Even Santa Claus and his reindeer circled the blue sky and dropped gifted packages down from his sleigh. When he opened the present they had given him for all of his toil, he discovered a perfectly round blue ball of yarn beneath the wrapping—custom-made from the yarn-maker's factory.

"C'mon, my young man," said his father, with his radiant mother holding his hand on his other side. "Let me show you around."

A CIVIL WAR TALE

That his farm sat near the Mason-Dixon line didn't seem to matter as much as his wife's refusal to take herself and his daughter further West where they could be safe without him. Dallas Moonbeam had gotten word late last night that the Union Army would soon descend upon the frozen fields of their land where they would then confront an equally anxious Confederate battalion trying to advance further into the North. And since there was no telling what may happen to his family should they stick around for the musket and cannon fire that would coat an already bleak Virginia sky with soot from exploding gunpowder, then he just better tell his wife that tomorrow morning was the day when they'd finally have to abandon the fruits of all of their hard work and labors and set a course over the mythical Western ridge where they could escape the collision of these two armies and rebuild their lives from scratch.

"But I don't understand it, Dallas," said his wife. "You still haven't given me one good reason why you can't come too."

"I just did," he said, sitting at an old oak table that his grandfather had carved by hand.

"You mean you refuse to share, is that it?"

"That's not it at all."

"Then what is it? You trying to prove something?"

"I'm not trying to do anything of the sort. I'm just looking after what's best for you and Charlotte."

"What's best for me and Charlotte is if you come with us. I don't really care if we starve or not."

"There isn't enough food for all three of us and Jethro combined. There just isn't enough."

"Well, maybe Jethro has to make his own way."

"Let's think about this for a second," said Dallas, pressing his fingers between his eyes. "You expect me to believe that I'm going to bear witness to all we have here today being lost to some dumb war, just because I'll be a little delayed in getting over that ridge?"

"We're not talking about a delay here, Dallas. If any one of those soldiers catches you, there's no telling where you'll wind up."

"The important thing is not where I'll end up. It's where the three of you will end up. Not me so much. Now as head of this family I have to make a decision here, and all of us will starve if I don't head east and get those supplies. Simply put, if we all leave here together—and I mean every one of us—we'll starve before we get over that ridge. Right now we only have enough for you, Charlotte, and Jethro."

"Y'know, honey, Jethro has to find his own way."

"I can't believe you're saying that. Jethro is every bit as part of this family as you or I am."

She approached him where he sat, the flickers of candlelight against her body reminding him of how beautiful she was, her slim body underneath her bellowing nightgown representing the entire beauty of their farm and the nice things they had. And soon it would all mean nothing. All would be laid to waste.

"I know Jethro is a part of this family," she said more consolingly. "Jethro is indeed every bit a part of this family, but Jethro is not my husband. Nor is he father to Charlotte. You are. That's your job."

"—And so it's my responsibility, as your husband, to keep this family safe, which is why I've got to do what I've got to do. I'll only be a couple of days behind you, that's all."

"What's this 'got to do' thing?" she said angrily. "You don't 'got to do' anything but leave with us at sunup. And as far as Jethro is concerned, we can all eat less then—all four of us. We don't need to eat that much. We'll just take turns."

"You'll be eating less even if I don't go with you, which I'm not. I tell you, woman, I'm not going to argue with you, and this is for the final time. I'm not going with you, and that's final. I'm tired of fighting about it."

"You think you're some kind of hero or something? Do you want to die, is that it?"

"It has nothing to do with that," he fired back.

"Oh horseshit it doesn't. All I ever hear from you lately is how your granddaddy did this, and your granddaddy did that, as though you're trying to live the same kind of life they had."

"It has nothing to do with that, I told you. I'm just being as sensible as I can be."

"—something about how they were all men, and somehow you're less of one, is that it? You never felt like you could measure up."

"That's not true! Now stop saying those things!"

His wife bent down to him as he sat at the table. Their shadows as husband and wife expanded along the curves of the sanded timber that was used to build their farmhouse. Her hand now stroked his arm, her skin like a newborn's smoothing over the severity of burlap, and while there was much comfort in her soft palm running along the roughness of his skin, in no way would it loosen the obduracy of his plan.

"I know you have to be a man about this," she said. "I know you have to do what's right. You've always had to do what's right, even when you try not to, but baby, going off all by yourself in the opposite direction just isn't a good idea. It's foolish. Those soldiers get a hold of you, and I might never see you again. So put all of that 'got to do' stuff behind, because right now I don't need your granddaddy's bravery. I don't need a hero either. I need my husband—please, dear Lord—I just want my husband to come with us tomorrow. Please."

"I'm sorry, honey," said Dallas firmly, "I just can't do that. My mind is made up."

"Damn you, then!" she said, before running off into the bedroom and slamming the door shut.

It left him in the cold clamminess of their sitting room, wondering if he should have decided differently now that her radical ounce of female reasoning had permeated his mind, her protest implanted there like a the glow of a flame edging out the darkness of what he knew must be done to get his family over the ridge successfully.

And while his wife and his daughter slept, he knew he had yet to pay a visit to Jethro's cottage across the front yard. Dallas looked out of his window to see if Jethro was still awake, and judging from the glow of the firelight through his windows and the hazy, muted smoke that exhaled from his chimney, it appeared that Jethro was busy making his evening supper.

He had told Jethro earlier what he had planned to do, and while Jethro disagreed, Dallas still wanted to confirm their plans one last time before he set out for the missing supplies in the morning. Dallas donned his coarse woolen overalls and a pair of old work shoes and then trod the half-mile or so to Jethro's cottage while taking note of how cold and blustery it had become, the brittle brush on the ground snapping under his shoes as he went.

Jethro had been living in the same wooden cabin on the Moonbeam farm since his birth. Dallas' grandfather had owned Jethro's parents, but ever since his father became more fervently supportive and involved in the abolitionist causes that had spread down from New England, he gave Jethro's parents the full freedom to do anything they wanted with their lives. As a young man, Jethro decided to remain on the farm after his parents had passed, and in return for his farm work and general handiness on the Moonbeam farm, Jethro shared in the profits of whatever the farm made. This wasn't a lot of money at all, but it was enough at least to provide for what they needed day in and day out. It was a simple but hardworking life that this patchwork family made for themselves, taking only a few days out of the year to stop their work and pray together. But otherwise it was a hardscrabble and labor-intensive life that at least granted them the good fortune of contentment and protection from the harsh winters that tended to blow down from Arctic North. And regardless of how unsatisfied and unenthusiastic Dallas' wife had been about being married to a farmer, Dallas had at least met all of her needs by preserving the same farm that his parents had handed down to him. But this was all about to end. The Union Army and the Confederate soldiers would soon descend upon their land in just a few short hours. There was no telling if he'd ever be able to sink his hands into the same dark soil ever again.

When Jethro answered Dallas' call at the front door, his fingers were planted in the middle of a leather-bound book he was reading. Jethro smoked an old pipe that let off a pungently sweet tobacco smoke into the cold air. He looked at Dallas as if he had seen a ghost.

"Sweet Jesus, Jethro, this is no time to read," said Dallas, stepping into the small cottage. "What is it you have there?"

"Just something I picked up a little while ago. It's poetry, you know."

"That stuff will just confuse you."

"Melt, melt away ye armies—disperse ye blue clad soldiers,
Resolve ye back again; give up your good deadly arms,
Other the arms of the fields henceforth for you, or South
or North
With saner wars, sweet wars, life-giving wars," Jethro
recited.

Dallas planted himself in Jethro's old rocking chair next to
the mellow fire and said quite plainly, "now I don't know what
in the hell that means, but you know there ain't never been
anything like a life-giving war."

"Not yet," said Jethro after closing the book and taking a
seat across from him. "But it sure would be nice if there were
some day, wouldn't it?"

"Oh, Jethro. Still chasing those pie-in-the-sky dreams. I
just don't know what you get out of all that reading. I never
really took a liking to any of that, and here you are—reading
every book on creation—and for what? We're losing damn-
near everything in this transaction."

"I know," said Jethro solemnly. "It's just God-awful."

Dallas looked at him with a sadness he couldn't define
just yet. The smooth blackness of Jethro's face, his wrinkles
more pronounced and his hair graying at the temples like
some prescient scholar who had been sentenced for years to
their small farm, gave him the comfort, at least, of beholding
someone kind and familiar, his dark face leather-worn from
tilling the soil in the wind, his hands gnarled from all of his
toil, and Jethro somehow chose this night of all nights to read
a book that made absolutely no sense to him at the moment.

"Well, you must get something out of those books that I
just don't get," said Dallas, "because those Yankees will be here
any day now."

"I still don't agree with what you're doing," said Jethro all of
a sudden.

"No one does—not my wife, not my daughter, not you, not even me most of the time—but damnit, it has to be done. News got to us late, and there's really no choice in the matter."

"You're a stubborn fool," said Jethro matter-of-factly.

"Now you're taking her side, is that right?"

"I'm not taking sides here. Dallas. It's just that you belong with your family—not riding around like some lunatic."

"Really? Is that right? And are you going to tell me just how the hell we're supposed to rebuild once we get over that ridge if you're not there? Can you just tell me that, please?"

"It doesn't matter," said Jethro, taking a puff from his pipe. "What happens afterwards doesn't matter. You're thinking too far ahead of yourself. We're in the middle of a goddamned war here. You should be satisfied if just the three of you make it out of here alive. And here you go thinking already about what's going to happen once we get there. I tell you something, Dallas—we haven't made it over that ridge yet. You three will be lucky enough if you make it there one your own—even without me."

"I'm gonna make it if it's the last thing I do, but we can't do it without you, Jethro. We have to think at least three moves ahead. All great leaders think that way. There's just no way we can do it without you."

They sat there silently for a time mulling over their disagreement by the glow of the fire. He saw worry etched on Jethro's face, but Dallas had already made up his mind.

"Jethro," he said, "before we part ways at sunup tomorrow, I've been meaning to ask you something."

"What's that?"

"Charlotte and my wife."

"What about them, Dallas?"

"Well, it will be just the three of you out there tomorrow."

"As we've already established, yes."

"Well—and this is a little hard for me to say—but I've been thinking about it a lot lately."

"What's that, Dallas?"

"Jethro, if I don't make it back—"

"Awww hell! Nonsense!" whispered Jethro hotly. "Don't even think about it."

"I mean it, Jethro. Just hear me out for a second."

Jethro was so bothered by the idea that he immediately jumped to his feet and paced the room, wringing his hands as he marched back and forth in front of his heavy bookshelves.

"I mean it," said Dallas again. "If I don't make it back with those supplies—"

"Then what, goddamnit?! What?! Have you truly lost your mind? Have you gone completely crazy?"

"I mean it. You'll be the only one who'll have to watch over them. You'll be the head of the family if anything happens to me."

"You're crazy, you know that?"

"I'm just being sensible, that's all."

"Yeah, well, there's nothing sensible about it. In the history of creation there has never been a human plan that's ever worked."

"I just wanted to make things plain to you, that's all."

"Well, you're going to make it over that ridge, because if you don't, I'll come find you and kill you myself."

"Better you than the musket fire from those good ol' boys, right?"

Dallas smiled weakly at his own attempt at humor. He slapped his knee and finally peeled himself of the chair. When he reached the door, he said, "I just wanted to make things plain, that's all. You'll be leaving with them first thing in the morning."

He left Jethro standing there, his poetry book loose in his fingers, his lean body curled up to the ceiling of the cottage, his gnarled fists clenched, and his eyes shut so tightly as though there wasn't a single force, divine or otherwise, that could pry them open.

"Just get the hell out of here, Dallas," he said in a low whisper. "I've had enough of you for one lifetime."

"Hopefully I'll be there with you for the next life over that ridge," he said before heading back to the farmhouse.

Perhaps there was something that he secretly liked about driving the people in his life crazy. With all of his best laid plans, his farfetched theories, his good intentions that never panned out, his new inventions that never worked, his get-rich-quick schemes, his ideas that never touched the surface of any known reality, he must have driven his wife and Jethro crazy over the years. But this time there wasn't very much to laugh about anymore. As his feet broke the short, sharp stalks that rose out of the field on his walk towards the farmhouse, he considered that there was something about his craziness that he no longer wanted. He promised to the midnight sky on his way back that he'd never again try to outsmart the way things worked. The seriousness of what he was about to do had finally worked into him, like mink oil into stiff leather, and maybe he was wrong to have a mind that wasn't fully aligned with the way things worked—how there were no easy shortcuts to anything but only the path that gave the most resistance and not the least—or plans that were more straightforward and plain, and not the crooked or winding plans that cut corners or utilized anything other than what the scriptures had ordained. And so he no longer found his tinkering mischief very funny—those tall-tales and magic potions and inventions that usually blew up right in his face—these were no longer very fascinating or funny to him. He would no longer tease his family with them, now that there was a good chance he may never see them again, and yet he still had to give his dauntless mind one last chance. He decided that after all four of them make it over the ridge in a few days that he would listen to whatever his wife had to say from now on. The moon hovering above him somehow heard this promise as its watchful light illumined the narrow path in front of him.

When he returned to the farmhouse, he inspected the stacks of wooden crates that his family would soon take with them on their journey over the ridge. They were piled high in the living room and stuffed with nearly all of their clothing and other such belongings that could be readily transported by wagon. All of their furniture, all of it handmade, would have to stay behind for the soldiers to pillage. The house was quiet and still. His wife and daughter slept soundly. He could hear their breathing. He could only curl up with a blanket on the cushioned rocking chair and hope to get by on only a few hour's sleep until morning.

He didn't sleep very well that night and spent a good deal of time trying to tackle some farfetched dream in which they had all made it over the ridge successfully. But his sleep was fraught with the unrelenting twists and turns of trying to rest on a hard surface, as he didn't want to disturb his wife's sleep by climbing into bed with her. His wife, however, was up much earlier than he was, as his sleep had set in too late. He awoke to the smell of frying bacon, but he wasn't at all hungry. His wife, he figured, wouldn't want to talk to him anyway. He sensed her anger as she moved about the living room, making sure to pack the looser items that hadn't been packed yet. He was right that she didn't want to talk to him. She did the best she could to avoid him while preparing Charlotte's breakfast. He heard them whispering in the kitchen as they ate. But when his daughter emerged from the kitchen after breakfast, she rubbed sleep from her eyes and weakly stumbled over to where Dallas napped in the chair. She simply climbed into his lap without saying a word and put her small arms around his neck and buried her head into the hollow of his shoulder. She didn't want to leave. Her limp and fragile body now cradled in his arms was like an egg shell. His daughter feigned drowsiness. It was her way of silently protesting his grand plan, just like her mother protested it.

"Charlotte, come on in here and finish your breakfast," called her mother from the next room.

Dallas found it slightly humorous how his wife didn't invite him in to sit with them. Sometimes he liked it when she was angry with him. But his teasing her had come to an end. She would no longer engage in bantering. Their rapport had changed ever since he announced his intention to head in the opposite direction. And while he knew she loved him deeply, especially when he tried to convince her of his crazy new farming methods that would make him a million dollars, or how they should abandon the farm to sell snake-oil from town-to-town, or how he wanted all four of them to move to Mexico and dig for gold for a few years, he couldn't be so sure how she felt about him anymore.

Jethro's demeanor that morning matched his wife's in many respects. When they met outside and began loading the crates into the wagon, he acted as if Dallas weren't there. Jethro kept silent as he methodically helped him move crate after crate into the back of the wagon. He didn't even look at him while loading, and as a result, he didn't know quite what to say to the man who was now taking responsibility for the wellbeing of his family. And when his wife and Charlotte walked across the hard frozen field, their feet balancing themselves over the muddy patches of soil that were more like divots in an otherwise smooth field, they too remained silent, as though Dallas were merely a strange ghost who was already a part of their memories and in no way touched the future life that existed for them over the ridge. It didn't anger him so much as sadden him that they reacted so childishly towards him. And when the horses were ready and the musty blankets were thrown over the crates and secured tightly with rope, there was nothing he could say or do to ease what he perceived to be their premature bereavement over his loss. As Jethro struck the reigns, the horses, with plumes of hot breath streaming through their wet, runny snouts, stepped ahead, and the wheels of the wagon jutted forward and turned in the frozen mud. Dallas' entire life was heading in the opposite direction. But there were no tearful goodbyes. There were no kisses or hugs from Charlotte. Dallas was simply exposed to the back of Jethro's head, a head that refused to turn around to bid him farewell. And then there was his wife who sat in the seat next to him. She did turn around, finally, but only to offer a cold stare from her icy blue eyes that had reified their many years of marriage in this one singular act of betrayal on his part, a betrayal that she would never forgive, and what's more, Charlotte did the same. She was growing up to be just like her mother. The two women simply looked upon him with the kind of ruthless disdain and detachment that could only be explained as the innate cruelty of women for all the right reasons.

'She's just like her mother,' thought Dallas as he watched the wagon drift farther beyond the boundary of their farm and through a trail that snaked through the forest. And when they were finally out of sight, he could only sigh into the open air as if to tell his wife that she took life much too seriously and that one day, after he had finally retrieved the supplies and had met them over the ridge, they would all be able to sit down in front of the fire they had made with stronger and more durable kindling and laugh over his ridiculous and dangerous plan that had actually worked for a change. He imagined saying, 'I told you it would work,' as his family gazes into the farfetched fire with him, Jethro's sweet tobacco smoke as pungent as ever as they all laugh and slap their knees at having forever outsmarted conventional wisdom—just as it used to be. But he would first have to make it over the ridge himself to have the luxury of proving that they should never take things so seriously as they had that morning and that a man could slip his way out of anything if he simply had the capacity to a smile and laugh more than he wept and despaired.

Such a proposition took lifetimes to prove, he figured, as he breathed in the air of his country farm one last time. He gazed at his farmhouse as though trying to engrave it properly into the depth of his memory. It was a weak ceremony. He then walked behind the house and saddled up the old, reliable horse that would lead him in the opposite direction of where he wanted to be, towards that vast flatlands that lay to the east. He would try to make it to the supply depot in two-day's time. All he had with him was a change of clothes, some camping gear and food he prepared, and his rusty old shotgun to protect himself from thieves and bandits that he may encounter on the road. All of his belongings were now with his family, and now that he was left all by himself, he carefully reviewed the pre-plotted route he would take. And quite honestly he didn't know what to expect—only that he should move quickly to avoid any confrontations and simply slip through the remainder of the day like a fish insulated by its own twitching cartilage, pulsating and warm within the slick of its cold scales, its independence and freedom from all of the things he had ever known twisting, turning, and slipping itself loose from the predatory forces that the never-ending circumstance of war had brought.

As a light snow began to fall over the sullen landscape, the amber stalks short and sharp like a balding scalp, his horse and wagon flattened the grass beneath as it lurched forward. The sun became a blurry white spot in the sky that shed no warmth, the heavy clouds girdling it refracting dull light over the bare trees that had fallen on either side of him. For a while there wasn't a human soul in sight. Although he cherished such an independence, he couldn't help but wonder what he would actually do with such a freedom, now that he was set loose upon the world. There wasn't much to think about without his wife by his side. There weren't any plans he could concoct or intensely imagine, as his purpose was as clear as the trickling brooks and tiny meandering streams that the wheels of his wagon bridged and now crossed over, his steady movement towards the next village like the steady movements of a clock, a methodical push along the ground that didn't require any extraordinary skill, just a slow dependability and a progress towards a destination that had been measured by the clomping of his horse's hoofs in a monotonous, linear pattern, his rotating mind empty and inspirationless, as though he wandered alive through all that had already died. The wilderness gasped and suffocated under the weight of increasing snow, his hands getting cold and his horse like a great solitary engine fixated on its rote task. He couldn't help but feel exhausted, even though his horse did all of the work. He couldn't help but feel as weak-boned as the creaking vacancy of his wagon that rolled along the dips and ascents of the trail he was on. And while he had looked forward to this day where he would finally be free for a time, he had to admit that the romantic lust of being all alone remained as unfulfilled as the hollowness of the logs that had fallen to the forest floor.

He actually missed Jethro and the damned stink of his pipe smoke, as scent that was now buried into the fibers of his clothing. He missed the way he had always quoted lines from his senseless poetry books that only introduced other-worldly confusions in their simple minds and distracted them from their singleness of purpose of working on the farm. He missed his family, damnit, and he was only a few short hours into the journey, the white of the snow reminding him of the pallor of his daughter's cheeks when they drained of blood when she didn't know whether to side with her mother or her father during a routine argument at the dinner table. It seemed like a blow to his dauntless mind just then that he should miss these people. It was a blow to the carefully constructed manhood of the fathers who came before him. He thought of it as a weakness that he would have to overcome if he were to rejoin his family over the ridge.

The sky slowly darkened as the day dragged on and the wagon moved forward. He decided that he should make camp soon, but only if he could push a little bit farther into the wilderness he could make better time. It wasn't until he had to make water that he did stop. He steered his horse to the side of the trail and tied it to the bark of a rotted tree. He then humped and stomped through the snow to an area deeper into the forest that had sprung up on either side of the trail. The sounds of the forest had returned, as he had been conditioned only by the sound of his horse's clompity-clomp along the trail and also by the creaking of his wagon. But all of a sudden the forest seemed much more alive to him. Squirrels raced atop the branches that hung over the trail. They scurried through the blanketed surface of the forest. Even a raccoon or two moseyed lazily between their lairs at the base of tree trunks, protecting themselves, he figured, from the plummeting temperatures. As he relieved himself, he stepped on a dead branch that immediately startled a flock of snow finches, their light, feathery bodies erupting and then darting from one naked bush to an adjacent one, their tiny claws and short wings grazing the top of his head as they flew. It made his heart jump a little. He recognized that his ride to the east was no longer a solitary journey at all but a part of the wilderness around him. Perhaps he was guilty of being too self-involved to notice how he was now an interactive player in all that occupied the spaces around him. He usually thought of himself apart from nature, as the trail that carved out the space was already too well-defined to give the wilderness too much credit. But now he thought differently.

As he finished and thought for a quick second how fascinating it was to have the warmth inside of him color and melt through the crust of the snow's surface, he thought he had stepped on yet another dead branch. He prepared for another flock of snow finches to erupt and fly passed him, but this time nothing moved. It wasn't a branch that he stepped on, he recognized after a moment or two, but there was definitely the click of something that he couldn't quite place. He turned around slowly and found himself facing the round hollow of a musket aimed directly at his head.

"Easy there, boy," said the Southern voice on the other end of the musket.

The soldier's gray uniform was threadbare. His moustache was untamed around his mouth and covered with wet ice.

"Just easy does it there, boy," said the soldier again, his eyes squinting down the length of the musket, his finger tense on the trigger.

Dallas' insides sank suddenly, as though his being discovered gutted all of his bodily organs and sent them crashing through his lower extremities. He carefully raised his hands up in a show of surrender.

"Now just hold on there, brother," said Dallas. "I'm unarmed. You can see that, can't you? I have no weapons on my person. Just take it easy, brother, okay?"

The man continued to press the steady aim of his musket at his head. Luckily, though, the soldier, perhaps feeling a little differently about him, uncocked his gun and moved it away from his head.

"Now that's better," said Dallas slowly. "Just take it easy."

He stared into the soldier's cold face for a second. The soldier flashed what he swore was a mocking and knowing grin. It was the twist at the edge of his smile that put the soldier in complete control of him. Dallas, not knowing how else to react, returned the same grin.

"Now that's better," said Dallas, as though taming a bear on the verge of attack. "Now maybe we can talk this over like two sensible adults."

It was then that the soldier grabbed a hold of the fat end of his musket, and with a speed that sent Dallas careening into the land of the unconscious, the soldier sent the blunt end of his instrument full-force into Dallas' soft skull, blinding him from all of the wilderness he just bonded with. His body dizzily dropped to floor of the forest like a sack of flour dumped from the back of an exhausted slave.

When he came to, he found that his hands were bound by a twine that rubbed away at the skin of his wrists and that they had tied his hands behind him to lessen the risk of his running away. He lay prone on the snow. The whole of his forehead throbbed in pain. He couldn't feel most of his body, as the cold had numbed most of it. Luckily, the soldier who caught him didn't strip him of his overcoat. The soldier at least permitted him to wear it through the mild storm that now covered the ground in a thicker blanket of snow. After he had a better grasp of his surroundings, Dallas determined that he was only an acre or two away from where was caught. He flipped himself over in the snow, the weight of his body now on top of his arms, so that he could better see the two Confederate soldiers that now held him prisoner—the one who caught him and the other one who seemed more like a lesser assistant. They warmed themselves over the small fire they had made, their horses and rucksacks emptied of their supplies that were spread out along the perimeter of their encampment. He also noticed that he wasn't the only prisoner being held hostage there. Another middle-aged man, tall and reedy and wearing a black outfit with a black pastor's hat, also sat manacled in the snow. He too looked too haggard and frost-bitten to run away. The pastor stared into the fire as if entranced by the dance of its flames, unable to do anything else but stare.

Dallas let out a loud moan that was the consequence of being left in the cold for too long a period of time. The Confederate assistant warming himself against the fire announced to his boss that the new prisoner was finally awake.

"Get him up," said the soldier who had caught him, and without much delay his assistant grabbed Dallas by the arms, flipped him over, and dragged him several feet to the edge of the fire.

There, Dallas managed to sit upright. The fire's warmth thawed his feet and legs and slowly licked away at the numbness of his face. His skin started to itch wickedly, and he coughed a few times as though something in his lungs had broken. Perhaps, he thought, that he had caught pneumonia or was on the verge of a high fever. Whatever it was, the warmth of the fire came just in time. His body pricked and tingled all over, as it was a warmth that felt both uncomfortable and foreign.

The man who head-butted him with his rifle, a soldier far too young to be so humorless and solemn in his duties, squatted down before Dallas who was just feeling the blood in his fingers return. Dallas didn't pay much attention to him at first. The soldier looked him over carefully, but Dallas was more interested in the heat the fire gave.

"Where do you think we are?" asked the soldier.

When Dallas didn't respond, he said, "Oh, I get it. You don't want to talk, is that it? Well, we have ways of making you talk, that's for sure."

Dallas only stared into the light like the parson across from him did, as though the fire alone could melt the frost from his eyes and deliver its warmth straight to his tired soul.

"What should we do with him, captain?" asked the assistant, his broken teeth and whiskeyed breath sliding into a grin that most of these backwater Southerners wore when they were on the verge of lucrative gain.

"This boy doesn't look like he's talking," said the soldier. "Ain't it funny how they never talk at first?"

"Well, what do we do now?" asked the assistant.

"Get my sword for me."

Judging by the stripes on his uniform, the man who caught him was indeed a captain in the Confederate army, and his assistant was a corporal who traveled with him and saw to his needs.

After the corporal fetched his sword, the captain unsheathed it and rested its length into the heart of the fire. He let the sword sit there until its lower half glowed red and hot.

"You gonna make him talk now, ain't ya, captain?"

Dallas was still stunned that he had made it through without freezing to death. He didn't know what was happening to him at first, but he finally reoriented himself when the Confederate captain drew the glowing end of the hot sword within an inch of his nose.

"You're gonna tell me where they're coming from," said the captain in a long Southern drawl that intended to scare him into confession.

"I don't know what you're talking about," said Dallas, feeling the heat radiate off the end of the sword. "I swear, I have no idea what you're talking about ."

"C'mon, Yankee. You know exactly where they're coming from. You better let it out before this here sword burns a hole through your skull."

"I swear it. I don't know anything. I'm not with the Union. I swear it. I'm just headed east."

"Where to, Yankee?"

"Just east to the supply depot."

"Awww, c'mon now," laughed the captain. "With that Northern accent of yours? I thought you'd be a better liar."

"No, I swear it. I'm not a Yankee."

"Well, you certainly aren't a good Southerner either."

When the captain tapped his arm with the blunt side of his sword the first time, Dallas could only yell up into the sky, and when he did it a second time in a spot further up the length of his arm, Dallas fell back into the snow and buried his arms into the layers of white powder beneath him.

"That will get him," said the corporal looking on excitedly. "Them folks from the North are just like cattle when it comes down to it."

"You remember now?" asked the captain of Dallas.

"I told you," yelled Dallas, "I don't know anything! I don't know a damned thing! I'm on my way east! Please."

61

The captain again touched his arm with hot sword, and it sent Dallas screaming into the snow, as though he were eating it, his arms twitching behind his back.

"You tell me, where they headed?" asked the captain again more fiercely than before.

"Can't you see—the man doesn't know," piped up the pastor watching the scene from the other side of the fire.

The captain stared him down from across the small space that divided them and then threw his sword into the snow. He walked around the small blaze and moved within inches of the pastor's face.

"And I take it you'd know where those Yankees are coming from?"

"I don't know either," said the pastor. "Now stop torturing the poor man."

"Your God doesn't have any authority here, old man. You abolitioners are no better than them nigger beasts as far as I'm concerned."

"It's abolitionists.—Ists, not abolitioners."

The captain immediately smacked him harm with the back of his hand, sending the pastor back into the snow.

"Just shut up, before I tear you a new hide," yelled the captain.

He then walked around the fire again and tended to Dallas who by this time had his arms buried deeply underneath the snow, his face writhing in pain. The captain grabbed him by the collar and said, "Look, I don't want any more trouble out of you. You tell me their exact location, or this time I'm gonna cut off that pretty Yankee nose of yours and burn your eyes out."

"Fine," gasped Dallas, "I'll tell you. They're about ten miles out of Pleasant Valley, and their marching southwest towards Lynchburg. They'll make a couple of stops in Oakville and Concord before they move on to Roanoke."

"Don't you see," said the pastor again, "the man doesn't know. Let him go."

"Shut up!" yelled the captain from across the fire. And then to his assistant, "see, I told you so. This trash ain't nothing but a Yankee spy. Them Yanks are heading right where want 'em."

The captain pushed Dallas back into the snow after he was through with him.

"I told you so," said the captain. "Now we know."

He marched around the fire excitedly, relishing in how he was able to scare the information out of his prisoner.

"I've got to hand it to you, captain. You just might save the South after all."

"Damn right. Now the question is, what do we do with these two?"

"I dunno," said the corporal. "I just assume we leave 'em here. We don't need 'em anymore."

"We can't leave 'em here. They'll just continue doing what they're doing, and that might be the end of us. We have to get rid of them."

"Get rid of 'em?"

"Yes, corporal. I want you to take these two and get rid of them down by those yonder trees. We'll keep the horses and that junky old wagon. We'll get the Southern Cross for this."

"You really think so, captain?"

"I know it so, just as long as we get rid of these two. And what's so good about it is that we have this old fool's Bible to read 'em their last rites."

"Ain't that a saving grace," laughed the corporal.

"Get 'em up then, and take 'em down to those trees back there."

"Yessir."

The corporal gathered his musket, while the captain pulled both Dallas and the pastor up off the snowy floor of the camp. The corporal took them from there and pushed the two prisoners forward. They now headed into the thick of the forest where they're corpses would soon be hidden from view and most likely lost to the wilderness and all who trudged through it.

"I'm telling you, I'm not a spy! I swear it," yelled Dallas.

"Shut up, Yankee!" said the corporal who pushed them deeper into the glade with the end of his musket. "Keep moving."

The captain behind them soon became a grayish figure in the distance. All about the forest the birds chirped in the snow as though the day were actually a merry one to them, but Dallas knew that he was suddenly on his way out of existence, and so he began praying for the well-being of his family as he trod through the snow and stepped over the branches that blocked his path. Out of the corner of his eye he caught sight of the pastor who by this point was shivering in the cold. The pastor's skin had gotten even paler, and the white stubble covering his sunken cheeks suggested that he had been with these men for at least a couple of days.

The corporal stopped them at a tree and told the two men to stand facing it. He then loaded his musket and prepared for what seemed to be the inevitable—or at least that's how Dallas thought of his circumstances at the moment, the forest around him still chirping and moving with life, the dead trees and branches moving along with them.

"Don't you want me to read him his last rites?" asked the pastor.

"What?" asked the corporal.

"I'm the pastor. You should really let me read him his last rites in a proper fashion. You forgot the Bible back at the camp. It's a sin if you don't let me do that."

The corporal looked at him for a moment as he puzzled over the new wrinkle in the task he was about to carry out. He stood there for a moment or two quite motionless, wondering what he should do.

"Awww, shit," said the corporal. "Move it, both of you!"

He pushed them back in the direction of the camp again, and when they returned to the fire, the captain's lips snarled in his response to the delay.

"What in God's name is happening, corporal?!" asked the captain angrily.

"The pastor wants to read the spy's last rites properly."

"Goddamned it, corporal, do you think it was really necessary to bring them all the way back here to do that?"

"I dunno, captain. It seemed like the right thing to do."

The captain thought about it for a moment and said, "well, damnit, take the old man's Bible then. You should have taken it with you in the first place. Do it quickly. The sooner we get rid of 'em, the better."

The corporal fetched the black, leather-bound Bible that the pastor had kept with the few supplies that remained near the fire. The three men again headed back into the thick of the forest, but this time the Bible was in the corporal's possession and ready to be used. The corporal again lined them up against the same tree, their faces planted against its rough bark.

"You've got to tie me loose if I'm going to read from it," said the pastor out of the side of his mouth. "You want to do this right away, don't cha?"

The corporal sighed heavily. He was no longer as carefree about killing them but once again seemed to be working on the same puzzle of how to proceed.

"I'd like him to read from the Good Book," said Dallas. "You can at least grant me that."

The corporal thought about it for a few moments longer, apparently confounded by what he should do. And fearing that he get yet another scolding from the captain if he headed back to the camp to ask him, he simply took out his knife from a sheath at his side and cut the pastor loose from the rope that bound his hands together. The corporal then handed him the Bible, his beady eyes watching the pastor's every move.

"Thank you," said the pastor. "You did the right thing. Now we can do this properly."

The pastor opened the Bible and thumbed through it until he found the right page and the right psalm to deliver the last rites. He faced Dallas and said, "Are you ready, my son."

Dallas said, "if you can please pray my family too, father. I never thought I'd leave this precious earth without seeing them again."

The corporal looked upon this with the same befuddlement that he had had before, but then he snapped out of it and rechecked his musket to make sure it was ready to fire. And in the middle of rechecking his gun, the calm pastor, after looking at Dallas squarely in the eyes, swung his arm around and began beating the corporal senseless with the blunt side of the Bible.

"For God's sake, man," yelled the pastor, "run for your life!"

The pastor beat the corporal several times over with the Good Book. He did so while screaming, "Damn it, it's abolitionist, not abolitioners! Abolitionist, you stupid moron!"

The pastor then forced the musket away from the beaten corporal who by this time had cowered to the ground. In the midst of this chaos, Dallas simply ran as fast as he could away from the camp, his hands still tied behind his back and his feet kicking up the powdery snow behind him as he ran. When he was but a few yards deeper into the forest, he heard gunfire, as the pastor must have killed the corporal already and was now busy firing upon the captain back at the camp. Dallas knew he still needed his horse and wagon that had been waiting for him near the camp, and after running wildly for several minutes straight in the blind hysteria of dead branches and the low stumps of trees that made him stumble all over the forest floor, he decided to turn back to rescue these items and perhaps to take the pastor away with him to freedom as well. But as he made his return, he heard even more gunfire, and when he finally made it all the way to the camp, he found the bodies of both the pastor and the captain dead in the blood-soaked snow that surrounded their corpses. The corporal was also dead, his body deeper in the forest.

All of a sudden, Dallas found himself completely alone. He simply heard the wind whistle through the spindly overhead branches and the last snaps and hisses of the fire in the middle of the camp. It was a moment of eerie serenity apart from the mayhem that had transpired. He located the captain's sword, still warm in the snow, and cut his hands loose from behind him with its sharp blackened blade. The moment his hands were freed, he ran straight for his horse and wagon that had been tied to a tree a few yards beyond the clearing. He leapt onto the wagon's seat and tore off down the same dirt trail that would ultimately lead to the supply depot several miles east of where he was. He had never whipped his poor horse so hard in his life, but as he rode, he beat his horse's back as hard as he could, sending the poor creature whinnying through the darkening forest, the wheels of his wagon kicking up powder as he sped along.

The sheer adrenaline rush of breaking free from the Confederate encampment slowly wore off when his singed flesh began to miserably sting, and his forehead, now a red-purplish knot that covered half of his face, throbbed as the cold wind eroded his spirits and sank him into a greater desperation. He had forgotten his overcoat back at the camp. And while his horse flew against the oncoming wind, he felt the need to slow the wagon down. He jostled in his seat for a ways and then brought his horse to a more manageable trot along the trail, just so he could think more clearly. He realized that he had to make it to the supply depot soon or else he would freeze to death without his overcoat. Already his wet flesh felt weak, and his body sweated and ached from what seemed to be a more developed fever. Yet he slowed down for only a few minutes, and in that short time it felt like death was overtaking him. He flung the reigns hard against the horse's narrow back, and off he was again. He hoped to make it to the supply depot before the darkening sky bled into night.

When he finally saw the town ahead of him, it appeared as a small hamlet nestled in the snowy-gray distance. He knew he couldn't stay there very long, lest the Union Army find him there. The threat of their entering the town at any time even found him wanting to turn around and head back in the opposite direction, but surely the Southerners with their cannons and muskets must have found the dead bodies by now. He had little choice but to continue forward, and the town came as a welcome sight. The houses in each acre of field, however, were all but abandoned due the near arrival of the Union soldiers. His immediate thought was simply to run into one of these silent homes and collapse on one of its living room floors, as he was already too worn out from the journey. Instead, he headed straight through the center of town to the depot itself, which was a large warehouse beneath a top floor where the storekeeper kept his living quarters. Dallas had been doing business with the storekeeper for some time now, and he knew that the storekeeper wouldn't leave until his supplies were picked up.

When he got to the entrance of the warehouse, he peeled himself off of the wagon's seat and rolled out of it, falling a few feet to the wet ground below. He couldn't stand so straight when he lifted himself off the ground. He stumbled into the warehouse in his wet and dirty rags, his shirt torn and his flesh febrile. Once inside, his eyes met the storekeeper's. He collapsed to the floor layered with sawdust. The storekeeper stood over him with a look of surprised concern, but Dallas couldn't hear what he said. He blacked out as the storekeeper patted his cheeks in an attempt to revive him.

He remembered that he dreamt of his wife, and how a week or two ago he had held her in his arms in their bedroom at the farmhouse. They had been arguing over the plan he had made, and the exhaustion of their argument and her pent-up frustrations with him caused her to surrender her body as an act of letting go of the deep-seeded fury that she held towards him and their marriage. Perhaps she couldn't believe it herself that she had married such a man. Perhaps she could have done better with someone else, as though before surrendering to him, there was little chance of ever escaping him. Surrendering to one's husband was the only clear path a wife can ever take, she must have thought.

He awoke from the dream with the taste of her on his lips. He didn't know how long he had been sleeping, but he found himself in a bed in what must have been the storekeeper's living quarters on the top floor of the warehouse. His forehead had been bandaged with gauze, and the burn wounds where the Confederate captain had tapped him with the sword were also dressed and bandaged. He wore a white flannel nightgown, his old clothes pressed and folded on a chair next to his bed. He didn't feel like sleeping nor staying awake. Instead he simply lay there, wondering when he would be able to head back west with his supplies.

A little while later, a young teenage girl entered the room. She headed straight for the closet that was near the iron bed that Dallas lied in. When she noticed he was awake, she dropped her things and called down the hallway, "Pa! He's awake! Dallas is awake!"

He then sat upright in his bed, his health and his strength returning to his somewhat, and soon the storekeeper arrived. He was a short and portly man with a handlebar moustache and woolen trousers held in place by buttoned suspenders. He looked more like a barbershop attendant than a storekeeper. His name was Walter, and their business dealings had gone all the way back to when Dallas' father ran the farm.

"Dallas, damn you, you made it out alive," he said.

Dallas hardly recognized the sound of his own voice when he replied, "those Confederate soldiers really know how to treat a guy."

"You're damn lucky, Dallas," said Walter, taking a seat on the chair beside him. "We thought you were gonna die for sure."

"Who fixed all of these bandages to me?"

"That would be my daughter," smiled Walter.

Dallas smiled at her as she finished up her work with the closet.

"But, damn it, we all shouldn't have been here. You've been knocked out for a good day and a half."

"A day and a half? Is that right?"

"Yeah."

"Oh, no. This is not good, Walt. This is not good at all."

"Hell, we were about to lock up the store and leave with everybody else until you came along."

"You waited for me?" asked Dallas searchingly.

"Of course we waited. We couldn't just leave you here. The Yankee army has already taken over the town. They're already here, Dallas. They keep coming in droves. A lot of them soldiers are now at the saloon getting drunk and sleeping with old Chauncey's whores."

"Interesting. Why would old Chauncey want to leave all of that? It's good money for him."

"But we're pretty much stuck here is what I'm trying to tell you. They've quarantined all of my supplies. They have two guards posted in the warehouse. It doesn't look like we're leaving any time soon."

"You mean you all waited for me to get better, and in that time the Union army took over the town?"

"That's what I'm trying to tell you," said Walter.

"I'm sorry. I'm so very sorry."

Walter looked down at his feet for a moment and said, "think nothing of it. I'm a good Christian first. A prisoner of war second."

"You mean they won't let us leave?"

"No sir, they won't. In fact, I was told that as soon as you regained your health that you should go see the colonel at Town Hall. We're all stuck here for now, whether we like it or not."

"And what about my supplies? You still have my supplies, don't cha?"

"They're on the wagon ready to go, but your horse and wagon are under guard in the warehouse. There are two soldiers who are at the front door making sure no one goes in there. I was told that, when you're ready, you should get your pants on and head to Town Hall to see the colonel."

"Shit," he muttered. "Maybe my wife was right."

"What do you mean?"

"All I know is that I have to get out of here, Walter. I need those supplies, and I need to head west towards the ridge."

"The ridge? Well, you're mighty far away from the ridge, if you ask me. You would have to go through the forest all over again. Maybe you could work something out with the colonel."

"Are you kidding me? He'll never let me just walk out of here."

"Maybe he will, and maybe he won't," said Walter, scratching an itch on his bald head.

"But Walter…thanks for waiting for me."

"Think nothing of it. Just get your pants on and head to Town Hall."

When Dallas stepped out into a resplendent sunshine that had melted much of the snow that the previous storm had brought, he was immediately accompanied by two Union guards that had been stationed just outside the warehouse doorway. The supply depot itself stood at the end of the town's main avenue as it marked the final boundary before the rural landscape continued far and wide to the east behind it. The front door opened to a main avenue replete with blue-uniformed soldiers visiting the open shops in town. These soldiers now occupied the small town as they wandered about the streets in droves, just as Walter said. They talked loudly and seemed to enjoy their occupation, their horses tied to posts along the main avenue in a long row, the local saloon open and ready for their business even though it was still so early in the day. Large wagons carted a few of Walter's supplies to and from the warehouse. It was an amazing sight considering how silent and peopleless the town had been when Dallas had first arrived. And now it was alive with the Union army en route to Lynchburg, he presumed. But it was clear that Dallas' status in the town was that of a prisoner, and while the two soldiers didn't manhandle him at all, they still made certain that he didn't run off anywhere. They saw to it that he walked directly to Town Hall, which was in the middle of the town. It was a squat, stone building that distinguished itself by being the sturdiest structure in the town. The other shops and eateries whose structures were made of worn wood were flimsy and vulnerable by comparison.

The two soldiers accompanied Dallas all the way through to where the colonel of the army that had been managing the town's occupation sat behind the mayor's desk in an office whose walls were dressed in dark oak paneling. Apparently, the town mayor had fled before the Union arrived, leaving a collection of plaques, awards, and citations on the walls that showed his strong ties and loyalties to the Confederacy in nearby Richmond. The colonel himself, a somewhat menacing but sturdy specimen with a scar that cut straight along the right side of his face, from his temple to his lower jaw, didn't seem too bothered about briefing yet another prisoner as to where he would ultimately wind up. His blue Union uniform, however, was perfectly pressed and free of any lint, dust, or wear that typified the threadbare gray uniforms that the Confederate soldiers wore. His stripes, gold braids, and epaulets were proudly displayed, his brass buttons brightly polished, and the blue cloth tailored tightly and snugly against the muscular size and shape of his body. If a daguerreotype were shot of him with his face hiding the fierce scar that wandered down the side of him, one would think he exemplified the model army officer— fierce and menacing though he was. His hair was cut terribly close to his scalp, and his cold black eyes looked at Dallas with a quiet aplomb of disgust that he must have reserved for most of the townsfolk who didn't get to leave in time. Dallas took a seat in front of him, and rather than leave the room, the two soldiers simply stood behind his chair on close watch, as though the colonel was about to hand down a verdict.

"Your name?"

"Dallas."

"Your full name."

"Dallas Moonbeam, sir."

"Why didn't you leave with the rest of the residents of this town? How come you're still here?"

"It was never my intention to leave from anywhere. I'm just passing through the town, that's all."

"Where are you from if you're not from around here? Because it doesn't look like you're from here, from what I know."

"I'm from a town just west of Appomattox," said Dallas, now uncomfortable with how fiercely the colonel stared him down.

"That would make you a Southerner."

"I'm not a Southerner—no sir, colonel."

"Then what are you, because you're certainly not a Northerner by the looks of you."

"I'm just on my way to pick up some supplies, that's all."

"Not anymore you're not."

"What do you mean? I'm just a visitor in this town. My intention was to head back towards Lynchburg."

"With all of these bandages on you? How'd you get all of those?"

"I was beaten up by bandits along the road. They took all of my things. I barely made it here alive."

"Don't try to bullshit and bullshitter," said the colonel abruptly, rising to his feet and pacing behind his desk. "We already know you must have had contact with the Confederacy. No one gets those kinds of wounds from bandits alone."

"I don't know what you're talking about. I mean, they may have been Southerners alright, but I certainly had no contact with Confederate soldiers—not that I know of anyway."

"What kind of answer is that?" scowled the colonel. "Either you had contact with them or you didn't. There's no in between."

"I might have," said Dallas nervously, "but I can assure you that I have no part in the Confederate army. I'm just trying to head back west with my supplies."

"You're not going anywhere," announced the colonel, "except further up North."

"North? But I'm not headed that way."

The colonel sat back down again and said, "you see here, we're a nation of laws. And unfortunately, I have no authority to beat the whereabouts of their position out of you. Since we're more of a civilized breed than you're kind, I'm bound by the law to send you for further questioning up to Fort Dix in Jersey. They'll be sure to beat it out of you there."

"Now wait a second!" said Dallas. "I told you I have no idea of their whereabouts, and I certainly can't go all the way up to New Jersey. I don't know anything, I tell you."

"You'll go where we tell you to go," barked the colonel. "The transport leaves first thing tomorrow morning. In the meantime, consider yourself under house arrest over at the supply depot." And then he said to the soldiers behind him, "make sure he doesn't leave his room. Get him on that transport with the other convicts first thing in the morning."

"Yes, colonel," said the two soldiers in unison.

"That is all—and, Mr. Moonbeam, enjoy the ride, because no matter how law-abiding we are, we always get what we need. You may be able to fool everyone else, but you're not fooling me. Not one bit. And when you get up to Fort Dix, don't be surprised if they don't draft you for a much holier and more righteous cause than the one you're pursuing now. Dismissed!"

"But colonel, I assure you, I don't know anything! I swear it!"

"Get him out of here!" ordered the colonel.

The soldiers behind him picked him by the shoulders and pushed him out the colonel's sight. He stumbled into the lobby of the Town Hall, the soldiers following directly behind him. He returned a bright sunshine that strained his eyes, the melting ground opening deep divots and craters along the main avenue that soaked his shoes in mud. The soldiers pushed him so hard on their way back to the warehouse that he slipped and fell a few times in the large puddles of water that the thawing had brought. Other blue-clad soldiers on either side of him caroused about the main avenue, laughing and spitting on him as he passed. It was a miserable march back to the third floor of the warehouse where he simply doffed his mud-caked shoes and slid back into bed, the same two soldiers stationed just outside of his room. And as the sunshine blared through the windows just behind the iron grate of his bed, he knew he had to use whatever acumen and whatever wits he had left to hatch a plan that retrieved his horse and wagon that very night and break out of the town even more quickly than he had stumbled into it. But there was nothing in the room he could use—nothing except the window behind his bed that had a view of the vast, flat landscape behind the town. The sky was so clear and blue that he could see eastward for miles.

The view, however, didn't fascinate him for too long. He looked directly down from the window's ledge and saw how he could have easily broken his legs if he dared jump three floors down. And yet he would take that chance in the middle of the night, because in no way would he allow them to transport his sorry shape of a body all the way to New Jersey. All he needed to do was to jump and land without breaking anything. He would then find his supplies and take off into the darkness. His plan was that simple, and even if it didn't work, it would still be well worth it than the consequence of not trying at all. Being drafted into the Union's service would be a fate all too tragic to bear. His determination to make it out of the town alive suddenly matched the confidence he had in the new plan he weaved, only this time his plan would work—he was sure of it—just as long as the soft mud below cushioned his fall...

As the evening fell over the town and the sun set on the opposite side of the main avenue, he was again fortunate enough to hear how the soldiers who were just behind the door of his room had been running, yelling wildly, and carousing with another group of soldiers who had been drinking at the saloon in town. They brought the two soldiers a couple of pints of whiskey from the saloon-keeper's special stock. Apparently their party had moved in-doors, and beyond his small room he heard the two soldiers talking loudly and drowning their sorrows about being two unglorified lackeys in an endless war in the bottles of bitter, distilled alcohol the other soldiers had given them. As Dallas tried to get some sleep, the two soldiers trashed about the third floor hallway, sometimes laughing hysterically and at other times weeping over their fate. He couldn't make out exactly what the soldiers were saying, but he could tell that they were pretty drunk and that they would probably fall fast asleep by the time Dallas made his escape through the window.

He stayed as still as a corpse in his bed, only to rise after they had stopped yelling and thrashing about. The floorboards of the hallway soon stopped bending and creaking with their footfalls that seemed to shake the entire building for a good two hours straight. The view from his window was now darkened completely by the stain of night. Dense clouds had obscured the moon's glow upon the town. Dallas tiptoed about his room and pulled his socks and muddied shoes on in the darkness, making sure not to make the slightest sound, lest he wake up the two soldiers just outside his door.

He carefully unlatched the window behind his bed, opened it wide, and squeezed his body awkwardly upon the window sill. Without much more thought or complaint, he simply rolled his body from the ledge of the window and fought the temptation to yell out loud as he free-fell from the top floor of the warehouse all the way to the soft ground below. He was lucky enough to land on the meat of his back, but he had the wind sucked out of him when he hit the ground. He struggled in the darkness to regain his breath, his body writhing in the cold mud but still making sure not to utter a single word or make a sound that might alert the other soldiers in the vicinity.

His body lay supine like a struggling animal with all four of its paws upended in the wind. His breath, however, gradually returned. His ribs pained, as he feared he had cracked at least two or three of them. But as determined as he was, he finally lifted himself off the ground, fearing that the slow wheezing of his lungs might alert the guards. He then immediately spotted a window on the ground floor that lead directly into the warehouse. He stumbled to this window and climbed through it by rolling his body awkwardly across its ledge where he then dropped a few more feet to the floor again, perhaps cracking another rib in the process—he wasn't sure. But now he was firmly in the warehouse, and the windows on either side of the building permitted the moonlight to illuminate the interior of the warehouse and guide his walk around the many crates and barrels that had been sitting there and gathering dust. In no time at all, he spotted his wagon and his horse in the far corner of the room. His horse appeared to be asleep while standing, his mouth fitted with a bag of oats that the soldiers must have given him. And now that he was again reunited with his trusty horse, he had a decision to make: either break out of the warehouse with his horse and supplies or simply to escape without these things, climb back out the window, and run wildly into the darkness never to return and heading in no particular direction until the morning sunlight could guide him.

He rested his paining body against one of the wheels of the wagon. The sliding door to the warehouse had been shut tight, and if he were to leave with his supplies, he'd have little choice but to surprise the guards outside by bolting down the main avenue with his horse leading the way. Quite frankly, he didn't know what he should do, but considering that his family over the ridge wouldn't survive very long without the supplies, he made a decision right then and there to surprise the guards in front of the warehouse by sliding the door open very quickly and riding down the center of town in a mad sprint out of town. He thought that if he could use the element of surprise to his advantage, he would be able to make it out of town before any of the soldiers knew what was happening. Most of them were drunk or fast asleep anyway, went his line of reasoning. He even peeked through the windows of the warehouse and noticed how the guards in front of the building had been snoozing while on duty. Empty bottles of whiskey were strewn all about their posts. He thought, 'now's the prefect time.'

With what little strength he had, he carefully hitched his horse to the supply wagon. He then saddled up his horse in the darkness as quietly as possible. He needed to ride on the horse itself and not the wagon seat in order to slide open the door that would release him to freedom. After climbing on the saddle, he positioned his horse and wagon against the frame of the door, and although it pained him tremendously, he leaned over the head of his horse to slide the front door of the warehouse completely open. Before he did so, however, he muttered a small prayer that he learned as a child. He realized after reciting it that there was no more need to put off the inevitable. God would work his magic that night, as he grew confident that his escape was simply the will of God operating in his life and that God wouldn't fail him this time, now that his finest hour had arrived. With a hard heave, he pulled the door open and exposed himself to the dark avenue that was sparsely dotted with drunk Union soldiers both laughing and stumbling about with the local women from Old Chauncey's whorehouse.

The door's wide swing and loud squeal immediately awoke the guards on either side of it, but by this time, Dallas had whipped the reins, and his horse flew down the main avenue heading west towards the town's limits where he hoped to lose the army in the dust the wagon created. And as he rode, he heard the soldiers by the warehouse shouting curses in the darkness. On either side of him the closed shops and the lightly-peopled saloon flew past. The horse madly sprinted by the stumbling soldiers who looked back to wonder what the shouting was all about. He passed the stone-built Town Hall, dark and empty in the moonlight, and all about the town he heard the clamoring and the shouting that ensued, as they slowly reawaked from their drunkenness and slumber. The entire town sprung back to life in hot pursuit of him and his wagon. He soon heard other horses galloping in the far distance behind him, the Union soldiers now on full alert.

When musket fire broke the still and once-silent night further down the long half-mile of road he had to go, he noticed how the high wall of forest at the town's outer edge stirred with small ovals of flame that weaved in and out of the trees. As shots were fired behind him, he suddenly heard the cry of a bugle down the road in front of him. Out through the dense wall of forest came the Confederate army. They had secretly slipped through the trees and descended upon the small town from where Dallas was heading. A row of gray-clad soldiers blocked the route in front of him. The Union army closed in on him from behind.

He knew he needed to slip a little—slip through the two lines like a fish chased by two sharks, slippery like an eel or a swordfish that tries to avoid its predators. He immediately yanked the horse's reigns and steered his wagon of supplies southward, flying at full speed through the gauntlet that both armies now forced him to ride. His horse found an opening in the wide field on both sides of the road, and his horse galloped through it. The rough terrain, however, dashed half of his supplies to the ground. And suddenly the bullets from both the advancing Confederacy to one side and the pursuing Union army on the other hit his wagon and sent even more of his supplies into the tall grass. Nevertheless, he continued to beat the reigns of his horse, as he noticed that both armies weren't necessarily shooting at each other but were instead shooting at him. He heard bullets whizzing by his head until two shots hit him directly in the back. His hands were paralyzed as a result of these direct hits. He was unable to control the reigns of his horse any longer. He suddenly lost control. His body shook and jostled in the saddle. Another shot then hit him in the shoulder. He quickly lost his balance on his horse and went tumbling to the ground below. He rolled for a few feet in the thicket of tall grass. There was no escape anymore. The supplies on the back of his wagon were now scattered along the trail he had blazed through the field. He could only hear the ceaseless firing of muskets and cannons, charging the moonlit air with the destruction he so mightily tried to outwit.

As the night sky flared and quaked amidst this melee of bullets, bugle calls, and shouts of soldiers engaged in the never ending cycles of war, Dallas Moonbeam crawled through the tall grass, his clothes soaked with his own blood. And through the grass amidst the flashes and sparks of momentary brilliance, he landed his sights on a ghostly woman in a long, flowing nightgown ahead of him. She peacefully observed the ensuing battle between the North and South as though watching a parade from a distance. In the hazy and fuzzy haloes of light the artillery had soon made, Dallas recognized the woman as his wife. She smiled down to him as he crawled towards her. He crawled as close as he possibly could in the hopes of avoiding his own death through her mysterious protection.

"I'm sorry, darling," he said as she bent down to receive him. "You were right, and I was wrong. You were right all along about me. I just wasn't good enough. I never listened to you, and I'm sorry."

She smiled from her steep height above him, and by the look of her sweet smile, he knew she had forgiven him for all of his shortcomings. Dallas Moonbeam then clutched at his heart and died in the field as many more soldiers did that very night.

A MEETING WITH DR. FITZHUME

I had been studying the importance of having choices in life for some time now, and as a young student at the college, a little too ambitious and a little too naïve, I had been called in by one of the older professors in the political science department who somehow thought that my latest paper on voting behavior had some potential within the broader scope of political theory.

Political theory, quite plainly, is the science of creating different political worlds, or models, if you will, of political systems that are both practical in their application and also predictable in that they ought to follow the direction of a society's movement. The more practical and predictable any given model of society is, the more palatable, and therefore, the more successful and attractive these models become, mainly to a group of venerable and finicky intellectuals and politicos whose job it is to pick and choose among the many theories that are out there vying for attention. While some theories argue for no government at all, other theories argue that all property rights ought to be owned and managed by a strong centralized government that dictates the daily lives of the masses. Some theories even walk the fine line between these two extremes and hope to persuade its readers that a balance is sorely needed in the perpetual shift between less government on one end and more government on the other. In fact, it is this cold civil war that has become the hallmark of our own American political system and the manner in which we are shaped by its methods of governance.

As I sat down across from this professor, Dr. Fitzhume his name, I noticed that he looked a bit more pale and sickly than when I had seen him last. The thin strands of his lightning white hair stood on end, and the deep wrinkles and creases cutting into his face had fossilized almost every facial expression he had ever used. It made me consider that he may have had mixed and varied reactions to the theories he had studied in the vast libraries of books he had read, and that lately he had been spending his twilight years pondering all he had learned over the course of his thirty-year tenure at the college.

His office was lined with books in mahogany bookcases, many of them ancient volumes, the subtle colors of the mahogany weighted down by a heavy dust that seemed to be ubiquitous and born out of the air. I could see these fine, white particles dance and wave in a single stream of light that cut through the one small window the department allotted him. He kept an old-fashioned typewriter on his desk, and his fingertips, calloused and swollen with sores, revealed the many years he had spent banging away on its stubborn, oval keys. The thudding taps of block letters on thick, flaky paper were now part of his inner world, a sound following him wherever he went.

I also noticed my latest paper of voting behavior tucked beneath the base of his green banker's lamp. Apparently he had read my paper and was poised to impart his thoughts on it. He reclined in his leather chair, taking my paper into his bone-stricken hands and licking his fingers before peeling back each page. It seemed as though he struggled to remember what our meeting was about.

"Yes, yes, yes," he said, "you certainly are one of our more promising students. I recall your last paper that specifically stated that the choices laid at our feet are more plentiful now than ever before, is that right?"

"Yes, professor," I said nervously.

"Well then, when I was a young, handsome scholar like yourself, I too thought that the world was full of amazing possibilities. They even gave me a few awards for proving that these possibilities existed, and while I discovered hordes of complicated equations and exotic philosophies to prove that these fantastic choices are all around us, just waiting to be plucked like apples from the devil's tree, I've learned over the years that, in life, we only really have four choices to choose from."

I chuckled at this, but apparently Dr. Fitzhume didn't see the humor in his statement.

"In other words, you are missing the bigger picture," he said, as his frail body arched across his desk and slid the paper back to me. "When you leave this college you will be confronted with only four choices, and these four choices represent the four types of people you will soon become. These choices are a direct consequence of this grand, antiquated, and problematic civilization of ours."

"I don't understand," I said in response.

"Oh, I know you don't, which is why I'll explain my simple theory to you in the short time we have left together. Again, because we have four different choices, these choices are mere reflections of the four types of people who inhabit this society of ours, as great as it is and also as limited as it is. Let's take the first choice, or more appropriately put, the first type of person you will inevitably become."

"Okay," I said, swallowing difficultly.

"The first choice you have is to be a strong and fiercely moral being. You take whatever knowledge you have collected from the few moral texts that your parents and your grandparents had read, and for every problem or issue our society faces, there usually is a set of very simple solutions to work with. The moral, upright being is usually the type of person who sees everything as a black and white issue, as there are very few gray areas in anything. They are also quite arrogant and abrupt, as they tend to believe that the stronger they are, when it comes to both numbers and muscle, then the greater their abilities will be to control and direct life's unrelenting uncertainties. They have very little tolerance for others and will see only those of their own ilk as allies in their quest to dominate the spaces and materials they had once inherited from their generous forefathers, until, of course, they have no more room left on their farms and plantations and decide at their convenience to break treaties and expand, conquer, and enslave.

"The more intelligent of this type of person does most of the planning, and so they take most of the profit when they send the children of other families off to war in order to plunder whatever treasures they need. And while these profiteers convince the rest of society that such an imperialism is based on just causes, many of our citizens are so shocked and awed by their unbending will that they are usually forced to comply with whatever cruel and unusual methods they use. This, in turn, keeps the average citizen safe from the thugs these profiteers hire to defend—not the rest of society—but mainly those planners who reap the profits in the first place. And again, while some of these planners and profiteers have some glint of wit in their sparkling eyes, it's a shame to say that those who benefit from this type of perversion will use fear and coercion to enforce their particular brand of what may or may not be their intelligent design onto the three other types of people who must either fight back against them or flee to distant shores. Whatever advances their intentions becomes the right, the good, the just, and the intelligent, as their planning almost always mimics the few books, scholarly or otherwise, that miraculously define life's unending complexities in a few short volumes.

"And while most of them are cautious and forthright in their daily lives, they usually stick to what they know to be true while hoisting up pictures of the evil cartoon figures they want the rest of us to destroy. And while these types of persons are generally the products of the union of two carnivorous Neanderthals somewhere down their nativist line, their way of going about things are relatively harmless when compared to the underhandedness exhibited by the second type of creature I'll discuss next. At least this first type is more direct and honest in his cannibalism, while the second type smiles at you happily before sinking his or her fangs deep into your neck.

"This second type of creature is usually raised as a spoiled brat, and in his or her younger years of intense wanting, this person is then abused in some way by the very people he or she loves. He is then unsure about how to survive or in what direction he should go. At first, the creature is lost and confused, only to dabble in many different intellectual and artistic pursuits. As he gets older, he calls this confusion "open mindedness" and thinks himself smart, highly sophisticated, or imbued with a futuristic prescience, and soon this person joins other free-spirited free-thinkers who in unison complain about and criticize anyone who doesn't eagerly volunteer to live in the castles they have erected high in the sky. They can't live in these castles themselves, so they'll convince young students like yourself to live in them instead, and when they turn you insane with all of their complaining and arguing, all of their bitterness, darkness, and cynicism, all of their lofty talk directed at undermining the cruelty of the world, you then realize that their visions have no practical grounding in any reality other than their own. They then realize that those very castles they've built have all burned to the ground by the few Neanderthals whose duty it is to light the fuse whenever their chatter, gossip, and debauchery become too irritating to bear.

"And from the ashes of their fantasies, they learn to confront a reality they can't for the life of them stomach. They then feed off of your money, your materials, your good nature, and your charity if only to bite the hands that feed them. They then dust off the blueprints of these same flimsy castles once again, as these castles are the sum of their passions and ambitions.

"And just like the many dangerous parasites we find in brutal nature, this type of person then stabs you in the back when you least expect it, sucking your blood while developing some new answer to the riddle of life, or putting forth some new, imaginary theory that puzzles most everyone else. They then preach the high value of their new alternative and all-natural lifestyles to you, as it ends up costing you three times as much at any store check-out counter. And when you refuse to eat what they want you to eat, don't clothe yourself with whatever chic fashion they want you to wear, and don't think like they do, they then inject your life with the same poisonous cocktail of bitterness and cynicism that rules out any other possibility.

"It should be noted here that this second type of creature is the fierce enemy of the first, only these second free-thinking and left-leaning types may indeed hate you more than they hate themselves, and thus the lot of them complain and vilify anything that smells of righteousness while selling their ideas and wares to the beautiful Neanderthals they secretly despise. They even sing symphonies of cacophonous anger and complaint amongst themselves but end up cowering before the very people towards which their anger is aimed. It's no wonder why Plato wanted these types of people expelled from the city gates, as they neither have the constitution nor the nobility of character to confront the source of their problems. Their main function is to bleed you dry, so that you too can be one of them and join in on telling your friends and family how they should improve their lives while you are nowhere close to improving yours. They like to call this "being aware and informed," or they hide their true intentions behind "the public's right to know." And in the process they burrow their "open-mindedness" deep within your flesh. At least you will remain open-minded long enough to discover interesting and creative ways to repel them after your blood has been gorged by their plump, sated bodies.

"But wait, don't leave!" said Dr. Fitzhume. "There's more! Sandwiched between these unimaginative realists and impractical idealists, between the Neanderthal ape and the ornamented parasite, we find the third type of creature who conforms to the thoughts and ideas of whichever side dominates the day. When among Neanderthals, this third type will say he is a Neanderthal, and when dining with the parasites who dream of their castles, he will be the first to say that he too is an architect of them. This third type survives only by following the latest trends and has no allegiances to any political thought, simply because their spines are not hardened enough to believe in anything substantive. Nor do they have the wits to investigate these thoughts and ideas for themselves, and so these changelings are always shifting and altering their true colors to conform to whatever trend or idea the first two dominant creatures force-feed them. If everyone is buying Hummers from the Neanderthals that week, let's say, then he too will buy a Hummer, only to ditch this costly, gas-guzzling vehicle for a Hybrid vehicle when the parasites nearby get anxious the very next day.

"You can say that this third type of person walks a fine line or travels the length of a sharp razor, vacillating between the first and second types of creatures whenever he or she is pushed one way or the other. They remain silent and cautious and jump on only when others have jumped on. They also represent a paradox that drags the weakest of them into lunacy and the happiest of them into drunkenness. They are both happy and sad, responsible and irresponsible, assiduous and lazy. The paradox within them ultimately integrates over time to form that animal who acts only when it is in his or her self-interest to do so. And this rational self-interest is both the pleasure and the pain of their existence. He is moral when everyone else acts morally, and a sinner when everyone else sins, and so silently monitors the pendulum that sways from left to right, and right to left.

"Interestingly enough, the silence and the scheming calculations of this third type of creature can often turn inward, and instead of being conformists who find healthy balances and equilibria between the brute Neanderthal and the blood-sucking parasite, they are still objective enough, or in other cases lame enough, to assert their full non-cooperation against this system that forces us to become one of the three types of creatures affore-mentioned.

"This fourth type of creature, which is an off-shoot of the third, is known as the outcast, the pariah, the misfit, the loner, or the scapegoat. This type of creature understands that he will soon be shaped and molded by the machinery that pinches and narrows his existence as time goes by, and through his awkward understanding of the system of things he helplessly tries to avoid being body-snatched by the other three types of people who are always actively recruiting. This fourth type often wanders alone and lost, vulnerable and marginalized, running from the social engineers and thought-shaping factories that pump out a pro-active, self-interested, and aggressive citizenry.

"And if it happens to be a man or a woman who is unable to become one of the first three types, mostly due to some disability or weakness or confusion or psychological disfigurement, then he is looked upon by others as weird or strange or is seen as the type of person that is better off separated, ignored, and rejected. This person is the stranger cackling in the alleyway and taking up valuable space when he is rudely told to move it to the next block, because he can't sleep there. His condition plunges him into a darkness and despair so visceral that when he discovers his society has no use for him, he begins his terrible war against the paranoid suspicion that he too will be culled from the population when the first three types of creatures discover that he is not one of them. He or she knows way too much for his or her own good and so must always look for an escape, as the manufacturing process that shapes and moulds his very being spits him out prematurely for the rest of the world to chew up, as he is unable to withstand the severity of such a rigid socialization.

"So there you have it, young scholar, there you have it. Out of infinite possibilities we come to know only four, and these four choices will keep you awake in the darkness as you grope for answers and try to defy your fate."

"And what about you, Dr. Fitzhume?" I asked angrily. "Which one of the four creatures is you? The ape, the parasite, the chameleon, or the skunk?"

"It's funny you ask me that, and this is the best answer I can give you. As we move through life's machinery, or as we grow older over time, we discard our own objectivity and cling hard to the ideas and beliefs that are beneficial only to ourselves and to our own survival. Having lost this objectivity a long time ago, I am only what you see me as being. I am defined, not by what I think I am, but by how others perceive me to be. And since I have determined that there are four types of people in this society that we inevitably become, it must also be clear and plain that I am also one of these four types of creatures who also has no idea which one of the four he is. That, my young friend, is for you to determine, because I have lost the capacity to see which one of these creatures I am."

"I heard his dark laughter echo through the hallway of the department building soon after I fled from his shadowy office. When I got to the bathroom, I threw my paper on voting behavior into the trash can by the door. My limp body, hot and feverish in one of the bathroom stalls, then kneeled against the cold porcelain of the toilet bowl and vomited up every word Dr. Fitzhume had said to me.

A MOTHER AND HER SON

As her ten-year old son slept soundly in the cot next to hers, she awoke with a start in the cold sweat of the dark desert night only to have a vague premonition, or perhaps it was an hallucination, of a shiny, black cobra slithering its way through an opening in the tent. Her bed under a draping white canvas burned as hot as a prison cell in summertime as she saw the snake's black-scaled body slide underneath her cot. By then she had understood that the snake had found a new home beneath her and that the only way to do away with it was to wake her son and ask him to kill it. Only then would it no longer interfere with the bliss of the otherwise serene life they shared together.

But before she could ask this of him, she considered that perhaps her own fears towards the snake were the greater problem and not the snake itself. Perhaps she shouldn't be so afraid of a slinking beast she couldn't control. Maybe she should wait patiently until it decided to slither back to the desert on its own.

She tried for hours to sleep that night but continued to hear it coil and uncoil, rattle and hiss intermittently, as though it had slid back out into the open, its slick body on the verge of slipping through one of the looping ridges in her tangled bed-sheets. At one point she even felt the reptile's forked tongue probe her soft brown cheeks with all of the slime and wetness of a diseased French kiss, and when the slithering of its body and the rattling of its tail became too much to bear, she disentangled herself from the sheets and reached over to her son who slept soundly on the next cot.

She loved her boy deeply and wanted nothing more but for him to rest before the laborers took him to the oil fields later that morning. Yet the snake continued to fester in the sand beneath her, and images of bloody snakebites up and down the length of her arms provided enough incentive for her to poke the boy's back until he too awoke from the snake's loud hisses.

Her son then looked at her with all of the timidity innocence usually gives a boy at such a tender age, and he trembled at the thought of venturing underneath his mother's cot to quell what had threatened them. But his mother had been suffering all night as a result of the snake's stubborness, and while the boy certainly didn't want to fight this poisonous creature, he understood that he must fight it in order to save his mother's flesh from its razor-sharp fangs. The boy took one look at her suffering, and suddenly no other option existed but to do battle with the snake. With nothing but a bed-sheet tied around his waist, he crawled underneath his mother's cot to where he immediately confronted the opacity of the cobra's milk-white eyes scanning him through the darkness, its fangs dripping wet with bone-yellow venom.

As his body vanished beneath the bed, the mother prayed and prayed for the safety of her only child. She wailed and chanted old ghazals in the traditions of her ancestors and promised to be a better mother to him, should he emerge from the darkness alive. She heard his body struggling in the sand, the snake's coiled tail rattling uncontrollably, and the ubiquitous hissing as it spit back its corrosive venom in its own defense. She cried long, soft tears, gnashed her teeth, and pulled out her hair in anger, fear, and regret. At one point she covered her head with pillows, if only to dampen the sounds of the hissing, spitting, and struggling that soon became a waking nightmare that slowly chewed on the fragile fibers of her soul. The cot then quaked, its steel frame banging frantically against the wall, until suddenly, all became quiet and eerily still.

The tired body of her son soon crawled out from under the cot, his hair caked in dirt, his back and spine poked with fresh bloody holes, his joints swollen, and his skin febrile with sweat. There was no more hissing or rattling. Nothing could be heard but the cascading desert wind outside. Her son slowly crawled back to his side of the room. He lay on his back as his mother rushed to his side to check if he were still alive.

He seemed to be half-sleeping or in some sort of trance. He didn't move much. He lightly breathed in and out, in and out, his thin eyelids closed and his muscles trembling. His mother then called his name softly and even went so far as to shake him a little. And when the boy finally awoke, his two opaque and milk-marbled eyes beamed at his horrified mother who gasped at the sharp, white fangs that filled the spaces where his teeth should have normally been. His fangs dripped with the blood of a cobra, and with his forked tongue he hissed, "Yes, mother, I killed the snake. I finally killed the snake."

ALMOST HOME

He walked into the bar on a Tuesday night with the few, wayward wisps of hair at the sides of his scalp dripping wet from a rain that pounded the city streets and soaked his clothes straight through to his skin. The old regulars were there, milking their drinks, but the bar lacked the vitality of the younger college crowd that sometimes overran the place, and there was no doubt that an immediate beer or two would enliven the otherwise dull mood that had settled over the regulars like a thin shroud.

The few who were there sat on the other side of the bar and nodded their heads to deliver a tacit greeting, but they soon went about the business of watching one of the many television screens that showed the infield of Yankees Stadium with a green tarp and puddles of water over it as well as the never-ending reruns of the first few innings. It was too early in the season for anything exciting, and the game was just one of the many the Yankees were losing that month. He figured the regulars would have rather watched the delay than be at home with their wives, and he smiled a little knowing that the loneliness of being a bachelor was much better than the irritation of being married, although the jury was still out on that one.

After he shook himself dry and hung up his sports jacket, the two girls working the bar took their time putting his usual pint of beer in front of him. They didn't say hello but only did their duty before returning to where the regulars were. He had always liked the blonde barmaid, Lisa her name, and she avoided him in favor of the middle-aged men on the other side of the bar. He had tried flirting with her once before, but it was something she just couldn't take. There was scorn and disdain for him in her pretty blue eyes, and he had little idea what put these things there. Perhaps it was the way he talked or just the look of his portly body that she didn't like. It never occurred to him that she may have liked him better had he not gotten drunk every night and closed the place down with an insult or two before leaving. He hated being ignored, certainly, but after all, he did think of himself as a good man, only that he wasn't good enough for reasons only the truly beautiful knew.

Granted that his job in customer service didn't pay very much, and his Japanese import looked like shit most of the time, but Lisa could have at least been sophisticated enough to notice the tenderness behind his eyes or at least the music beneath his serious talk, and it seemed to him that women generally stayed away no matter how hard he pushed them.

There was something about him they didn't like, some sort of deficiency they refused to accept, and instead of being nice around him, they usually just filled his beer, took his money, and insulted him behind his back, or at least that's what he thought they did. And the regulars, well, they were just losers all the same who talked about things so trivial as to make the barmaids giggle like girls, and it didn't make much sense to him why he couldn't be as superficial as they were. He instead preferred politics and all sorts of ponderous intellectual rubbish to which the women in the bar had a fast aversion.

No one liked politics and religion with their beer, but for some reason it was something he couldn't let go of, and on a few nights when he would corral one of the young college kids sitting on the next barstool over and talked about the possibility of a draft for the war spreading in the Middle East, the kids would politely listen to him, sure, but the talk immediately got the attention of the barmaids who sometimes had the gall to yell at him for what they considered to be his unpatriotic leanings. They were, after all, fierce patriots, and he a liberal intellectual, and that didn't sit too well with anyone at the bar. He had faith that they would one day know what he was talking about, but until then his words fell upon deaf ears, kind of like Noah before the flood, and they were sorry souls if they didn't see such a thing coming. But that still didn't change his status as a bachelor that night. And in order to get himself back on Lisa's good side, he decided not to engage in any of his political and philosophical ramblings for the time being. He wanted Lisa to like him after all and tried to get in a few words edgewise as she put the beer in front of him.

He said, "you're looking mighty nice tonight, Lisa," to which she gave a curt little smile. The next time she came over, he said, "how about I take you out after your shift," but she wasn't having any of it. She poured him the beer and then went to the other side of the bar to chat with those whom she thought would win the game of life with their smooth talk of the popular trends that still managed to captivate the young and the beautiful.

He had showed up at the bar alone that night, and perhaps this is what Lisa didn't like about him. He remembered when she used to fawn all over him during his first few months there, but then his usual sweetness took a turn for the worse when the war came, and after a week or so of heavy drinking something within him became fascinated by the bloodshed overseas. For a while he wouldn't shut up about it. His once good nature turned to pessimism and cynicism, and this, he figured, was one of the reasons why the regulars didn't like him anymore.

He was a man of principle after all, and when Lisa figured this out, she quickly did an about-face and never really returned to his side of the bar. He figured some people were that way and couldn't be helped. Yet he wanted to be liked again by the people assembled there, and maybe for once they'd forgive him for the sorry ass he had become and slowly allow him back into their quaint little social circle that had formed ever since his negativity took hold. It seemed that nothing could arrest their good spirits, no matter how hard he tried, and somehow he would have to try to win them over again.

But being a single man fast approaching middle age didn't attract too many women into his corner. The others must have noticed how lonely he looked, how pitiful and sad he looked, and one would think that this would merit some kind of attention from the barmaids working the night shift, but it got him the exact opposite. They never said anything to him directly, and there was always the overpowering suggestion that he should leave and never come back. Every bar needed a scapegoat, or at least someone who could keep their conversations going if only to give their own spite something to chew on, and he was the one they had selected that month. Maybe he did hit on Lisa too much, but it was only because he thought her pretty, and getting too drunk over her meant that in some small way he did, in fact, love her.

She should have seen that he loved her, he thought, as a sipped his beer. Going to the place night after night became a punishment, a battle to be won, and he wouldn't stop until they all respected him for his knowledge on the subject of war. The war, though, never came up unless he was drunk enough to bring it up. No one liked a spoiled-sport. People liked him more when he got along, and to be so left out and on the outside of everything stung bitterly, especially when young Lisa, a twit as far as he knew, smiled upon those who made her laugh instead of think about the bigger picture, which he hoped one day would include him.

He finished off his pint of beer and thundered out of the place thinking they would miss his company. The rain darted down as menacingly as before, and he drove off a little drunk, making sure to keep on his side of the road. He soon found himself in his studio apartment with very little to do but watch television, a bland and monotonous universe of electronic nothingness that filled an intimate need, not to know more about anything in particular, but to be closer to the beauty and good fortune that had blessed the fictional characters on the screen. He felt a little less lonely with the television on, as it brought women who looked like Lisa into his living room. Old laundry had been sitting in small piles on the floor, and small, irritating crumbs from a turkey sandwich he ate at dinnertime stuck to the back of his thighs as he lay on his couch flipping through channels.

It wasn't long before he realized that television no longer filled the void but only served as something to get angry over. He tried reading a newsletter his company sent him by mail, but this only put him to sleep for a few hours. He awoke in the middle of the night to a captivating silence that normally would have demanded the ongoing chatter of the television but instead gave him an awkward feeling that he could do nothing else with himself but wait his boredom out until morning. Yet he preferred the fluidity of night, a time when the earth seemed to stand still and the quietude of the city streets tranquilized whatever anxieties the daylight brought with it.

The window in his studio offered a view of a narrow alleyway two-stories down where several cars slumbered, and this, he thought, must have been part of his overall problem. Like a rat he was caged in and didn't have the capacity to gnaw his way out. His aunt who lived about an hour away suggested that he find a new hobby, but hobbies sucked away time and too much money, and anything that did interest him, aside from war and politics, only held him for a few days. He usually abandoned these new hobbies and reverted to the sedentary lifestyle that had been with him since childhood. He also thought of traveling to some far-off island, but winced at the sight of himself in a bathing suit and so put off the idea of such an adventure until he had lost enough weight to look good without a shirt on. Unfortunately, he only put on more weight by drinking beer every night after work, thus ruining his plans.

He again tried reading the newsletter but was overwhelmed by the nighttime silence. It didn't put him to sleep a second time around but only created this awkward feeling that his life should be much more, if only he had a good woman.

And with a good woman perhaps his life would have been much different, or so his thinking went. Perhaps he had been too busy making a man out of himself by talking the way he did at the bar. He only acted a little rough around the edges because he figured that that's what women wanted—the hero on the movie screen who saves the maiden in distress—and because he could never live up to these heroes, who always seemed to win the fair maiden's love, he got his revenge by eating too much red meat and too many French fries, hoping to combat the fascism and poison of such fairy tales. From childhood he noticed that the women loved these heroes, no matter the era, and that he would be the first to make the ugly beautiful by being a hero himself, as this was his ultimate ambition.

But being so revolutionary in his approach brought him a special kind of loneliness he couldn't shake, and while reading the last lines of the company newsletter, while craving the steady stream of chatter another round of television-watching would provide, he instead picked up an old magazine he kept around the house just in case he needed it.

A young stripper with long brunette curls and a see-through tank-top graced the cover of the magazine. Her fishnet stockings and black leather miniskirt provided some relief, but not enough to shoo away his loneliness. Her legs were long, and her chest abundant, and he couldn't mistake the power of her image, even though it was something he wanted to be deprogrammed of. His plump fingers caressed the spaces of skin the glossy magazine cover permitted him, and while doing so, he came to the firm conclusion that it was time he take some sort of action, or else continue living like a rat in cage. He couldn't stand thinking about it anymore, and he quickly rifled through the magazine to find a list of classifieds in the back.

He found the section that read 'adult services,' and with careful deliberation read each of these ads that offered a sexual experience without actually saying that sex would be performed. There were Asian women available, two for the price of one, exotic Russian beauties who looked like runway models but barely spoke a word of English, and big-busty women with their measurements printed in bold typeface, their names similar to the girls he wanted in high school but was always too afraid to ask. There were many possibilities, even ads for a she-male and a dominatrix, but he found these ads to be too outlandish if not distasteful. What he really wanted was a girl like Lisa, and she would be hard to find among the names of women listed in the classifieds.

Then came an entirely different rationale for making the call, and it concerned his needs as a man. It went along the lines that a man needs sex, because he is, in fact, an animal in many respects, and without sex he would surely perish and do damage to himself. Having sex, then, is as natural as eating food or drinking beer, and because the women in his life, like Lisa, cut him off from this essential activity, he should then avoid becoming something unnatural by conforming to his own nature as a natural man. A man hungered in this respect, and to deny him would be to repress him. Repression would then lead him to violence or some other deviance that would stall his evolutionary development and keep him a child. A child certainly can't survive the bitter city streets like an adult can, so he better call a woman and have her come right over if only to cheat death and affirm his own life. To deny him sex would be to deny him life, and since the women somehow stayed away from him no matter how hard he tried to improve himself, paying for the service would have to suffice, even though it was a last resort. And like tuning up an engine that needs to perform better, so sex is that lubricant that makes the engine run up to standard.

He had heard many times before the arguments used against hiring women for this kind of service. The argument went that these women are usually of the abused and victimized sort who really don't want to have sex with strangers but must do so in order to survive themselves. These women are the immigrants sold into slavery by underworld crime bosses, or women so terribly abused in childhood that they must prostitute themselves in order to bolster an otherwise shattered self-esteem, yes, he had heard all of these arguments before. The women only get a percentage of what the Johns pay them, as the rest would go on to their abusive pimps, and maybe he should steer clear from taking advantage of these young and impoverished souls. He knew better than to give into lust at that hour. Neither did he want to drain his bank account and plunder the couple of the nicely-sized paychecks that took over a week to clear. He knew it was wrong, but couldn't stop the urge. He needed a woman right then and there, no exceptions, as this one time would somehow make up for all the times Lisa had ignored him at the bar. There was really no other choice.

Finally he made the phone call, dialing slowly and hoping not to feel too embarrassed when discussing such an intimate proposal with a complete stranger on the other end.

"May I help you?" said the operator, a female.

He immediately hung up the phone in embarrassment. He waited a minute or two and then tried again.

"Hello, may I help you?" said the same operator.

"Hello," he sputtered, "I would like a date for the evening. I've never done this sort of thing before, so I hope—"

"Don't sweat it sweetheart," she said. "What type of girl would you like?"

"Oh, just any girl, I suppose."

"Well, we have black, Hispanic, Asian, and white."

He wanted to say 'white' here, as that's the type he preferred, but he knew he should remain open and balanced about wanting only a white woman, in keeping with his 'equal opportunity' stance on the matter, although in this case it was a perversion of that stance.

"Anyone would be fine, but if you have a white woman, I'll take her."

"I have a white woman. She's 5'4" with brown hair and hazel eyes, 34C-24-36, and her name is Randy."

"That sounds fine," he said nervously. "How much does it cost?"

He surrendered his credit card information to the operator, and she promised to call back after the information had been verified. He hung up the phone and noticed that his palms were sweating. The operator called back after he waited by the phone for a couple of minutes. He gave her the directions to his studio and then was told the driver would call him when he was near.

"It'll be about a half hour," she said.

When he hung up the phone, he could scarcely believe that the process of ordering a woman was as simple and hassle-free as ordering his favorite dish at the take-out Chinese place down the block. He also couldn't believe he didn't make the call sooner. He found that waiting for Randy was incredibly difficult, and he found himself pacing in his room, struggling to form a mental picture of what she looked like. He imagined someone in lingerie underneath a trench coat, as it was still pouring buckets outside, and he imagined taking her in his bed and fulfilling every erotic desire imaginable, as it had been ages since he'd been with a woman. In fact, he was comforted by the fact that he lusted for her. His lust proved, above all else, that he was indeed a heterosexual man, a wild beast who couldn't be restrained, and not some freak everyone slandered at the bar. Randy would give his manhood back to him, and although there were moral implications involved with paying a young woman for sex, comforting the raging throb inside of him that would otherwise lead him to kill an innocent man on the street outweighed such implications. In fact, he was taking the high road on this one, and if a man couldn't have a women due in part to his natural ugliness or lack of a higher paying job, then paying her for the service was the next best thing. And so his thinking went.

As the minutes slowly passed, he tried to find something to occupy the time. He watched television a little, but only found the programs he had been used to watching at such a late hour both bland and vapid. Nothing compared to the real thing, he figured, and yes, he deserved at least one hour of happiness in his life. He would never be successful at anything other than making sure his boss didn't fire him, although he had at one time tried to get promoted, or at least as a younger man he had dreams and ambitions so wild as to merit their blundering pursuit. But success in the conventional sense, much like the success of those he constantly watched on television and the ones he read about in the glossy magazines, he would never achieve. A man needed to slide once in while, or come to terms with his own ugliness every now and then, in order to feel that he's really alive. If he flirted with a little danger now, he wouldn't have to be consumed by it later. There were so many reasons why this was the right thing to do, and from all angles of his conscience, this was the best thing he could do for humanity at the present.

His pacing became furious, and every few moments or so he glanced at the digital clock above his microwave. He thought about having a drink or something to eat, but his heart was racing now, his impatience driving him to lie on his sofa bed and sink his head deep within his pillows and grind his teeth at his maddening impatience. He thought of calling the service again, just to remind them that they had a desperate client waiting for a girl, but he didn't want to ruffle any feathers his first time out there. Better to keep it casual and discreet, as they may not deliver her due to his agony.

The phone rang after he had given up all hope. His heart leapt from his chest, and the call just may have been the greatest gift the Gods had bestowed upon him during his time spent alone in his cruddy apartment. He picked the phone up slowly, so as not to disconnect the call accidentally.

"Hello, we're on the highway now," said a rugged man's voice in broken English. "Can you tell me how to get to you, because we're lost right now."

He assumed the guy was from Eastern Europe or somewhere close to there, but he carefully gave him directions on how to get to his apartment from the highway they were on. To his disappointment, they were by no means close, and the driver promised to call him back once they hit city limits. And once again he was forced into waiting. It something that would drive him to drink, but he refrained and decided instead to sweat it out and build up whatever reserve of desire lurked inside of him. It took nearly an hour before the driver called him again, and he had almost fallen asleep, only to wake up to the surprise of the phone call.

"I'm in the city," said the driver.

"Where?"

"On Main Street and Mercer," he replied.

"Good. I'm just a block from there," and he gave him further directions.

It was not long before the downstairs buzzer rang. It was close to three in the morning, and the rain had slowed to steady drizzle. He buzzed them in, and after a couple of minutes he heard loud talking in the hallway, something that might disturb his neighbors, but at this point he didn't care very much. He opened the door to a tall, meaty figure smoking a cigarette and behind him a brown-skinned woman of average height wrapped in a faux fur coat. It wasn't the Randy he expected, but he still found her somewhat attractive. She had long brown hair and hazel eyes like the operator said, but she was by no means white. She looked Hispanic or Latina, and she was a little under the weather. She smiled coyly, and he smiled back.

The driver took a seat on his sofa bed and asked for an ashtray. He gave him a plastic cup filled with water in lieu of one. The driver carried a metal clipboard, and he began the painstaking process of filling out the paperwork required for a credit card transaction. He assumed the driver worked with the mob or was some hit man when he wasn't busy driving these young girls all over the area, but he nervously handed over his credit card anyway and hoped he wouldn't charge anything on it fraudulently. He remembered watching a news segment on identity theft and cringed at the idea of surrendering the number, but he did so, because he was tired of waiting and wanted the young girl in his bed as soon as possible. He didn't have the patience any longer to entertain the worst case scenario. The driver also asked him for his drivers license, and he readily surrendered that as well. He then signed a couple of innocuous forms. All in all, it took about ten or fifteen minutes for the driver to etch his credit card onto a blank transaction slip, and at one point he was about to lose his cool due to his uncontrollable impatience, but he persevered, and soon the immigrant driver was gone, leaving dank cigarette smoke in his place.

Randy, who had by this time seated herself on the other side of the sofa bed, got up and locked the door. They were all alone now, and he couldn't have felt more relieved. She doffed her faux fur coat. She wore a white, skimpy spandex top that clung to her waif-like curves along with a short leather mini-skirt that barely concealed what hid directly beneath it. He was overwhelmed by the trashiness of her clothing, as this was a woman he could easily see himself fucking in some back alley on any given urban street. She turned him on her clothes were so tight, and she casually took a tour of his small studio, studying some of the pictures on the wall and the old paperbacks on his bookshelf.

"So where are you from," he asked, relieved that the driver was gone.

"I live nearby," she said. "So, what do you do?"

"I'm in customer service," he said humbly.

"So am I."

She took charge at this point, and when she sat him down on the edge of the sofa bed, she took off her clothes.

"You know, you're kind of handsome."

"Really? You think so?"

"I bet you've had plenty of women."

"Actually quite the opposite is true, unfortunately."

"Well, why don't you take off your clothes."

He undressed in the soft light of the kitchen just a few feet away. He also drew the blinds so that the neighbors across the alleyway wouldn't intrude. It was the last hurdle that separated him from the girl, and as she took hold of his hands and ran them over her chest, he could scarcely believe that he had never before purchased a gift such as this for himself. Her skin was as soft as butter and her scent as sweet as wildflowers in a springtime garden. They fell into the bed together, and after a few short minutes it was all over.

"I do have you for the full hour," he said, after he caught her reaching for her clothes.

"I know, but I only allow you to come once," she explained.

He didn't want her to leave just yet. He wanted to keep her for a while, and suddenly money seemed like the last thing on his mind. It was no object as far as he was concerned. Having her lie in bed with him had to be the most comfortable thing he'd experienced in a very long time, and it was too soon to let her dash off like that.

"What if I wanted you to stay?"

She smiled, kissed his cheek, and whispered, "I'm negotiable," in his ear.

"I want you to stay with me until later tonight," he said to his own astonishment.

"That's a lot of money."

"I have it. I can take an advance on my next paycheck."

"Don't you want to think about it a little more?"

"No. I'm as certain as I'll ever be. I want you to sleep here and then go out with me this evening."

"I'm not going to stop you, but wouldn't it be better if I left after an hour or so and then returned at, let's say, eight this evening?"

"God, you're smart."

"That's because you're thinking with your dick."

"Yes, I see. Okay then, let's do it your way, but you should stay for an hour more and then leave."

She fished her cell phone out of her purse and called the driver downstairs.

"He'll have to come up if you want me for another hour."

He nodded in full agreement, and it wasn't long before the muscled driver knocked on the door again. He did another etching of his credit card, and it didn't really matter at this point how much he spent on the girl. The driver grinned at him lasciviously after he finished and then left the two of them there. They undressed again and lay on the sofa, awkwardly holding each other. He didn't know if he should kiss her or not, as he had learned from an old movie that it was too personal a gesture, so instead he kissed her cheeks and the length of her neck. His body rubbed against her softness, and he couldn't imagine anywhere else in the world he'd rather be. He wanted to run away with her.

"I'm Puerto Rican," she admitted after he had asked, and he couldn't think of a place more perfect for a getaway. "I want to move back there once I've made enough money."

"It's hard in America, no?"

"Very hard," she sighed, "but one day I will make it out of here."

"On my salary I'm pretty much stuck here."

"Oh, my poor baby," she said, kissing him.

"I'd really love to go there one day," he said.

"Puerto Rico? It's a beautiful place, and my family is there."

"What brought you here, by the way?"

He didn't mean to talk of things so personal, but perhaps she would reveal something that would make him believe that she truly liked him, although it must have all been an act on her part. He sensed she was pretending, but he ignored it. He suspended his disbelief, as though the two were star-crossed lovers going their separate ways once the daylight intruded upon their small bed.

"My husband, he's in jail," she said.

"Jail? What for?"

"Murder. He killed a bunch of people in New York."

"I see. Why did he do it?"

"He's a bully, that's why. He used to go to the clubs, and that's where I met him. He killed people over money, and then he kept doing it until they caught him."

"How long is he in jail for?"

"At least twenty or thirty years. I'm leaving him. I'm going where he can't find us."

"Who's 'us?'"

"Me and my two children. We're trying to make enough for plane tickets to Puerto Rico."

"I guess the American dream didn't work out, eh?."

"No, but I'm not bitter about it. Sometimes it doesn't work out."

"You're an incredibly brave woman. Are you running from him, or is it this place?"

"A little of both. I can't seem to survive here."

"Me neither," he said. "It had once been so beautiful. I was having the time of my life. But then it all dried up suddenly."

"Are you married?"

"No. I've been single for a long time now. I never had any children."

"Which is why you called me?"

"Yes. I can no longer stand being alone. I thought I could at one point, but now I realize I was mistaken. If I could, I'd go to Puerto Rico with you."

"You're just saying that."

"No, I'm not. I've never been so frustrated before, and I've never worked so hard for so little. And now I'm frustrated with this place."

"My poor baby," she said again, kissing him.

Her soft skin seemed to envelope the whole of his rough body, and his comfort in it was the closest he had come to divinity while living in his cramped studio. But he was a little afraid of the girl's boyfriend whom he imagined would murder him some day if he ever found out about their affair. He knew he should avoid any emotional attachment to the girl, but as he sensed his extra hour coming to a close, he couldn't help but want her to stay even longer, no matter what the dire financial consequences were. His sense of time was so acute, however, that he pulled away from her instead of taking advantage of the fifteen minutes or so they had left, as that was his nature. He always planned ahead, even to his own detriment.

"So I'll see you tonight?"

"I should come at eight o'clock?"

"Yeah, and wear something nice. We'll be going to a place I know."

She called the driver on her cell phone and said she was coming out. She left him in bed, sheets scented with wildflowers, an indelible reminder of their love-making.

He awoke with a start later that morning. He wiped the sleep from his eyes and casually glanced at the demonic red readout of his alarm clock, which told him that he was yet again late for work. He had been used to taking long showers, but his lateness wouldn't afford him such a luxury. He hastily put on a tie and jacket and sped along the highway with the nervous fear that he would be fired before lunchtime. Luckily his supervisor was at a meeting elsewhere, and so he was spared the humiliation.

His callers were of the rude and repetitive sort, and he must have spent nearly an hour explaining to one customer why her cell phone bill was so high. He knew at the same time that the company had a policy of terminating such calls, even if it meant not solving the customer's problem. After all, there were plenty of South Asians who could do his job just as well, and it wouldn't be long before his supervisor traded him in for one.

When he did get the chance to break for lunch, he felt much better that the supervisor hadn't phoned in that morning to check on him. He wouldn't be fired after all, even though most of his callers threatened that he would, and he blissfully looked forward to an evening out with Randy instead. He now knew what married people looked forward to after hard day's work, and he realized that it was this sort of bliss that gave them the courage to get up in the morning. No man could be great without a good woman behind him, he kept telling himself, and although he thought he was the last person on earth a good woman would want to marry, the evening out with Randy would surely suffice. And maybe she would fall in love with him, and maybe he should leave his job and fly with her to Puerto Rico where he saw themselves lying on a beach and sipping margaritas. Perhaps this was the American dream and not the constant buzz of the call center whose phones rang in his sleep. The good life was always somewhere else.

When five o'clock rolled around, he was happier than Fred Flinstone in the quarry after Mr. Slate blows the whistle. He signed himself out of the call center and drove along the highway listening to self-congratulatory music that hinted at another night of revelry and rebellion, but this time there would be a lovely young woman by his side. Drinking beer was meant for this, he figured, and he had been a fool for not hiring Randy sooner. He got home and immediately called her. She would be over at eight, and their date would continue despite the doubts he had. He took a shower, shaved, and put on a clean shirt. When he found himself in front of the mirror near the kitchen, he agreed with himself that he could look no better. He turned on his stereo and put on some of the same self-congratulatory music, and at the height of his happiness the downstairs buzzer rang.

First the driver entered with a cigarette dangling for the corner of his mouth, followed by Randy who wore a black, halter-top evening dress with a string of pearls around her neck. She looked much too elegant for such a dingy apartment, but the regulars at the bar would be impressed as hell with her, and it would make Lisa jealous enough to be nice for a change. But first came the business of paying her up front, and so it took a good fifteen minutes or so for all the paperwork to be filled out. He put her fee down on his credit card, and it amounted to about a month's salary. He didn't really care at this point. She looked like something he didn't deserve, and it didn't matter that he paid her for this. Once again he suspended his disbelief as though there was magic in the way she looked. He knew that she would be in his bed at the end of the night as well. There was no reason to struggle anymore. He had won the game of life after so many years of trying to play it the honest way.

"So where are we going?" said Randy after the driver left.

He escorted her to his car, and off they went to the bar about ten minutes away. The evening brought with it a splendid breeze that lifted the edges of her dress, and when they got there, he was saddened that she would have to leave at the end of the night. But he put on his best smile anyway and sauntered up to the bar with her in tow. Lisa was at the other end talking with the regulars, and when she saw him with Randy, her eyes lit up. They sat at the bar, and Lisa soon came over and introduced herself and smiled as she got the low-down on the beautiful young woman who fell for the man who had earlier been the butt of all of her bad jokes and snide comments. She liked him after all. Then some of the venerable regulars came over to be introduced, and Randy played along with it. They were impressed indeed, and one of them even patted him on the back and gave him a thumb's up. The regulars asked if they would join them at the other side of the bar, to which she replied, "no thanks. I want him all to myself."

He decided in the middle of his drinking to take Randy to one of the tables away from the bar area if only to give them the impression that what they had together was intimate enough to merit a separate table. They held hands as they walked in front of everyone's gaze, the spotlights shining brilliantly upon them.

"So what do you think?" he asked.

"I think they're very nice," she said.

"Really?"

"Yes, really. You have a very nice life. You're very lucky."

"I'm only lucky because you're with me. You know that don't you?"

She smiled at this.

"I was thinking," he said. "Do you really want to go to Puerto Rico? With me, that is?"

She again smiled and touched his hand.

"I'm serious," he said. "You and me. We can leave tomorrow."

"Oh, if only it were that easy."

"It is that easy. I'll pay for our tickets. It'll be you, me, and your kids would be flying for free."

"You're joking, right?"

"This is no joke. I've never felt this good before, and I want you to run away with me. I have some money in the bank, and I can take the advances from my paycheck, and we can both get the hell out of here. I know you need some time to think about it, but I tell ya, tomorrow we can be in Puerto Rico, with your children too, and we can make something of what we have here. You do like me, don't you?"

"Sure, I do," she said.

"Then, let's go for it."

"But we hardly know each other."

"Trust me. There'll be plenty of time for that."

"I need to make a few phone calls first," she said. "If we're going to fly away, I need to get ready, I guess."

He heaved his portly body across the table and kissed her lips in full view of the regulars, and frankly he didn't care about them anymore. Nor did he care about Lisa who seemed to watch his every move.

"Just give me a moment, okay?" she asked, while holding her cell phone. "The reception is bad in here."

She took her purse with her, and he ordered a bottle of champagne in her absence. Lisa served it chilled in a silver bucket. It was the most expensive champagne in the house, and he thought they deserved nothing but the best. The dream was real all of sudden, and so was Randy. Never in thirty-four years of living could he have imagined that his life would take such a dramatic turn for the better. He had a family to raise now and many moonlit nights on the beaches of Puerto Rico strolling hand-in-hand with his girl as a warm tide tumbles upon their toes in the sand. Never before had his life become filled with so much meaning, and for this great gift he swore to become a better man and forever love the woman who gave him the second chance of becoming the man he really wanted to be.

He must have waited for about half-an-hour before his epiphany brought him back to earth and his impatience rudely kicked in. He carefully got up and walked outside to check on her. When he realized that she had left him there, he didn't go back inside. He simply got in his car and drove off along the empty highway that fed into a dark, foreboding horizon. He was unsure if he would ever return.

AT THE CHELSEA RESTAURANT

My boyfriend and I decided on a late evening dinner down in Chelsea—to a restaurant we know that served an excellent veal scaloppini for me, and for my boyfriend, he would be having the filet mignon, as he hadn't eaten a good cut of steak in a while. We both left our loft around nine o'clock and caught a cab into the heart of Chelsea, not far from the well-known Chelsea Hotel that had been completely restored and remodeled in recent years. The evening was cool and dry with a slight breeze that tickled my cheeks and hair, and I really felt that I had finally arrived at what life was supposed to be about for a recent college graduate—a loving, committed boyfriend, a good job in advertising, a loft in the East Village where we shared our bed, and now a cool evening where we could dress up for a change and walk hand-in-hand down Seventh Avenue. It felt regal to put on a skirt. We could even see a star or two up in the sky despite the tall skyscrapers and many lights that kept the city eternally aglow.

The restaurant, we liked to think, was the perfect place for us. It was the type that had cloth napkins, Spode silverware, a decent wine list, and well-dressed people who were also on the younger side and starting their adult lives just like we were. We would leave the restaurant well before they dimmed the lights, as we no longer drank and danced so much as we did when we were undergrads in college. We had moved on, because it was our disposition to do so. But at night, by the time I'd be cozened up to my boyfriend in bed, the restaurant would attract a more fashionable crowd. But we were fortunate enough to have moved on.

When we had been shown our seats upon entering, we ordered a nice bottle of Italian wine with some bread and olive oil for starters. I then noticed that there was this one man at the middle of the bar who didn't seem to belong there. For one thing, he had a dark complexion, which was somewhat unusual for the restaurant, but not totally outrageous. But what's more, he looked like an immigrant almost, not only because of his foreignness but also because of his clothes. While trying to remain tailored properly to his body, his sports jacket was too tight on him, and therefore ill-fitting. He was an overweight man approaching obesity, and he had this depressed, haggard look on him that in no way matched the ambience of the restaurant. He looked like a character who had just walked off the studio set of an old movie, like a Fatty Arbuckle, an Oliver Hardy, or a Lou Costello. I actually found him quite amusing at first, because he sat on his bar chair as immobile as a stone, and he ordered beer after beer after beer. He drank pints of Amstel Light.

When our meals came, my boyfriend and I discussed some family matters. His sister was getting married to an investment banker, and his grandmother would be celebrating her ninetieth birthday up at the family's farm in Vermont. We would be taking the train, he said. And yet every so often, I would look beyond his shoulder and check on my project, this man I had been monitoring. By this time he tried to start a conversation with the woman tending bar. She was exquisite, by the way, and was the type of girl who would one day find herself working on Union Square. But she still had the job of serving her other customers, and so every attempt the man made at having some sort of dialogue with the woman, who had now become the object of his affections, I should think, failed miserably. She smiled at him when he spoke, and for some reason, he talked about the things you're never supposed to talk about in bars, namely politics and religion, and this woman, who probably wasn't interested in anything remotely connected to the gravity of the topics he discussed, had to stand there and take it all.

Soon his voice grew louder every time she came by to serve him. I overheard him talking about women and their nature, the daily newspapers and what they had printed, political conflicts in third world countries, and the supposed sorry state of American literature. She was flabbergasted and had to move away from him frequently just to avoid talking to him. But she did return every so often to serve him his pints of beer. Soon after, though, she would quickly move to the other side of the bar, finding relief and comfort in the other customers who hopefully didn't talk about the same frightful things. And the man looked on quite jealously as she paid more attention to the others and not him.

By the time our desserts had arrived, (my boyfriend, the apple pie á lá mode, and myself, the chocolate soufflé), quite a few people had entered the restaurant, and there were several similarly exquisite women at the bar who had ordered cocktails, some of them with male companions, others without. But from what I could see, a lonely bubble enclosed the man I had been monitoring in the middle of them all. He still sat like a stone, quiet and sullen. The patrons seemed to be mingling quite well on their own, but it was very clear that he was not. He knew this, because every so often his drooping head swung from left to right in the search of someone to spend the rest of the evening with. His eyes were bloodshot by now, his face unshaven, his clothes bursting at the seams, and yet he still tried to fit in somehow.

He finally fixed his sights on two women chatting at the far end of the bar, and at that point, I thought that he'd make an attempt, perhaps, at reliving some past moment of former glory. Sure enough, he slid his weighty body off of the bar chair and wandered down the length of the bar. Fortunately, he wouldn't be driving that night, because he certainly couldn't walk evenly. He nudged himself up to the two women who were much too well-dressed for him, and since he stood there, he had interrupted their conversation.

At first they were polite and respectful, but for some reason he interpreted this as an unconquerable coldness that could only be defeated if they loved him completely in return. He tried to smile—I'll give him that—and I couldn't hear exactly what was exchanged, but then I overheard the women respectfully saying that they were having a private conversation and that they wanted to return to it. The man, however, just wouldn't leave them alone. I couldn't say that it was harassment exactly, but the man was so incredibly persistent with them that the two women told him to get lost after several agonizing minutes of his badgering.

Well, the bartender had been watching this display the entire time, and by the time more people had entered the restaurant, the man had returned to his seat to order yet another beer. The bartender served a few of her other customers first, and it seemed that the more formal evening of the restaurant had been gradually coming to a close and being replaced by the more fashionable and club-like atmosphere that defined its later hours. The music played a bit more loudly, the lights were dimmed even further, the styles of the women's dresses were even swankier, and the din of the place grew heavier.

Our waiter presented my boyfriend with the check, because we really didn't want to stay any longer. We had tired of all of this long ago. He slid his credit card into the leather valet and got up to use the washroom. I now had a complete view of the man I had been watching all night. He still waited for the bartender to serve him another beer, and he was getting anxious about it, as though his senses had been stirred by the lack of it.

The bartender finally returned to him, and I heard her say, "You're cut off. You're going to have to leave. I'm sorry."

What followed was both sad and amusing, because the man started berating her from his side of the bar. He had been instantly transformed into a third-world tyrant, an irate mobster, a disenfranchised thug, as he growled at the top of his lungs, calling her actions unfair, unlawful, and altogether unconscionable, and that one day she would be haunted by the very same act of unkindness that she showed him. I think he called her a bitch too. He slammed a few twenty-dollar bills on the bar and dizzily left the restaurant.

When my husband returned and finished signing the bill, I looked into his blue eyes dreamily for a moment. I noticed the curves of his smile. I thanked my lucky stars that he was truly my boyfriend and nothing remotely like the man I had been watching all evening. He would never be like him, I thought. Never in a million years.

CLANCY'S TALE

Two German shepherds, wearing helmets and black K-9 bands strapped to their legs, escorted Clancy from the back of the squad car to the dog house behind the police station. A mist of rain from the nighttime sky barely made an impression on the black, muddy puddles that reflected the bright klieg lights and sagging barbed wire surrounding the precinct, which was the only place alive in the middle of the night for several miles around. The dog house shielded him from the cold wintry mix that had just hit the region, and they took him through a back entrance just to avoid the flashing cameras of the newshounds who barked uncontrollably on the precinct steps. The hallway leading to the interrogation room was menacing at best—all of these German shepherd K-9s staring him down as though he were some mutt who just skipped parole. But he knew himself to be an innocent dog. His black fur was slicked wet with rainwater, and his limp body shivered all over. They wouldn't even let him shake the wetness off his fur.

The interrogation room smelled like dog shit and stale pet chow. They led Clancy to a table and a hard chair and left him there alone for a while. He could hear both the whimpering and the barking of the other dogs they had dragged into the kennels that night, probably for petty crimes, like urinating on a fire hydrant or noise complaints for barking too loudly. Clancy sat at the table facing a large mirror, and the pale green walls of the rest of the room, both pockmarked and peeling, showed a previous layer of white paint that had been clawed through by the paws of the other criminals who had the terrible misfortune of sitting in the same spot. But he wasn't a criminal, he said to himself. Black Labrador Retrievers like him were hardly ever brought in. He was of good stock, a pure breed, and the K-9s would see that. Sure they envied dogs like him— always so obedient and pampered, always living on the sunny side of town, always the first choice of good-looking owners with well-manicured lawns, places to play in the backyard, and large shopping malls nearby that were stocked with only the finest gourmet dog food. But he was registered, and he was hardly a stray, and he had been to obedience school, and he earned his certificate. Clancy hoped they saw through to his innocence, even though these K-9s had been trained from birth to sniff out the guilty. But he had done nothing wrong, and maybe they just wanted to ask him a few questions.

It wasn't long before the doors swung open and a large Doberman Pincher flanked by two German shepherds walked calmly into the room. The Doberman was a handsome dog who kept his fur cropped close to his skin, and the narrowness of his snout suggested that they brought him in from the city to handle the delicate cases that were politically sensitive. He must have driven the bitches wild, this Doberman. Clancy could have sworn he had seen him before, perhaps on one of the news channels late at night when they busted up that ring of Mexican canines importing heroin in their bellies across the border. The German shepherds left the Doberman in the room with him, and for a short time the Doberman just circled the table, sniffing him down as he passed, the claws on his paws long, sharp, and strong, and his perfectly tapered mouth hiding teeth that could have easily ripped out his throat. The

Doberman also seemed sophisticated enough to recognize his innocence, but maybe they would stick him in the kennel just because they wanted to, or because they needed a patsy or a fall guy out of all of this, or because Clancy unwittingly got involved in some sort of canine conspiracy he couldn't for the life of him figure out. Clancy's nerves flared just thinking about these possibilities when the Doberman finally took a seat across from him. He also pulled out a brown lunch bag from under the table.

"Milkbone?" asked the Doberman, as he slid over a doggie treat.

Clancy was hardly in the mood to eat, but he took a couple of biscuits anyway. They certainly didn't taste like anything special, and they certainly didn't make him any happier like they would have made a Scooby-Doo, but they at least calmed his nerves for the time being.

"Do you know why you're here?" asked the Doberman in a highly inflected voice. His accent sounded almost European.

"I've done nothing wrong," said Clancy, chewing on the biscuit. "I'm an innocent dog, and you have no right to keep me here."

"Then why did we find you running out on the road in the middle of the night? Were you in a hurry to get somewhere?"

"I was just taking a walk and doing my business."

"At one in the morning?"

"That's when my owner lets me out, yes."

"Your owner," said the Doberman, "is dead. He came dead-on-arrival at St. Anthony's Hospital just a couple of hours ago."

"What? That can't be."

"Yes, I'm afraid it's true."

"Dead? Oh, God. I had no idea."

Clancy wanted to whimper out loud, but he kept this urge to himself. A puddle of haphazard tears slowly gathered between his paws on the table. The news of his master's death came all too suddenly, but somehow he already knew that Jack had suffered a terrible fate.

"Can you tell me a little more about your owner?" asked the Doberman. "Where, for instance, did you first meet him?"

"He's not my real owner," said Clancy, gazing into the pale green of the wall. "He was never my real owner. My real owner was his girlfriend, Melissa."

"Ah, yes. Now we're getting somewhere. How did you come to know this man? How did you come to be his pet and not hers?"

"It's a long story," said Clancy.

"Start from the beginning. We have plenty of time."

"We used to be so happy," he said.

"Who used to be so happy?"

"The three of us—Melissa, Jack, and myself."

"I see. So the three of you were a family, I take it?"

"Yes, and I was never the happier. Melissa, you see, adopted me when I was just a pup. She took me out of that horrible place, like a prison it was. Just being close to these kennels again gives me the shivers. She took me home, and I stayed with her in a beautiful house overlooking the lake. On sunny afternoons we would walk along the water's edge—the other dogs were so jealous of us, really they were—and when she pet me and brushed me, and even when she washed me, there was no other feeling like it on earth."

"So you loved her?"

"Yes, I loved her very much. I ate nothing but the finest dog chow—none of this stale, nutrition crap—but as close as any dog gets to real human food. And the Alpo wasn't too bad either. She also let me swim in the lake every now and then, and the poodles watching me were always so impressed at the way I paddled in deep water. Melissa always dried me off with a towel, and she even bought a bed for me to sleep on in the living room."

"Sounds like you had it good for a time," said the Doberman. "But what happened?"

"We were living just fine, she and I, when one night she had a party over at her place. It was a real drunk-fest with hours d'oeuvres and as many doggie treats as I wanted. The guests must have pet me and played with me a thousand times over, and they even poured wine into my bowl and kept on blowing smoke from their marijuana joints in my face. That's when Melissa met Jack, on that very night. It was a magical night for all of us, and when I got up the next morning, I found Jack and Melissa sleeping together in her bed. I jumped on the mattress and snuggled my body between theirs, and from that point on, I knew that I had finally found a family. I had such high hopes, you see."

"So all three of you lived together?"

"Yes. Those were the happiest days of my life. Jack used to get up early in the morning, and he took me for jogs around the lake. He was a good runner, an ex-athlete. I remember we used to run around that lake rain or shine, even in the winter when the ice on the lake looked like patchwork on a quilt. He sometimes brought an old tennis ball with him and threw the ball a mile-high in the air for me to catch. Of course all during this time I ate like a king. They even got me a big white bone that I chewed and chewed on in the backyard, all by myself. There were other dogs in the area too, but I never got lonely. Melissa petted me plenty, and Jack always played with me. It was perfect."

"So how does Jack wind up dead in a three-story walk-up and you running for your dear life along a dark country road in the middle of the night?" asked the Doberman.

"It just all fell apart," said Clancy.

"I'm afraid you'll have to be more specific than that."

"Something changed in him."

"Who? You mean in Jack?"

"After a while he wasn't the same man anymore."

"How so?"

"I don't know. I don't know how to explain it."

"Well, you better try," said the Doberman. "You're facing three counts of abandoning your owner, obstruction of canine justice, and roaming without a leash, so you better stop reminiscing and start remembering, because right now you're also a suspect in a murder case!"

"Hey, wait a minute. I never killed anybody. I never murdered Jack."

"Then start talking. What happened to Jack after he moved in with Melissa?"

"He just started to change. He came home angry all the time."

"Why?"

"How should I know?"

The Doberman barked loudly, and in an instant two beefy German shepherds entered the interrogation room.

"Take him out back," barked the Doberman.

The German shepherds surrounded Clancy at the table. One of them even grabbed Clancy's dog collar by the teeth to drag him outside.

"Alright! I'll talk!" yelled Clancy. "Jack was gambling, okay? He was a compulsive gambler. Are you satisfied now? Take away a lab's loyalty to his owner, why don't ya."

The Doberman called off the German shepherds who seemed disappointed that they wouldn't be having their way with him.

"What was his game?"

"How should I know? I never went gambling with him. I just saw him meeting some men at the front of the house a couple of days a week."

"Bookies, you mean."

"Call them what you like. He handed over whatever he took from Melissa's purse. Melissa would come home from working her desk job in the city, and all Jack did for a time was steal from her. It was horrible. I tried to stop him, but what's a dog to do? The guy kept on losing, and when he'd lose, he'd go straight for the bottle and drink himself silly. It was awful. Just awful."

"Did he ever do anything to Melissa when he drank?"

"They'd kick me out of the bedroom on some nights, sure. Every neighbor down the block heard them hollering at each other. Sometimes Jack would leave for days, and when he left there was calm. But then he'd come back after a three or four-day bender and start up with Melissa again."

"Were you and Melissa on good terms when he left?"

"She'd ignore me. She'd lock herself up in her room and cry. I tried to cheer her up, but she didn't want anything to do with me after a while. She said to me one night that I reminded her of Jack, just for the way I carried on, I guess. After she said that, she left me alone to do as I pleased. She wouldn't take me for walks anymore. She'd just open the screen door and let me roam around the lake for hours. I'd go and visit a few poodles I knew down the road, and sure, at first I had a fun time, but I wound up feeling so miserable, lonely, and bored. Melissa started drinking too, and she stopped going to work. And all this time Jack still drifted in and out of her life, right on schedule, every few days. They made love in the bedroom, but they always ended up fighting to the point where Jack just got up and left."

"How long did this go on?"

"I'd say about six months," said Clancy, resting his head on the table.

"When did they officially break up?"

"Jack came home one night drunk as hell, and Melissa, well, she had had enough of him by then, and so did I for that matter. She ordered Jack to leave, but he wouldn't. Melissa then started throwing things at him—plates, glasses, silverware—everything she could get her hands on. I'm surprised the neighbors didn't call the cops, as the lake is usually a quiet place where all you can hear at night are the crickets chirping. But that night, Melissa must have screamed a thousand times, until Jack finally packed all of his stuff into the pick-up truck and yanked me by the collar too. I remember that night well. We sped along the lake as Melissa stood on the front steps of the house screaming at the top of her lungs for Jack to bring me back. I even tried to bite Jack a few times, but he hit me so hard in the head that I had no choice but to stay in the truck and hope that Melissa found me after a few days. Days turned into weeks, and it turns out that that was the last time I saw her—screaming at the top of her lungs on the front steps of the house."

"So you were kidnapped?"

"Yes. Jack took me to this apartment he was renting on the side. It's about twenty minutes from the lake. It's right in the center of town. It must have been a week before he fed me anything. I got very sick. I was starving, you see, and whenever I tried to go out, Jack threatened me with a rolled-up newspaper."

"Did he use it?"

"Plenty of times."

"You must have been shitting all over the apartment."

"At first, sure I was. But I couldn't help it," whimpered Clancy. "He wouldn't let me leave the apartment. Not even for a few minutes."

"When was the last time you ate something?"

"Jack left a lot of garbage lying around. I usually had to tip over the garbage can in the kitchen just to eat. What other choice did I have? I'm a dog for Chrissakes. I'm not some insect or rodent. I have needs too. You think I liked shitting all over his apartment? Do you know how embarrassing and humiliating it was for me to have him come home and find my shit all over his Persian rug? I did everything I could not to shit on that rug, but I was eating out of his garbage can, and he wouldn't let me out. He was drunk every night. How can you call me guilty for that?"

"Just calm down, Clancy."

"I'm an innocent dog, damn it," he said, pounding his paws on the table. "As much as I wanted to kill him, I didn't do it."

"Why didn't you do it, then?"

"What do you mean?"

"Any dog worth his salt would have killed him, isn't that right?"

"Now wait just a minute—"

"You had the motive. Why didn't you attack him in his sleep or rip his throat out?"

"Because I'm not that kind of dog!"

"Sure you are, Clancy. You had all the reasons in the world to kill him. He was beating you night and day, wasn't he?"

"I didn't kill Jack!"

"Like hell you didn't," barked the Doberman. "He wouldn't stop beating the living shit out of you, and so you had to tear him to pieces."

"I never laid a paw on him. I swear it!"

131

And just when it looked like Clancy would be arrested for a crime he didn't commit, the doors to the interrogation room swung wide open. A squat, grey Bulldog, flanked by two German shepherd K-9s, walked in and pulled the Doberman aside. The Bulldog looked like a city official of sorts, and while the K-9s kept a close eye on Clancy, both the Doberman and the Bulldog traded whispers in the corner of the room. Something had changed. The Bulldog then left the room as abruptly as he entered it, leaving Clancy alone with the Doberman once again.

"What happened this evening when we found you running on the road?" asked the Doberman calmly.

"There were two of them who visited Jack tonight. They came up the stairs, one after the other."

"Did you get a good look at them?"

"Yes," said Clancy. "They went into Jack's bedroom and started to beat him up."

"And why didn't you stop them?"

"Jack had told me many times not to step on his Persian rug, and he'd hit me if I even looked at it. His Persian rug is spread right in front of his bedroom door. Damned if I shit on that rug again."

"And so these intruders, these henchmen, if you will— would you be able to identify them in a line-up?"

"Why? Have the humans found them? Is that what you and the bulldog were talking about?"

"Just answer my question, blackie."

"Yes. I saw them enter the apartment, but they left the front door wide open. I fled the apartment while they were roughing up Jack. I had no idea they were going to kill him."

"We'll see," said the Doberman, "we'll see. For now, though, there's someone waiting for you out front. You're free to go. The guards will show you out."

Clancy was half-way out the door of the interrogation room when the Doberman put his paw on his back and said, "and blackie, don't even think about skipping town. You're a witness to a murder, and we'll have plenty of questions to ask you later. So don't go anywhere."

"Oh, I won't leave town. And the name's not 'blackie,' you asshole. It's Clancy."

Two K-9s followed him to the exits of the doggy precinct. Clancy soon found himself on the front steps above a swarm of newshounds, their cameras whirring and flashing brightly every few seconds. The rain had started to come down harder, but the crowd didn't budge. The press was busy making him out to be some sort of celebrity witness, even though Jack's corpse was still warm.

Clancy searched through the crowd of newshounds who were being held back by a line of towering K-9s. He searched through the lightning-white flashes, and within that frenzied mob of reporters who barked and bayed in the middle of the night came a tall blonde woman whom Clancy immediately recognized as Melissa. He immediately jumped down the steps and leapt into her soft arms.

"I'm so sorry, Clancy," wept Melissa as she held him. "I'm sorry for letting him take you away from me. I swear it won't happen again, you good boy."

And as the flicker-flashes of light descended upon them, Clancy couldn't help but notice that his tail was wagging as it did many moons before Jack ever violated their lives. Melissa soon pulled away from the precinct in her car with Clancy riding in the front seat, his big, wet tongue hanging out of his mouth. Although he knew he wouldn't be able to leave town, as the Doberman had warned him not to, he also knew that there was no longer a reason to leave. He had everything he wanted next to him in the front seat.

FIRST LOVE

Although I'm a young man, I'm clumsy with women. It's a clumsiness that has driven me, for much of my short life, into the depths of a self-imposed exile. Loneliness is more suited to my needs. I can get by feeding off myself—inventing activities like going to the movies on my own. On dark Saturday nights I watch men and women collide perfectly on the screen. These movies taught me what women expected of men. The actors were never clumsy, and so I felt less of myself.

Considering my clumsiness, I never expected a woman to take my overtures seriously. I shied away. Love became a concept fiercely imagined, and in no way did I ever expect love to permeate the wall I had built around myself, until I accepted an invitation to a gathering at the Supper Club.

I thought this another foolish endeavor, because at parties I'm always the one who sips my drink off to the side, unable to get involved. I am reluctant to admit who I am, what I do, or where I come from, because I actually don't know who I am or what I do, and as a child we moved around so much that I can't express to anyone where I'm from. But I went to the club with my neighbor down the hall, because I had nothing else to do on a Saturday night. Neither could I escape how people socialized. At parties I'm always the first to leave.

When I arrived, a hostess guided my neighbor and me to people I had never seen before. I shook hands, and for a moment I thought myself transported to another time and place where they did the jitterbug and listened to the Andrews Sisters on Voice of America. I did have a choice, however, on where I could sit—either behind a pillar, where I'd get drunk alone, or up front where a solitary woman dreamily listened to the swing music. I couldn't decide at first, because I had nothing to talk about. There was nothing I could do to lift this curse of clumsiness. I didn't know how she'd react to a strange man sitting next to her. I sensed she was alone, but I didn't know if she'd be kind to a stranger. Being without a woman for so long had humbled me. Reluctantly, I did sit next to her, because I blocked everyone's view by standing in the the aisle where the showgirls streamed through and filled the theater with a heated expectation. I asked if I could sit next to her, and she surprisingly nodded her head.

We didn't talk. The golden horns of the jazz men muted whatever greetings we exchanged. Her perfume caught me off guard at a time when I needed to be vigilant about everything I did, said, and believed. Her blonde hair surprised me, not because it was natural, but because I never saw blonde hair so up close before. It reminded me of Connecticut for some reason, but after the trumpets sounded, I found out she moved to New York City from California. She knew very little of New York but mentioned an address in Midtown. She said people in New York were very abrupt. She traveled from coast to coast for a living.

Even though I couldn't relate to her lifestyle as a busy executive, I could relate to what she said about being, at one time, seventy pounds overweight. Her willingness to talk to someone like me must have been one of the products of her struggle. I never would have known. Her black evening dress hugged her body in ways that made me want to touch her, or at least sweep her blonde locks away from her lips when she spoke of her exercise routine. I hesitated touching her, though. She missed her family and friends in California, and for a moment I thought she lived a charmed life, as any life other than my own was charmed. I did see in her, however, an incredible sadness, as though she didn't want to be out all alone. She opened up her sadness to me, and I couldn't help but notice how beautiful this sadness made her.

The floorshow ended, and I asked her to dance. It was the next logical step, and I asked her without thinking of the consequences. I expected her to say "not right now" or "maybe later." Women usually said that to me. They could tell that I didn't know what to do on a dance floor. They saw right away that I had resigned myself to loneliness. She then said she would love to dance. I followed her onto the floor, both of us a little embarrassed.

When I pressed my hands to her back and held her close, I lost sight of the big band on the stage. A soft, violet light bathed us. I told her how fantastic she looked, and she said that I got that line out of the 'guy's handbook.' Somehow men like myself mysteriously knew how to open a woman's heart. I confessed that I was not privy to such a handbook. She laughed at this and let me twirl her. To my surprise the twirl worked. She said she had taken dance lessons before and felt more comfortable when men led. I pretended to know what I was doing.

I could have stayed with her for the rest of my life, and it wouldn't have mattered. For the first time I felt what it meant to have a woman accept my clumsiness. I had built my life on the hoax that there was something forever wrong with me, and that women would forever shun my love, because I didn't know how to love. She proved me wrong, and I wanted even more of this validation from her, that I did belong with a woman and that I could be the man she hoped for.

I did the unthinkable that night. I fell in love with her. She kissed me after the music stopped and left me on the dancefloor. I finally realized that night that I am indeed cursed, but not because I'm clumsy. I'm cursed because I let her get away.

FREDDY KATT

Maybe he had been too caught up in his own little world to give anyone else a moment's thought, and perhaps it was silly of him to be concentrating on the deal he made with an affiliate of the pharmaceutical company he worked for, but Freddy Katt would no longer be sidelined by his own weakness to feel bad about things over which he had no control. There was a time when he felt guilty about almost everything, stuff that went back to his high school years, and these events still lingered in him and haunted him all the same.

He remembered a time at the academy when the school's chaplain took him aside after he had punched another student during soccer practice, an incident he recalled as clearly as the blue sky above him. From that moment on he vowed never to hit anyone in the same manner again and swore that he would commit all of his energies towards good thoughts and a few vague moral rules that would somehow get him through life unscathed. Such a commitment would lead to good deeds that would set the goodness of the universe in motion. Nothing but goodness could result from thinking positively, he thought at the time, and maybe from that point on he could avoid sucker-punching people at play and getting into trouble over it.

But his deal with a well-known distributor to buy truckloads of a new anti-psychotic drug that had gone through rigorous testing and FDA approval just a week earlier needed only a signature by the vice president of the company, or basically, the consent of his boss. Freddy's boss, a man he had gone to school with back in the mid-80s, was also a good friend who had engineered his promotion to head sales representative just a few years ago. The man lived on an elaborate estate just south of Innsbrook Harbor, on a sprawling palatial retreat where he took his wife and two young sons to sunbathe and swim in the ocean.

The manor-home sat upon a high dune that sloped into the beach. Freddy thought of the water and how just one visit to his boss' home could cure him of the many ailments that stole the innocence from his life.

His boss seemed to have it all—a beautiful wife, two brilliant sons, who would probably attend Ivy league schools when they got older, and of course, he was wealthy.

Freddy also had money, but not the kind that his boss had. His boss was old money, the kind that came with disposition. Freddy, on the other hand, had at one time been flat broke and had to crawl his way to the top by working harder and faster and longer. He lived in the city, while his boss lived in both town and country, making him a well-balanced man altogether, and it seemed that nothing would stop his boss from one day becoming the CEO of the company he worked for.

Freddy stuck with him, as though he could get to the top also by riding his coattails. But because of this strategy Freddy always played second fiddle to his high school friend. That's how things worked, and it was something he accepted without reservation. He was lucky enough to be working at such a high level in the first place, and for that he should have been thankful instead of constantly wanting more, or at least this is what he told himself day-by-day at company headquarters as his boss hung around the beach house in his swim-trunks and holding an afternoon cocktail.

He pondered this relationship with his boss as he drove his Porsche convertible along a coastal highway that snaked its way over jagged mountain rocks on either side of him. The sun splashed its warmth over him, and he tuned his satellite radio to the type of easy listening station that would normally put any other person to sleep but somehow excited him that afternoon.

'There's nothing like commercial-free,' he thought to himself, as the wind tousled his hair.

Secretly he had always looked forward to spending some time at the beach home, and his suitcase full of paperwork was good excuse for a road trip. He was lucky enough to get out of the office on such a brilliant afternoon, and he didn't need anything else but a drink and a view of the ocean.

The highway ducked into a valley, and he was soon in a quaint town that bordered the beach and vast flatlands to the east. There were a few restaurants that served vegetarian specialties, a few jewelry stores that advertised in the fancy men's magazines he had subscribed to, and also a small eatery that served all sorts of coffee and teas, the type of place where one could see a music school dropout playing Bob Dylan or a poet reading from a tattered journal book. But there was hardly anyone in the town that afternoon. They all seemed to be at the public beach a few blocks down, as there were several cars and mountain bikes parked near there.

The road split at a dead end, and a long, narrow trail curved down to the beachfront. He was happy to see a few long-legged women in bikinis sunning themselves on the sand and also a group playing volleyball at the ocean's edge. The only noise he could hear were the sounds of the ocean beating on the shoreline, the wind, and the occasional squawking of seagulls that had suspended themselves midair.

The trail itself was unpaved, and he drove slowly so as not to ruin his car's suspension. The road was made more for an SUV than a sports-car, and he turned the stereo low to hear the movement of his car along the bumps, sharp dips, and ascents that typified the beach's changing surface. The beach road ended at another paved road embellished with lush lawns and gated homes on either side of it. The homes were well guarded by walls of ivy-covered stone too tall to look over. One could only sneak quick looks through the bars of the gates to find meandering driveways that led to pillared mansions, the ocean their backyards. Movie stars lived on this road along with a host of other famous people who had played the game of life skillfully enough and seemed to have everything he didn't. Even though he envied these people, he couldn't deny that he really wanted to be a part of their crowd. He only got as far as his boss, though, who invited him over every so often like it was a charity event. He could taste the cherry on the Pina Colada already, and maybe he could even stay over if he played with the kids long enough.

His boss' estate was well fortified and secure, almost like a castle that kept the strangers away, and an intercom with a surveillance camera beamed right at him and followed his car onto a circle that curved into the house. He parked his car on the gravel and checked himself in the rearview mirror before ringing the doorbell.

The maid let him inside with a slight grin, and immediately the two young boys, as blonde as sunshine over the beach, scurried up to him from another wing of the house and yelled his name over and over. It felt good to hug a couple of cherubs every once in a while.

Freddy didn't have a family as of yet. He chose a professional life over any sort of family, and while he did miss the company of a wife at home and children of his own, he became used to his bachelorhood and the long hours he put in at headquarters. His boss sometimes tried to set him up with other women, but his blind dates were usually one-night stands. On the next-mornings he had trouble talking of mundane topics, and the conversation always returned to work and his position at the company. His women were never surprised by his suggestion that they take the latest drug for any number of conditions they might be having. He then ran off and left them, usually as they slept.

Some people had to work for it, he figured, and women who talked lazily of their night's out with former boyfriends and far-off trips to islands in the Caribbean never really got the point that he would always have to climb mountains to be comfortable in his own skin, and the women were indeed incredibly beautiful, both in their looks and their girlish charms, but none of them wanted to commit to his kind of climb. They took the easy route, and they were probably better people for it. He saw his road, however, as hard and gruesome with no end in sight. He'd always be chasing something, and lately it seemed that he wanted everything his boss had. He even wanted the two kids at his knees who seemed a part of the same conspiracy of beauty that had always excluded him. It was an awkward feeling that never went away, and rather than fight the entire conspiracy against him, he went along with it and came to believe that more overtime at company headquarters would rid him of this misfit status within the club of the wealthy few who paid his salary. It worked for a time, but the kids at his knees, still yelling his name, reminded him of how far he had to go in order to become a part of something just a few notches greater than himself. And they were beautiful kids—the type of kids one would find on a cereal box or in a toy commercial. Their success had been predetermined, and patting their heads was the closest Freddy could get to something like that.

"Okay, guys, you don't have to hurt him," called a voice through the screen doors.

"Hello, Bill," said Freddy, fighting the kids off.

"Why don't ya come out back."

His boss was William Foxfield, the Harvard graduate, the second in his class, the Gulf War veteran, the youngest executive hired at the pharmaceutical company, and soon to be a member of the board. Yes, that was him in the pool area having lunch on the patio, his skin tanned by the ocean sun, his body carved of all body fat, the man who jogged three miles every morning, the man who ate three well-balanced meals and took efficient, fifteen-minute showers after his workout. Yes, that was William Foxfield. He seemed happy to see him, although Freddy didn't know why. Freddy only had a few papers for him to sign, and then he'd be on his way. He never ceased to feel clumsy and awkward around him, like a rowboat that leans too far into the water or a Martian who tries desperately to hide his true identity among the earthlings he recruits. Yes, it wouldn't be such an easy morning around William Foxfield. Conversing with him at his home was something he rehearsed on the drive down.

The kids followed Freddy outside. He then took a seat opposite him and unloaded his briefcase.

"You worked hard on this one, Fred."

"It's not a big deal. I was just looking at the bottom line."

"Yes, I know. You're bottom line is saving us millions with our distribution. What are we pushing again?"

"It's a new anti-psychotic, time-released, FDA approved last month."

"That should help with the high crime rate in our cities, don't ya think?"

Freddy smiled, but he didn't find the joke all that funny.

"There's always a market for us," said William, "the crazies and the criminals. Soon there'll be a pill for everything."

"Our research department says this is almost as good as a cure, or at least that's what they say."

"A cure?"

"Yes."

"What bullshit," chuckled Foxfield. "You and I both know that these pills don't do squat. R&D will probably get started on a newer version next week. These pills are more powerful than religion. It's amazing how they pay us to offer these lost souls just a tiny bit of hope. All you need is an alarm clock and a full glass of water, and presto!"

Freddy laughed nervously. His boss could have been joking or could have been dead serious; he could never tell. Foxfield's bronzed skin and bleached hair exuded a health that Freddy might never achieve, yet there was a bit of sadness in the eyes that seemed to look out over his shoulder as though he were reminiscing about some faint and distant memory.

"Is everything alright, Bill?"

"I'm a commander by nature," he said, "and sometimes I like to find trouble before it finds me."

"A lot of great men are that way," said Freddy, "but what's on your mind?"

"Oh, I don't know," he sighed. "There's something missing. I mean, look at all this, Freddy. One day you'll have something like this, assuming you lose a few pounds."

"Yeah, I'm still working on that," he said, patting his belly.

"But what I mean is that, well, how many worlds, let's say, did Alexander the Great conquer before realizing he could conquer no more?"

"There's a quote that says that Alexander the Great wept when he had nothing left to conquer."

"Y'know, Freddy, I tend to feel the same way. I mean, look at all this. You think all of this takes hard work?"

"I think some of it must come from that, yes."

"I think a lot of it comes from just being who I am. I can't put it any simpler than that."

"Yes, you certainly have had your fill at this stage of the game, no question. You certainly have an advantage at this point."

"And what do you think makes that?"

"Makes the advantage, you mean?"

"Yes."

"I guess it's because you've worked hard, you've made good decisions, you have a solid family."

"But many people have that."

"So, I guess what you're trying to say is that you're someone they didn't see coming."

"Not exactly."

"Then what are you trying to say, Bill?"

"I guess what I'm trying to say, Freddy, is that I'm thinking about leaving this business behind. I've made my mark pushing these pills, and I just think it's time to settle down a bit. Journey in another direction."

"Really?"

"Yes, really."

"Well, that certainly is news."

"It's just between you and me right now, Freddy. Just between you and me."

"Sure. I'll keep this quiet."

Foxfield's silver fork had poked at the few lettuce leaves left in his bowl when from the other side of the pool came a silhouette draped in a white Turkish robe drying her wet, blonde locks with a towel.

Freddy was keenly aware of her, Francesca her name, Foxfield's wife of three years and step-mother to his three children.

"We've been good friends, haven't we, Freddy?"

"Yes. I owe it all to you."

"Do you?"

Foxfield stared into his eyes. The stare startled him a bit. Freddy had never clashed eyes with Foxfield before, and the feeling was so painfully awkward that he couldn't help but pull away in embarrassment.

"What's wrong, Freddy? Is there something you have to say to me?"

Francesca then joined them, the kids running after her.

"You guys don't want to stay in longer?" she asked her children about the pool.

The boys then noisily ran upstairs, and Francesca took a seat next to her husband.

"Why hello, Freddy!" she said cheerfully.

"Francesca, how are you. You look as pretty as ever."

"Why, thank you."

Foxfield steadied his intense gaze on him, and Freddy felt the same feeling of awkwardness rifle through him before his eyes pulled away.

"I guess I can buy that new car now," said Freddy nervously after Foxfield signed the papers.

"And, oh, honey," said Francesca, "we could use a few more guestrooms for the house, especially if we're having company over so often."

"How about we fly away to the Islands, just the two of us," said Foxfield, kissing Francesca's bronzed shoulder.

Freddy couldn't help but look away at this point, Foxfield's piercing stare returning to him and still gripping him as awkwardly as before.

"Well, how long would we be away?" she asked.

"A month, maybe two."

Francesca laughed uneasily.

"But darling," she said, "what about work?"

"I think Freddy can handle the workload for a while, can't you Freddy? Or Freddy, how about coming along with us? It'll be the three of us. What do you say, old friend? Won't we have a nice time? I'll probably need you around to take care of some family business, and of course, my wife can have you around too."

"Darling," said Francesca, "I don't think we should commit to any sort of...oh, God, no."

Her uneasy smile broke just then. Freddy's eyes again clashed with Foxfield's, only this time Freddy knew that his old friend had known all along.

"I think I better get going," said Freddy, collecting the signed papers.

"And Freddy," said Foxfield, "don't think you're also getting away with taking a swing at me like you did when we were kids on the soccer field. When you get back to town, you can clean out your desk at the corner office too."

OVER THE SANDS

He searched beyond the hard plastic of the windows and noticed that the plane, although miles away from their destination, had started to descend at a slow, helpless angle, cutting through spongy clouds and gliding towards the desert sands below them. He worked hard to get to this place in time, he told himself, as one of the engines failed to restart. He looked to his colleagues seated across the aisle and wondered if anything could be done at this late stage. His colleagues were, after all, the leaders of a new energy exploration company that had soon become the darling of Wall Street after the price of crude shot up, and they were quick to make important decisions, manage the money, and please their corporate backers even as the jet plummeted at an even steeper angle towards the earth below. His bosses seemed stripped of whatever command they had over a situation that was now both new and uncontrollable. They shot back pale and startled expressions—a nervous twitching of the lips and flat-lines for smiles—yet they remained gracefully composed within their steely corporate shells. Trickles of nervous sweat moved down the temples of his immediate superior who clutched his arm rests with white, bloodless knuckles while muttering prayers for his dear life. They were as bewildered as he was by this new wrinkle in their plans.

"It's time to get into your crash positions, gentlemen," explained the captain over the intercom.

William Buford, the only black member of the board, disregarded what such a contortion would do to his suit and immediately tucked his head between his knees. He couldn't say if he were to live or die that afternoon, but he knew that he should hide even the slightest tick of emotion as he preferred holding his cards very close to his vest, and just like in the boardroom, his colleagues, both of them middle-aged white men, tried to do the same.

The plane rattled and shook, and although Buford couldn't see what was happening outside, he could certainly feel his back ache and his heart buckle as the plane gathered speed and dove through the air at a breakneck speed. A loud alarm sounded in the cabin—an annoying introduction to their scrape with death. It wasn't long before Buford thought of the family he had raised and the beautiful life he had built for himself. For all of this to happen now seemed like the cruelest of cosmic jokes. He had worked both brain and body to the bone setting up one of the most technologically-advanced oil exploration organizations ever to canvas the Arabian seas, and his bank account showed it. Money, however, didn't matter much to him at this point. He had always done the right thing and always minded his manners, ever since his business-minded father sent him to an elite prep school as a post-graduate on scholarship, and he chalked up his oncoming death to one of those absurd ironies that usually comes before the greatest of tragedies. He didn't know if he should laugh, cry, or shout. He always thought he'd have another chance to let his hair grow out, and even though such intimations shouldn't have mattered, it was one of the few things that did. His family, of course, he thought of first, but nothing could be done. He remained as poised as the quarterback he once was in college. He waited in a shallow pocket as brawn-stricken visions of Death closed in on him. He tried to accept his fate unflinchingly as all of his corporate heroes had done at vague points in their lives.

Sputtering and then grinding down to its last spin, the remaining engine squelched whatever whimpers, yelps, and calls for mercy these executives traded. When the engine sighed for the last time, Buford's heart crept up his throat, and as the ground rose to meet them, the plane soon nosedived and slammed face-forward into a massive sand dune in the Arabian desert.

The mid-section of the plane immediately broke off from both the cock-pit and the tail end where the engines were. The twin engines exploded upon impact. Buford's head banged hard against the seat in front of him as his body tumbled across the sand like a pebble tossed within the belly of an incoming wave. The cabin landed several hundred feet from the glowing burn of the wreckage, the wings snapping off the sides of the hull like chopsticks rended apart. The jolt was severe enough to knock him out, and when he woke up an hour or two later, he thought himself, not dead, but stuck in limbo between the unbearable emptiness of the spiritual world and the heaven his church congregation back home had always preached about.

Buford, however, wasn't dead. A splash of cold water pried his eyes loose, and before him stood both the CEO of the company and the other fellow board-member, their suits tattered, and their limbs, as seen through the tears in the fabric, smeared with patches of dried blood. Their cuts and sores and bruises and bumps were in plain view against the glare of the deadening desert sun, their hair in disarray and tousled by the wind. They looked like they had just walked through a war zone and had stumbled out on the other side as crazy and confused as zombies from a mass grave. At the very least, his two colleagues confirmed that he still lived. He became a privileged yet unfortunate survivor of a horrible plane wreck that had placed them somewhere between the coastal city of Jeddah and the blighted war-zone of Baghdad.

"The pilots were both killed," said the CEO, Perkins his name.

"They died instantly," said the fellow board-member, whom he called Richards.

Richards slowly felt for Buford's seatbelt. It had locked itself into place and wouldn't let go of him. Perkins had a pocket knife and cut Buford's belt off at the sides of the seat. As Buford lifted himself out, sharp pains stabbed at his chest and his knees. He had difficulty breathing.

"Your ribs are broken," said Richards. "Be careful."

The plane's hull opened into the desert like the mouth of a snared fish, and he wasn't surprised that his body was covered in layers of sand. He brushed off his suit, the back of it split down the middle, and he limped into the desert with Perkins and Richards helping him along. He could barely walk at first as his knees were banged up pretty badly, but after he reached the point where the cabin floor met the sand, he was able to limp on his own. They all saw this as a good sign.

"Ahhh, he's alright," said Perkins, watching him limp. "Just a little roughed up, that's all."

After eliminating the possibility that any one of them was seriously injured, they milled around the wreckage for a while and collected what they could, anticipating the moment when the sun would disappear. Thick black smoke billowing from the engines puffed into the sky like balls of shaved wool off a black-sheep's back, and since the tail end of the plane was where most of the food had been stored, Richards found only a few lunch trays that were saved from the explosion. They were still edible. He also found a few cans of soda and bottles of spring water, but the rest had been destroyed.

While Buford watched them from the sand, Richards and Perkins soon went searching through the cockpit. They returned with a couple of maps, a few signal flares, a first aid kit, and an automatic handgun. They had squeezed between the corpses of the pilots to find that the radio wasn't working along with everything else—no wipers, no lights, no navigation equipment—nothing. Although there was at least some relief in finding the first aid kit, the three of them couldn't deny, after putting everything into a small pile, that they were stranded in the middle of nowhere with the sun sinking quickly and the wind starting to kick up the sands on the desert floor.

"Well, this is all we have, gentlemen," announced Perkins abruptly.

It was clear to both Buford and Richards that Perkins, as their CEO, was still in charge, and this suited them fine, just so long as he could lead them safely to the next town. Buford's knees had pained him so badly that he unfurled his body on the sand, unable to move for a while. The other two took it as their cue to take a load-off with him. They then rummaged through the cabin of the plane and added pillows and blankets and the contents of their carry-on luggage to the pile of supplies. They were fortunate enough to find a lighter and a crushed pack of smokes.

"I didn't know you smoked," said Perkins.

"Only on occasion," said Richards.

"We lose billions a year in productivity that way."

"Actually, chief," said Richards, "we're damned lucky we found a lighter. How else would we keep warm tonight? We're definitely in the shitter until we find our way out. We have to sleep in the plane. I don't see any tents or anything around here."

"The plane probably's the best shelter there is right now," said Buford. "Who knows when the hell they'll find us."

"Find us?" said Perkins. "No one's gonna find us out here. We have to find them. Look around," as he searched the flat horizon. "There's got to be a town around here somewhere. We can't just sit around and wait for something to fall from the sky and save us, Buford. We have to take the fight to them. We have to get to the next town."

"Agreed," said Richards.

They unfolded the map recovered from the cockpit. They judged where they were by approximating their time up in the air and the position of the sun, which had now turned blood red and slowly dipped below the earth. Each of them studied the map carefully, as it was brand-new and up-to-date. They agreed that the plane went down somewhere inside Iraq, but where exactly they weren't sure.

"I'd say we're about fifty miles from Najaf," said Perkins. "We just head east, away from the sun, and we should hit something."

"I'd say it's more like a hundred miles from Najaf," countered Richards. "It'll take at least a day or two to get there. You see this sand?" as he dug his foot into the ground. "Walking on this stuff will slow us down. What would normally take us a day will take us twice as long. It won't be easy, especially with these supplies."

"Nothing of value's ever easy," said Perkins. "This is survival out here, and to survive we have to confront what may kill us. I say we gather this gear here and set out tonight."

"I don't think that's a wise idea," said Buford. "The desert at night is dangerous. We have these flares, so we might as well light them and see if anyone comes. My legs are killing me, and I think I have a concussion."

"Well, you've got to suck it up!" barked Perkins.

"I just don't see why we should risk it at this point," said Buford. "We have shelter and supplies. Everything's here. We just have to wait."

"And when we run out of this stuff?"

"Then we can move, but not until we give search and rescue a chance."

"But that's the problem," roared Perkins. "We won't have any of these supplies if we sit on our asses and consume them. We've each got to carry a pack and hope we can get to Najaf before the food runs out. We light the signal flares at the end of the journey, not before it begins. If a search and rescue team never shows, we'll starve. What do you think, Richards?"

"I think we should stay here for the night and give some time for Buford here to recover. We should set out tomorrow at daybreak."

"That sounds fine with me. How about you, Buford?"

"Agreed. Let's get a good night's sleep in the body of this thing. It'll give me some time to recover. We'll set out at first light."

They used whatever sunlight remained to stuff all of the supplies into their carry-on bags. They even tried the radio again, but it was as dead as the weight of their eyelids. As night descended, a cold chill tunneled through the open ends of the aircraft cabin. It was so cold at one point that they all awoke from their restless slumbers simultaneously and agreed to light a fire with whatever kindling they could find. Richards even poured the files in his briefcase over the fire. It was that cold.

Although the fire did keep them warm for a short time, it soon died out after they had dug a trench around it. They tried to build the fire again by pulling out the seat cushions and dumping them on the frail glow, but that too didn't prevent it from going out. Instead, the early death of the fire gave way to bright clusters of stars that hung above them. These were fat and bloated stars, too many to count. The ones that shot across the darkness were as discernable as Buford's dreams of being rescued. It seemed as though his circumstance was taken from the script of a farfetched fairytale or was at least a reminder of the summer camp his father had once sent him to on the lake. The analgesic from the first aid kit relieved his pains for now but also made him drowsy, which again pulled him back into slumber.

He awoke several hours later on the floor of the cabin, covered once again in the sands that seemed so ubiquitous. The pink sun in the east streaked its crimson-colored brilliance across the sky like rosy fingers gripping the skull of a child. Small animals stirred and moved about as the temperature steadily rose. Once-cooler breezes blended with heat to form hot gusts of air that burned his lips.

Perkins and Richards had woken up before him. They sat around the ashes of the fire and planned the perilous journey into what they believed to be the village of Najaf. They expected to find the usual landscape of bug-like vehicles choked with desert dust and sitting stationary along the mangled highways that headed towards Baghdad, their sharp horns prodding the many dark-skinned Arabs on the roadsides who walked patiently towards the bazaars. In fact, Jeddah, many said, was much more opulent than any of the cities in Iraq, and the three of them were confident that they could get to Najaf in a couple of days, assuming the sands weren't too deep.

Buford joined Perkins and Richards as they studied the map. His two superiors pondered over it while sharing a tray of cold meatloaf. After Buford ate, they rechecked all of the supplies in the carry-on bags. Richards listed these items in a small notepad.

It wasn't long before they reached the automatic handgun they had retrieved from the cockpit. It was at the bottom of one of the bags. They had packed it there the night before. They gathered around the gun and thought things over for a moment. In the nervous silence they knew that it was something they shouldn't leave behind. They traded looks— Perkins eyeballing Richards, Buford eyeballing Perkins, Richards eyeballing Buford—until Perkins finally broke them from the spell of what they all seemed to be thinking about.

"I'm the boss," said Perkins, reaching for the weapon. "I'll carry the damned thing if you guys are too scared to."

"Now wait a second," said Buford. "I think we should think this thing through."

"There's nothing to think about," said Perkins. "I'm running this show. I'm the one who should carry it."

"With all due respect, sir, this isn't the boardroom. We're not back at company headquarters. A gun becomes a powerful thing if something goes wrong out there. I don't think only one of us should handle the responsibility alone."

"What are you trying to say, Buford? That I'm not fit to carry the gun? Is that what you're saying? Because if that's what you're saying, you should know that I shot milk bottles off of fences long before your Mamma was changing your diapers."

"I'm not saying that at all, sir."

"He's not saying that," chimed in Richards.

"What I am saying is that a hundred things could go wrong."

"Like what?"

"Well—just things could go wrong, that's all. The gun is the only force we have out here."

"So how do you suggest we go about it then," asked Perkins, glaring at him.

"Well, I think we should shoot it out—odds and evens, that sort of thing."

"Oh, for Chrissakes! What are you? A child?"

"He has a point, chief," said Richards. "We should at least let the element of chance into our decision-making. Will that be enough for you, Buford?"

"It sounds good to me," he said. "Or maybe we can all take turns carrying the thing."

"I always knew you were a communist, Buford, but I'll go along with that if it'd shut you up."

"I beg your pardon!"

"Now, people, let's not get too emotional about this," said Richards. "We need to save our energies. Perkins should hold the gun first. He is, after all, running things around here."

"Fine," said Buford, picking up the weapon and handing it to Perkins.

"Now can we stop acting like children and get moving?" said Perkins, as he tucked the weapon under his belt. "It's good to know someone's still in charge around here, especially the guy who owns fifty percent of our stock."

"Hey, man," said Buford nervously, "I didn't mean any disrespect by my—"

"Let's move out," said Perkins. "We've wasted too much time already."

It occurred to them just a few yards into the journey that the bags they carried weren't exactly making things any easier. The sand was a foot deep, and their legs became weights that couldn't function without the same lightness and spring of step that accompanied their many walks to places like the office bar back home. The bar prided itself on serving twelve o'clock martinis that went down like silk. They weren't back home, though. They were deep in the desert with mountains of sand all around them. It made the sheer simplicity of walking as uncomfortable as their first dealings with the Arab oil executives they often courted. Although Buford was third in line back home, he happened to be the tallest and the best built of his two colleagues now that he was in the desert. He even volunteered to carry the heaviest two of the four bags. Perkins and Richards struggled with the other two, carrying just one a piece. Buford heard their huffing and puffing up ahead, the sun's rays on top of them like slave drivers beating their scarred backs, and it wasn't long before Perkins dropped his load about a quarter mile ahead and exclaimed,

"Well, damnit all to hell! We have to rethink this."

"I agree," said Richards, collapsing on his bag and struggling to catch his breath.

In a strange way, however, Buford was emboldened by their show of weakness. He calmly put down his bags, unzipped one of them, and pulled out a bottle of spring water.

"Hey, pass that over here," demanded Perkins. "This isn't a one-man show."

He found the two quite amusing just then. They were children when it came to marshalling their own strength.

"At this rate we'll never make it to Najaf," said Buford, a grin curving on his face.

"No shit, Shirley," said Perkins. "We need a little help, that's all."

"I'll second that," said Richards, watching Perkins gulp down the warm water.

"This is just plain inefficient," said Perkins, spilling some into the sand.

"What do we do, chief?"

"Well, we can't carry all of our loads. I've got a gun at my side, and the trigger doesn't exactly have a safety. What we have to do is do away with some of this stuff and consolidate, if you will. These bags are just too damned heavy to be lugging around all over this wasteland. And I don't find the humor in it, Buford, so you can wipe that shit-eating smile off your face. Not everyone's built like a friggin' linebacker."

Buford's knees and ribs still pained him. He sat on the sand with them and understood too that their inability to carry their fair share of the load would only mean more work for him.

"After all, I've got to carry this gun," said Perkins, "and I'd hate to have it go off while lugging these supplies around. Otherwise, I'd be carrying ten-times the weight Buford's carrying."

"And I'm navigating," said Richards. "No one else can read these maps like I can."

"So what you guys are saying, if I'm interpreting things correctly here, is that you two carry nothing at all, while I bring up the rear with all these bags? Why don't you just give me the map and the gun, and you two go off in any damned direction you want to?"

"This isn't the time to be smart," said Perkins, "and besides, it's impossible for you to be smart. By dint of your upbringing and family line, you just happen to be built like a horse."

"And this is while my knees are throbbing and my head is still spinning from the plane crash, right?"

"Listen, Buford, no one's begging you for help," said Richards. "You either do your fair share, or we'll all starve."

"And you'll be out on your ass as far as a job goes," said Perkins. "You can be sure of that."

Considering that Buford did most of the grunt work setting up the company anyway, he wasn't about to let all of his hard work go to waste just because he thought carrying all of the luggage himself was unfair. He remembered the many hours he spent alone at company headquarters pouring over endless files, crunching notebooks of numbers, and having to deal with a barrage of younger corporate lackeys who thought he didn't know his ass from his elbow, and this was not to mention the self-righteous Arab suits who had a knack of putting him in his place—based on their hierarchy of skin color, of course. He must have spent a year or two doing the board's bidding, and to risk all of that due to his reluctance to cooperate and get-along, well, that seemed a bit counter-productive. He had a hunch that they would eventually make it out of the desert, and he wanted to keep his options open should they manage to reach Najaf safely. He went along with their plan, seeing that he was indeed the strongest of them. Let them have their toys and their weapons, he thought, because once they escaped the cruelty of the desert, he'd buy himself a steak dinner at Peter Lugar's and a new Mercedes-Benz to take back home to his wife. He would once again become the man Perkins and Richards counted on, but only if he cooperated and complied now. And besides, carrying the bags would only make him tougher and stronger physically. Call it the first day of training camp all over again, if you will.

And even though he knew he would be giving in and sacrificing more than Perkins and Richards ever could, the satisfaction of knowing that they couldn't have survived without him was now etching itself into his ego. If Perkins and Richards were the dashboard of the operation, then Buford was the engine behind them. He was the first to end their ten minute break by declaring that he was finally in agreement with their plans for his inevitable tenure with the company. He grabbed three bags by his fists and set across the desert like an unknown soldier taking initiative.

"Now he thinks he's fucking Superman," said Perkins to Richards, who followed him from behind.

Carrying hardly anything at all, the two of them easily caught up with Buford, and within fifteen minutes or so, they easily outpaced him along the makeshift desert trail they traveled. With three heavy bags brushing up against his calves,

Buford brought up the rear once more. Rivulets of sweat cascaded down his forehead and stung his eyes. The unrelenting sun poisoned him with heavy fatigue, and his attitude soon turned lousy. His labors eventually forced the idea that these two colleagues of his had positioned themselves to be his sole superiors while treating him unfairly. Yet he knew he had a job to do, and on more than one occasion he felt like ditching the bags if only to enjoy the freedom of wandering the desert as aimlessly as they did. Visions of cold, sinewy waters washing over mossy stones came into distant focus. And for a time he clung to these visions as he dragged the bags across the sands, the blaring sunshine slowly losing power.

Perkins and Richards soon became two dots floating on the desert horizon ahead of him, as they were moving along at a much faster pace. Buford's knees, it seemed, had gotten worse. They were as swollen as grapefruits. The dizzying nausea that inflamed his concussion only reminded him of the intense pain of banging the crown of his head against the steel frame of the plane seat in front of him. Luckily for him, however, those distant dots gradually grew larger and more distinct. Apparently, Perkins and Richards had stopped to wait for him, or so he first thought. As he came closer, he heard bickering between them, and then shouting. Their loud voices became clearer and more defined as he approached.

"Look at the position of the sun, you fucking idiot!" yelled Perkins to Richards. "We're on the right track!"

"Not according to the map," fired back Richards. "We have to move north from here. You're getting us lost."

"No, you moron! You're the one who's gonna get us lost. You messed things up right from the get-go. We've been going the wrong way. Can't you see that?"

"Listen to me, and listen to me good," said Richards. "If we don't head north from here, we'll never get to Najaf. We'll still be wandering this desert long after the food and the water run out."

"And look at the position of the fucking sun! It's more important than that stupid map of yours. You don't have a basis on which to judge the nautical directions. Only the sun does that."

"This is the only map we have, and we have been basing the entire journey on this map. I am the navigator. I am in charge of steering us into Najaf, and I'm telling you now that if we continue to head east instead of north, we'll wind up at the Kuwaiti border, which is much farther away than Najaf."

They bickered like this for some time, or at least it seemed like some time to Buford who stumbled as close as he could get to them and then immediately collapsed to the sand with fatigue and exhaustion.

"Buford? Are you alright?" asked Richards.

"Don't worry about him," yelled Perkins. "We're moving away from the fucking sun, you got that?"

Clearly at an impasse, Richards directed his attentions to Buford who moaned as his body lay on the hot sand.

"Damn," said Richards. "Who's gonna carry these bags?"

"We're stopping here for the night," muttered Buford, his eyes half closed.

"Like hell we are. This isn't the time to be lazy, Buford."

"We'll head north in the morning," said Richards.

"I can't believe how incompetent you two fools are," said Perkins, clearing a space for himself on the sand. "Utterly useless you guys turned out to be. We might as well die out here right now."

"That's enough!" said Richards. "We camp here for the night, and we head north in the morning."

Perkins closed in on Richards. They stared each other down, eyeball to eyeball.

"I don't think you heard me correctly. I'm the one in charge here, not you. You do as I say."

"Take your company and shove it," said Richards defiantly.

Buford, watching this confrontation from below, came between the two after peeling his sweat-soaked body off the desert floor."

"Now just calm down both of you," he said. "We need to stick together on this."

"Not if he insists on heading east, which would put us back into the fucking desert!"

Buford wasn't aware of it at this point, but Perkins quietly un-tucked the handgun from his belt and pointed it at the both of them. Whether the gun was a mirage or not, both Buford and Richards couldn't believe their own eyes. They suddenly stared down the pipe of a loaded weapon that had now been co-opted by Perkins alone. Buford didn't move an inch, and Richards carefully contemplated this latest wrinkle in their plans.

"When I say we head away from the sun, that's exactly what I mean," breathed Perkins hotly, his eyes glowing like burning coals. "I want no more debate, argument, or discussion on the topic. Do we understand each other?"

It was only after Buford and Richards nodded their perfectly bewildered heads in agreement that Perkins then returned the handgun to the space beneath his belt and watched them as they got rid of a few, very essential supplies from the bags and made camp for the night. They lit a fire while the sun radiated its blood-red hue and gradually cast dark shadows along the desert's surface. Barring any run-ins with the many scorpions and sidewinders that took up space in the paranoia of their minds, they saw themselves leaving early the next morning and heading in any direction Perkins wanted them to. It was as simple and as plain as that. They would either end up starving on their way to Kuwait or celebrating the glory of their lives in the traffic-laden streets of Najaf, but hopefully they would move ahead before Perkins had a chance to kill them both.

Buford did manage to get in a few hour's of sleep. His mind's eye wandered to his country home about forty miles away from the glass monolith that was company headquarters at the center of a densely populated city.

In the backyard, his wife carefully prunes her small rose bushes on all fours, the ends of her short pink sundress rising above her upper haunches in the breeze. It was a glorious dream that delivered his trophy wife to him once more, as he is a man so terribly abused by the unrelenting hardships of the desert, and lately his superiors, that her body provides the essential healing he needs.

There seems to be no end to the abuse, no end to the fat red ants biting into his black flesh, flesh that had all the deliciousness of a cactus in a drought, and no end to the burns on his face and chapped lips, his knees still swollen and his lungs coughing up grains of sand like shards of asbestos. His wife's backside rising up to meet his torso seems like the only relief he can get, as entering her from behind and hiding his manhood whole in the security of her warm sweetness becomes its own form of security. It is a pathway to a more masculine completeness that has been broken to bits by two people he now couldn't stand. And in this dream he wraps his arms under her flesh and holds his chest tight to her smooth back as she begs him to push farther into her, as far as he can go. And just when his muscles slacken and all of the tension from his days and nights of wandering aimlessly and madly in the desert is on the verge of releasing, he suddenly feels a cold, uncomfortable dribble of lukewarm water flood his eyes and nostrils.

Buford opened his eyes to find himself in the desert again, only above him stood Richards who splashed water all over him. Buford summoned every ounce of tolerance and restraint to avoid tearing Richards' skinny white body to pieces and devouring his flesh whole.

"I'm sorry, Buford," whispered Richards, kneeling down to talk to him in the darkness.

"This better be good, or I'm gonna kill you with my bare hands."

"I'm sorry for waking you, really I am, but we have to act fast if we're going to get to Najaf in one piece."

On the other side of the extinguished campfire, Perkins' body rose and fell as he snored with his back towards them. The snoring came and went with the powerful alacrity of a buzz saw biting into stubborn wood. Dawn was coming upon them gradually, and Perkins showed no signs of movement. His body lay across from them like a stone, and it seemed his sleeping would outlast the action that Richards now proposed.

"The old man has lost it completely," said Richards, whispering hotly. "He has no sense of what he's doing or where he is. We've been traveling in the wrong direction. He doesn't have the map. Only I have the map, and I can swear to you, Buford, that we're not very far from Najaf, but only if we travel north from here and not further east. The man has lost his mind, and pointing the gun at us only confirms this. Something has to be done, and it has to be done before he wakes up."

"Let him go his way, and we'll go our way," suggested Buford. "If he thinks we should head east, then let him go east, but he'll go it alone. You and I will head north."

"But he'll never let us leave without the rest of the supplies. We can go our separate ways, sure, but he'll take all of the food and the drink with him. We need the rest of these supplies to get us to Najaf. Besides, he may kill himself out there. We can't leave him, since he has the handgun. Who knows what's still out here—snakes, wild animals, scorpions, cobras, Arab terrorists, you name it."

"So what are you suggesting? That we take the gun away from him and hold him hostage while we all head north?"

"Precisely. We need that gun. Who gives a shit where he goes afterwards, but we need that gun for our own protection. He had no right to hold us up like that. We have to get that gun before it gets lighter out. It may seem like he's sound asleep now, but that old bugger sleeps with one eye open, and he'll wake up any minute, I know he will. Either we get it now, or we'll have to follow him for hundreds of miles into Kuwait, only we won't be seeing Kuwait because we'll die of starvation before we get there."

"I would just feel a little awkward manhandling our CEO. I'll lose my job, and when we do get back home, he'll have us sent to jail. Have you thought about that?"

"You of all people know that that shit doesn't apply out here. Haven't you taken a good look around? We're in the middle of nowhere. You said yourself that this isn't the boardroom. And I can feel myself dying out here. All of us are dying out here. I don't care if there's all the oil in the natural-known world out here, and I don't care how holy this wasteland is to these towel-headed terrorists who will torture us to death when they find people like us out here, but I'm not willing to die out here, Buford. Not now. One we get back to the States I'm leaving this business behind. Yep, you heard it right. There's something so unnatural about our being here, so damned unnatural about what we're doing here, and to think we can just dip our beaks into whatever land we want has got to be the most foolish assumption we've ever made. I want out of this business, and you have to believe me. In order to get out of here all of us need to get to Najaf, and in order to get to Najaf we need to get that fucking gun away from the fucking boss-man.

"Help me get the gun back, Buford, and I'll sell you all my shares in the company for dirt cheap. You'd have a clear majority on the board and more shares than Perkins. You'd be able to do anything you want with him. You'd be richer than most rich men, and you can fire Perkins, and you'd never have to deal with us white trash ever again. All you have to do is hold him down a minute while I find the gun. You'd also have to carry most of the supplies into Najaf, but the weight of the load will be a helluva lot lighter knowing that your name will be at the top of the Fortune 500 next year."

The question of whether or not to trust Richards would probably have taken a lot longer to answer had the quickening sunlight allowed the luxury of an informed and well-thought-out decision. Buford, however, knew that the light, the heat, and the billions of crawling desert insects would soon wake Perkins up at any moment.

"First, I want something in writing about the shares. Then I'll hold him down. You just make damn sure you get the gun."

And as Perkins snored restlessly nearby, Buford grabbed him by the wrists and pinned his arms over his head. When Perkins came to, Richards smacked his face hard with the back of his hand."

"Where's the fucking gun, Perkins?!"

"Let go of me, you fucking twerp!"

"Just give me the gun, and we'll let go of you."

"Don't struggle," said Buford. "There's no one out here to hear you scream. Besides, you're not strong enough to break free."

"Damn right I'm strong enough, you black bastard!"

But as much as Perkins struggled in the sand, Buford's grip was too tight for him. After Richards smacked him around a couple more times, Perkins still struggled but could only toss and turn his body into similar, inescapable positions. The grip of Buford's strong hands holding his wrists above him was the straight jacket that eventually calmed him down."

"The gun's under the blanket," said Perkins after Richards started hitting him with closed fists.

They pulled him off the blanket and yanked the blanket free from under him. Sure enough, the gun lay on the ground, its metallic casing shimmering in the light of a new dawn. Richards quickly grabbed it, and Buford let Perkins' arms go. Perkins, having lost power and having been banged up by Richards pretty badly, could do nothing but cry softly in the sand as they held him prisoner at gunpoint.

"We're heading north," announced Richards. "Buford, get the bags. We'll leave after we've eaten the last of the rations."

As they wandered once more into a desert that stretched for an eternity in all directions, they knew themselves too damaged, both physically and otherwise, to utter even the slightest word to each other. What most surprised Buford, who was once more dragging the remaining supplies at the rear of their procession, was how quiet and despondent Perkins had become.

Perkins walked a few paces ahead of him, not necessarily so confused and bewildered about what had happened, but lost in his thoughts and deeply reflecting on the scope of the misery they endured. HE walked slowly, as an old man would. His unsteady gait tipped from side to side as he shuffled away from the straight line of their general direction. He seemed overwhelmed by the vast complexity of the desert, its indifference to his suffering, and its soullessness that now bred dark worlds in his mind. The desert, it seemed, had no feeling. It was both dead and barely living, which is why the Arabs must have submitted to this strange, invisible God that had haunted it. Only the wind and the rustling sands could be heard, as both the wind and the sand lived alongside the ghosts of warring clans vying for their own claims to righteousness.

Every so often some strange underground rodent would scurry from one side of a dune to the other, but after the three of them had wandered under the hottest of blazes, these critters became mere mirages that hinted at signs of life but never delivered the sustenance they needed. Still, they continued walking straight ahead for hours. It could have been days, as Buford had lost all track of time.

Every once in a while Buford sucked up the last beads of water at the bottom of a water bottle he carried. He hoped that Najaf miraculously appeared on the horizon. But day soon turned into dusk once more, and while fooling themselves into believing that they were on the cusp of some great but imaginary breakthrough, they all understood that such intimations were only symptoms of their general disease— that they had no chance of surviving the desert unless and until the punishing God that had menaced them all along had intervened on their behalf, just as He did the Arabs when they first cried out for Him.

Buford, however, soon got the idea that Richards had been reading the map incorrectly all along, and Perkins, who had busied himself extending his upturned palms to the darkening sky, muttered some of the same cranky insults he had earlier hurled at Buford in an effort to pray to the new God he had found. Both Perkins and Richards seemed as dead to him as the long famine they suddenly faced.

As he heard him mutter vague things to the sky, Buford knew that his CEO had lost it—mind, body, everything. Yet he saw Perkins walk faster to where Richards led the pack with the handgun and the navigator's map. He noticed, just as before, that Perkins and Richards were two dots on the horizon ahead of him, and it wasn't until night firmly set in that he saw, to his genuine surprise, Perkins running up behind Richards and slugging him in the back with the bag he carried.

'Oh, shit, not this again,' was the only thing Buford could think of, his brain dripping into the same slow pond of madness that had overcome Perkins. But he dropped his load a few yards away from the fight only to discover that Perkins had successfully wrestled the gun away from Richards. Richards was now grounded on the desert floor with a fist-full of sand in his eyes and the gun pointed at his head.

"You see that!" yelled Perkins. "You were asleep at the wheel. It was then that God came to me—when you were sleeping at the fucking wheel! How do you like that? That's the problem with your whole fucking life, Richards. You have no God, and you're always sleeping at the wheel."

Buford, too exhausted to do anything about this latest turn of events, still tried to tackle Perkins but was met instead with a hard strike to the jaw with the heavy handgun Perkins now controlled. He felt his jaw snap in two as he fell back to the sand, his mouth filling up with warm blood and pieces of his cracked molars slipping down his throat.

"You black sonofabitch! You think you can handle me?"

Perkins fired two shots at Buford. The first one strayed into the desert, but the other hit Buford's thigh. Buford fell to the ground in agony. Richards, however, didn't move a muscle. Perkins ordered him to get on his knees with his hands behind his back.

"Pray, you mother fucker, pray!" as he cleared the chamber and pressed the tip of the gun to what seemed to be a well-worn spot on Richards' forehead.

"Please," repeated Richards over and over again. "I'll give you anything you want. Anything. Just name it."

Half of Buford's face was in the dirt when he heard a slow, methodical din somewhere in the distance. He lifted his head just enough to notice a procession of mild yellow lights, almost like insects, marching against the darkness. At first he thought nothing of these lights, but when the din grew louder, he knew the din to be man-made.

"Say your fucking prayers, you weasel," said Perkins, as the yellow lights danced in the distance.

Unable to speak and coughing up blood, Buford propped his body up on his elbows and pulled himself to where the bags were. He unzipped one of the bags and frantically searched within it. He finally applied flame to the fuses he found, and soon enough brilliant sparks of electric-cherry light plumed up high from the sand. Trails of smoke from the wayward sparks dropped down from the sky and illuminated parts of the desert that couldn't be seen. Insects and strange animals with bulging black eyes scurried to safety as the signal flare burned in the chaos. The pressures at his temples, however, soon became so great that he slowly lost consciousness, but not without igniting a second flare. It was the only way, he reasoned, to ward off the spirits of the dead before they took his body into the depths of the underworld with them. Everything soon faded to black.

And as a white light danced above him, Buford's body was pained in its deliverance to the other side of the world. It was almost as though an angel was fitting a halo over him. At first he thought he had died, but after a good hard shake that brought him fully to consciousness once more, he opened his eyes to find himself prone on a stretcher staring into a ceiling light at the back of a moving jeep. He was sore from head to foot, his body wrapped in rolls of bloody gauze and his head pounding as though the bullet that had pierced his skull dragged his brain out from the other side. But as he found himself under the ceiling light, he soon noticed a dark-skinned Arab sitting next to him.

The unshaven Arab smiled down at him with a mouthful of polished teeth. They were like heavy slabs of marble, all in a straight line. He must have been the enemy, thought Buford to himself, but he was unable to move from his tight and narrow position on the stretcher. Apparently they had tied him down, his body jumping around like a dying fish.

"Jesus," he said, trying to lift himself up. "Where the hell am I? You're not the enemy, are you?"

The Arab smiled and immediately told the driver up front what Buford had said. The jeep then jumped with laughter, the Arab's thick, heavy accent mocking Buford's assertion. The Arab also wore what seemed to be dirty Army fatigues.

"Just relax," said the Arab in broken English. "You're in good hands now."

"You mean I'm not your prisoner?"

"On the contrary," smiled the Arab. "I am Colonel Saamdi Sualeh, Commando Battalion, Iraqi Special Forces, Najaf Province. We are your friends."

"You mean you're not going to kidnap me and torture me to death?"

The Arab laughed and immediately informed the driver up front again. Another round of laughter accompanied the jeep's loud engine, and the manner in which it continuously shook and jostled his sore body from left to right only worsened his pains.

"Ah, Americans!" said the Colonel, lighting up a cigarette. "You certainly are a very humorous people. But we are certainly not handing you over to the insurgency in Najaf. In fact, we are the ones saving people like you from the insurgency, Mr. Buford."

"How did you know my name?"

"We are part of the multi-national force that keeps the peace in Najaf, among the other things that we do. We were on a routine recognizance mission west of the province when we spotted your signal flares."

"Oh, thank God Almighty," sighed Buford heavily. "After all of this, we're saved. You've found us—"

"Please, Mr. Buford, just relax. We are on our way to the military hospital in Najaf, and we have a couple of hours before we get there. There's no rush to speak, okay? We were made aware of your plane crash just a few hours ago. Apparently you and your friends have been traveling the desert in circles."

"Oh, my! Perkins and Richards? Where are they? Are they alright? Tell me they're alright."

"I'm sorry, Mr. Buford. When we arrived, we found both of them dead. One of them had executed the other and then turned the gun on himself. I'm very sorry to have to tell you this, Mr. Buford, and I'm very sorry that this has come to pass. You were the only survivor of the plane crash, I'm afraid. Just try to relax right now. We're almost at the hospital."

"They were like, well, they were like two parts of the same mind, and they still couldn't make it out alive."

"Yes," said the Colonel, his glassy eyes retreating to the desert beyond the windshield. "There's only room for One mind in the desert, Mr. Buford, and people who adhere to the voice of this single mind fare much better than those who don't.

SLEEPER CELL

They said that learning the language wouldn't be the main difficulty, nor circulating among the American people, all of whom would be tolerable to live among, although barely so. They said the food wouldn't be so much of a problem as the alcohol, which they served like our own zum-zum water. They served it at every restaurant and bar, at every cantina and grocery store, but this was only a minor difficulty considering that one usually socialized while drinking, which wouldn't be a problem for me, because I was told not to socialize with anyone. The women, they said, wouldn't be a problem either, even though they didn't cover themselves and usually pranced around like whores. I wouldn't be tempted by them, they said. In fact, I would come to pity them but in a way that wouldn't permit me to interfere in their own demise. They were the wives and consorts of Iblis, they said, and they reiterated that point as though they had been through it already.

The police at the immigration checkpoints at the various terminals and small-town airstrips and at all disembarkation points would only be minor inconveniences, they said, just as long as I carried the documents they then presented me with. These documents would easily pass as authentic. The police may search me, but this wouldn't be difficult, since I wouldn't be carrying anything unlawful. I wouldn't be looking like a typical Arab, so even though the complexion of my skin would pose some difficulty, it wouldn't get in the way of my plans one way or the other. My clothing would be cheap but in a contemporary Western style that suggested some kind of colonial relationship that my country of origin had with the West, as my home country was one of the jewels in an imperial crown that protected me from those other types of Arabs who were much more devout-looking, and therefore, much more suspicious to the authorities.

Moving out to the country after I arrived in New York City wouldn't be so difficult either. People minded their own business, they said, and so I should mind mine. And when the time came to get the equipment together and to meet my other Muslim brothers who would be a part of my holy mission, this wouldn't be a problem at all. Neither would our ride into New York City be a problem. Americans will do anything for money, they said. The would sell me semtex off a street corner if they thought it would help send their kids to college, only that I should be discreet about it. Don't buy everything in one place, in other words. And what made things even easier for me, they said, was the contact I'd meet in Manhattan, about once every month. He was an older man whom I would check in with and have lunch with every so often. This wouldn't be so difficult, they said.

They said that the only difficulty in all of this—from the moment that they had conceived of their plan to the moment God would finally answer our most clandestine prayers—was managing the time it took for such an answer to arrive. They said that I may have to wait for years for God's divine plan to manifest. They said all of this to me in the summer of 1996, the time when I left Beirut to settle just south of metropolitan New York, to live in a suburb in central New Jersey where I rented a ground-floor apartment in a typical mother-daughter home. I was ordered to stay put until my contact called.

It took him about a month, but when he did call, he ordered me to Manhattan, to a restaurant near the United Nations on First Avenue to have lunch with him. He wasn't as I had imagined him. He was actually quite thin but taller and older than I was, his head balding, his moustache and beard cropped close to his face, his complexion a little lighter than mine. He dressed in a three-piece suit, and I'll always remember the red silk tie he wore. It was the only thing animated about him, that and the international edition of a British newspaper he read from, the name of which I can't recall. And I, of course, having purchased all of my clothing at a discount shop in New Jersey, looked like his servant or at least a distant relative whom he had sent to college here in the States. He ordered steak and a glass of red wine, and he permitted me only a small cup of tea, meaning that our discussions would be brief and that we were neither friends nor colleagues. I was simply his worker, and he was my superior.

"How do you find America?" he asked in a British accent.

"It's interesting," I said. "It has taken some adjustment."

"Is there anything out of the ordinary you'd like to report?" he asked.

"No."

"Your bank account shows that you are being properly compensated for your expenses? Your rent and food bills are being paid on time?"

"Yes."

"The accommodations we've provided you with are satisfactory?"

"Yes."

"Good, then. You will await further instructions, but if none come between now and next month, you are still to check in with me next month and every month thereafter at this same time and at this same location. Is that clear?"

"Yes."

"Good day to you, then."

And he went back to reading his newspaper. He hardly even looked up from it the entire time we talked.

I returned to New Jersey that afternoon, and it was only a week later that someone knocked on my door. It was a crisp autumn afternoon when, actually, two people knocked on my door—a mother and her young son, apparently. She was a young American woman with auburn hair and mysterious green eyes. I had never before seen such a bewildering combination in a woman before. And standing next to her on the porch was her young son who couldn't have been older than three or four. A small tot he was, standing there looking at his shoes. And I remember being a little annoyed at the interruption—not that I was doing anything important really. I was watching CNN. She also held a package wrapped in tin foil in her hands.

"Hi," she said. "I'm Angela, and this is my son, Alex."

"Hello," I said reluctantly, my English steadily improving but still a bit broken.

"We're your upstairs neighbors," she said. "We thought we'd bring you over some homemade apple pie."

"But I don't want any apple pie," I said.

"Oh. Well, we're not going to eat it, so if you'd like to try some..."

"I'm not hungry right now," I said.

"Okay. Well, we just wanted to introduce ourselves."

I knew I shouldn't have, because they were infidels, and no woman ever visits another man alone at his residence—with or without a child at her side. But there was something very sad about her that her green eyes hid very deeply within the folds of that American soul of hers, and of course her son didn't look all that jubilant either. They turned to walk away, but I just couldn't see them leave so quickly. Yes, I was rudely disturbed, but there was something very melancholy about them that I had to engage. Perhaps there was some part of her melancholia that I had to fight.

"Wait a minute," I called out to them. "Why don't you come in. I'll accept the introduction of you and your American child."

I remember her telling me that I needed furniture for my apartment. We all had to sit on the floor back then, until one afternoon she finally convinced me to buy a sofa and even a coffee table. I never expected her to visit so often, but apparently she was a lonely woman. The father of the child had abandoned them for some pleasure-seeking dream that she said probably wouldn't come true. She said he played guitar, and one morning he simply left her and the child at the breakfast table, never to return. He said he would be right back, she said. The woman had been moving from town-to-town ever since, finding work where she could. They seemed like such a lonely pair, but they were beautiful people, I came to believe. And even though I preferred to remain alone—because I wanted nothing to do with the enemy—I slowly began to look forward to her visits. Sometimes she would bring her son with her. At other times, especially when her son was off to school, she would visit me alone, and we would talk over tea.

She asked me about Lebanon, as that's where I told her I was from, and she grew fascinated by the life I had once lived there. At times we indulged and had coffee, and she sometimes brought some American pastries with her. But I'll always remember how sad she looked and how alone she was. She wanted more out of life, and I thought that this wanting of more is what made Americans the bane of humanity, their greed and corruption knowing no bounds. The rest of the world had to suffer because of it.

But after several straight months of waiting for my orders, I too wanted more for some reason, and I came to understand why the young woman suffered so much. Her eyes, it seemed, were always looking for an escape and perhaps a return to the places she once knew—places of comfort and security, the places where she was once happy, joyous, and free. But she had been cast out of these places, she said. And after several months of having coffee and pastries with her, usually in the afternoons before the yellow bus returned her son from the local elementary school, I came to see her wanting to move on to better and greater things as somewhat, well, as somewhat admirable. It was a worthy goal: to aspire to a better life, I supposed, and perhaps this was how Allah operated within her. She believed heaven actually existed on earth somewhere instead of it existing in heaven alone.

On one of our usual afternoons together, she asked me, "Would you look after my son tonight?"

"Why? What for?" I asked.

"I have a date tonight, and I'll be out for a few hours. I can't afford to hire a sitter."

"What do you mean you have a date tonight?"

"Well," she smiled, "in America, sometimes a girl is asked by a boy to go out to dinner and eat. And this time, I accepted."

"Who is this boy?" I asked, unable to calm the pang of jealousy that pinched at my nerves.

"He's a guy I met," she smiled. "He works at the Shoprite."

"And you like this boy?" I asked incredulously.

"I don't know. I mean, I just met him, so I really don't know all that much about him."

"I see. But now I'm thinking that we should do the same thing."

"You mean go out?"

180

"If that's what you want to call it, yes."

"Sure," she smiled a bit shyly. "But you're forgetting that I already see you almost every day."

"Yes, but we should go out for dinner too sometimes, don't you think?"

"Sure," she said.

For several years I must have watched her son grow. He grew right in front of my eyes, because from the first time she dropped him off, to the last time I had seen him, she trusted me with her son, and together he and I spent many evenings playing these silly American board games, all of them corrupt, and reading the silliest American children's books until he fell asleep on the new couch I bought for his small body. At times he was so filled with energy that I thought the child a jinn who would never know the virtues of patience. But over time, I taught him about God and the importance of submitting to His will. Of course, he usually fell asleep when I talked of God and only awoke to play another silly board game, but I figured that this was how Americans are—always wanting to play a game, or go to the movies, or read the cartoons in their books. He was certainly a restless boy, and he asked me so many questions that I couldn't possibly answer any of them myself. It was then that I admitted to myself that the only ignorant person in America was myself and not everyone else as I had initially believed.

It was in the winter of 2000 that I again met my contact in New York. He actually had something for me to do this time. He asked all of his standard questions as a matter of course, and these were the same tired questions he had been asking for four years straight. His moustache and beard had grayed, and he was no longer so thin. All of those steaks, cooked to perfection, must have finally caught up with him.

At this particular meeting, though, he slid a thick, letter-sized envelope across the table.

"Your time has just about come," he said.

"What is it?" I asked of the envelope.

"We're sending you to Florida for a couple of weeks."

"What on earth for?"

"You're going to learn how to fly."

"What for," I asked.

He folded his newspaper and looked at me for what seemed like the first time he had ever laid eyes on me. His eyes were dark and vacuous, as though there weren't a decent soul behind them—just a cold darkness that knew no end.

"Do you remember why we sent you here?" he asked.

"Of course I do."

"You didn't happen to forget why you were sent here, did you?"

"No. Of course not."

"If I were you, I'd better not forget. Have a good trip. All of the details are enclosed. That will be all for now."

You could say that the arrival of my orders was met with a bit of ambivalence on my part, but when I returned by train to New Jersey, it finally occurred to me what the plan was leading to. In fact, there was no doubting it. I simply connected the dots with the news that had been coming in through the television, and I could see that the world hadn't changed its attitudes very much since the election. I learned that my orders were, in fact, much bigger than my own paltry desires were.

When I returned home, I immediately asked the young woman to come down to see me, but I wanted to see her alone and not with her son. I said it was urgent, and being the good woman that she was, she came downstairs immediately. Together we sat on the small couch that I had bought for her son. I turned the television off, and I told her that I was leaving for Florida in the morning.

She looked surprised, only that I was more surprised by this admission than she was.

"Why are you going to Florida?" she asked, her green eyes wide and expressing a concern I wasn't used to.

"I don't want to go to Florida," I said.

"Then don't go to Florida," she smiled. "The beauty of living here is that you don't have to do anything if you don't want to do it. You may have to accept the consequences, though."

"I don't want to go," I said again. "I want to stay here. I want to take care of you."

She smiled at this.

"Now why would you want to take care of little ol' me for?"

I think it was then that I kissed her for the very first time, and that night she stayed with me after putting her son to bed upstairs. Her beauty infiltrated the ugliness of why I had come, because I finally recognized how ugly I was—how criminal and ugly I was capable of becoming—as though there were no end to my ugliness, just continual trap doors that kept me falling into regions that slowly pecked away at any ounce of soul that remained. And somehow it was she who would stop me from falling, always falling, into circumstances and conflicts that I couldn't for the life of me understand anymore. And as we lay together in bed underneath the single white sheet that covered our nude bodies, my heart exploded in confession—about the contact I had been meeting in New York, about why I had come to America in the first place, about the meetings I had with my Muslim brothers in Damascus before I left in 1996.

"Do you really hate us that much?" she then asked me.

I couldn't respond to this most essential question, a question I could have easily answered affirmatively several years ago, but now this question simply revolved in the furnace of my mind without any answer at all. I simply said, while gazing into those green eyes of hers, that I couldn't possibly hate someone I've grown to love.

"What will you do then?"

"They'll come for me if I'm not on that plane to Miami tomorrow morning. I have to leave tomorrow, but I'm not going to Florida. I have to go elsewhere."

We lay there for an hour or so before I asked her, "do you want to come with me," and to this she remained quiet and still for some time, her soft body entwined in mine, rising and falling as if in a trance.

"It's my son," she said. "I can't leave him."

"He'll be coming too, y'know," I smiled.

"It's not a good idea. He likes it here. His teachers are here. His school is here. His friends are all here."

"I see."

She then kissed me softly, almost sadly, as if to tell me goodbye.

On the next morning, after I kissed her mouth over and over again and stared into her green eyes for the very last time, I knew I had betrayed my cause, my Muslim brothers who had been waiting for me in Florida, my faith, and everything I had once believed in. Call it an insurrection against the madness of our conflict, if you so desire.

I packed my bags and headed west by bus into the heartland of America, never to return to New York again. I disappeared as many venerable imams of our Middle Eastern past have come to do many times over. It was only a year later, in the fall of 2001, that I woke up on that ill-fated morning to find, to my genuine horror and disgust, that my superior in New York had easily found a replacement for me.

THE ANOINTED

Lately I've been very concerned about my status as an advanced bachelor. There's no question that I often wonder about those who are lucky enough to be dating or involved in some long-term, drawn-out relationship that will eventually lead to marriage, kids, and the quaint suburban home in towns well-known for keeping out all undesirables like myself, because this where a lot of dating couples wind up. And lately I've ruled out the possibility of this happening to me, because I've now hit one of these very lonely periods in my short life thus far where I just can't seem to get a date or attract a woman for reasons that are almost mystical in their proportion.

I'm assuming that every man has a dry spell or two in their life, but my dry spell has extended way beyond what I even thought possible—which is why I'm so concerned nowadays that the options normally left wide open for most men are now closed for me. And so I must continue plodding along this road of life and try to forget about attracting a woman or getting involved in a relationship with one, even though not thinking about it is totally impossible to do.

At first I began to question what exactly was it that women found so wrong with a guy like me. I consider myself to be a good, decent person. I'm responsible in many ways. I'm a half-way decent conversationalist. For a man, I'm not that ugly at all. But then I started to wonder whether or not I was too short, for instance. Or perhaps I was too reserved and not anally expulsive enough. Or perhaps it's because my skin is a bit tanner than the average Viking. Or maybe there's something about my mind or my personality that women pick up on, thereby giving them some reason to turn me away when I ask them out. And considering that I'm neither too rich nor too poor, maybe it does have something to do with my income. Maybe it's not adequate enough. I guess I can't see anything that's too terribly wrong with me, and I figure that women do like me to some degree, as I am a fairly likable guy. The problem may lie in the fact that they just don't like me enough to date me. I've even tried exercising and lifting weights, but even this fails to attract them. And so this dry spell has lasted for several years now with no sign of it ending, and I can't for the life of me figure out why this is happening to me.

When I look out of my window on a typical weekend night here in the city of Albany, New York, I see plenty of evidence of men cavorting with women, men getting into romances, and men getting into highly-involved sexual relationships with women all along the small strip of avenue that I have a view of from my small apartment. And these men aren't exactly clones of each other either. I can't say that they fit the mold of some generic type of male, or some standard model of a male that is more likely to find a girlfriend in this city. Actually, the men here come in all different sizes, shapes, colors, and varying degrees of handsomeness. They all seem to be actively dating and having sex while doing it. And so I am still left wondering why I am the one who is left out of the running. This predicament has given me good cause to invent a theory regarding my exclusion from the dating pool, and lately this theory has given me some solace on lonely nights such as this but not enough solace to withstand the threat of a perpetual singledom that I can't seem to wiggle my way out of no matter how hard I try.

This theory I've invented is based on the assumption that, due to some mystical or quasi-supernatural force that I cannot see but can still detect operating in the universe, that there are men like me in a sexually-thriving and promiscuous population who are strangely 'anointed' by these mystical forces to attract women on a continual basis and, therefore, get involved in both romantic and even purely sexual relationships, reproduce, and fill the world with their eventual offspring as a result. This, in turn, leaves all of those who remain 'unanointed' with the problem of never attracting the opposite sex no matter how hard they try or how desperate or clever their strategies of pursuit become. And so there is a growing divide between those who can get laid any time they wish and those who are forever closed off from this possibility.

For instance, I once knew a man who, in his younger years, was an anointed male who could pretty much get any woman he wanted. He wasn't terribly handsome, and he certainly didn't make a lot of money either. But somehow the women flocked to him wherever he went, and from my standpoint, I still can't tell why the women seemed to fall at his feet. He was one of those rare birds that could walk into any local bar and pick up any woman he wanted for the night. And it wasn't the case that he possessed any special gift of language or speech. Neither was he any more well-endowed in a certain area of the male anatomy than any other of the males jockeying for women on any given night. But one thing's for sure—the women fell at his feet for reasons that most lonely men like myself just can't understand.

A story about this man that I once had the sad misfortune of hearing boldly illustrates the contrast between this man, who was mystically anointed, and another man who was not. One night this same man walked into a local Albany watering hole intent on having a few beers before heading home. It was no secret that many women from the local area hung out at this bar, and on that particular night in question, a local beauty from the nearby college was sitting alone at the bar and having a quiet drink all by herself. It was clear to the other male barflies who buzzed about her that this woman didn't want to be disturbed by any of their vain attempts to pick her up. She was there to relax, and she spurned all the men who propositioned her and who would have loved to take her home. This included a young man at the far end of the bar who had a crush on this college beauty but was always rejected by her.

For our purposes, we'll call this poor young man Kronski, which alludes to the famous Henry Miller character who suffers a similar plight in one of Miller's novels. At any rate, in walks the anointed man after a night drinking in a few other watering holes around town, and perhaps he is even thankful to be entering the bar alone. All he wants is a solitary drink before he calls it a night, and so the anointed man simply walks up to the bar, sits close to where the young beauty queen sits, and orders his nightcap. But for some strange reason, the beauty queen suddenly breaks her terrible silence, and she immediately starts talking to the anointed guy about God-knows-what. It turns out that the beauty queen and this guy really hit it off—to the intense consternation of poor Kronski at the end of the bar who is lost in the swill of his own misery and drinking himself to death over how this mystery stranger appeared out of nowhere and just picked up the woman of his dreams.

'This can't be,' says Kronski to himself, as he has been rejected by her too many times before. Kronski has offered her the world along with all of his devotion, and yet she has still refused him, only to find delight in this complete and obtrusive stranger. Well, it turns out that this anointed stranger takes the beauty queen home that night, and for every night thereafter the two are seen cavorting and feeling each other up at the bar—all of this to Kronski's slow and deepening madness, because it is Kronski who truly loves her and not this stranger. But what's very important to note is that Kronski has no idea why the beauty queen has refused him and why she suddenly gives all of her love to a slick-tongued stranger who just happens to saunter in one night.

It turns out that poor Kronski just couldn't take it anymore. One night, after voyeuristically tuning into the newly anointed couple at the bar and the romantic conversation they shared, poor Kronski soon left in a fury, got into his car as drunk as anyone his size could get, and rammed his vehicle full-speed into a retaining wall at the shopping plaza across the street. He died instantly. He just couldn't handle the fact that this other man was an anointed one and that he simply wasn't. He couldn't understand what made some men anointed and other men unanointed. The unanointed, like Kronski, are sentenced to a life of abject loneliness and despair for reasons they can't explain. Nor can anyone else explain it.

Let's take another example of this strange curse that haunts men who aren't necessarily as woebegone or as cruelly excluded as Kronski. For this, we take a turn to the literary world and reexamine the lives of the poets Phillip Larkin and Kingsley Amis, both of them good friends during their notorious literary careers, but alas!—one poet was unanointed while the other poet received all of the privileges that went with his anointed status. And while we often tinker with insanity when we actually try to compare the talents of two different poets, after a cursory survey of these poets' works, many in the literary world may argue that Phillip Larkin was truly an amazing poet and was even more talented at the craft than his good friend Kingsley Amis. And while it's true that Amis was cut from a more princely and perhaps a more physically attractive cloth than Larkin, let's make no mistake about it that Larkin wasn't exactly too ugly to be turned away by any of the women he pursued. Larkin, in other words, was certainly no Kronski in this regard but a well-known and talented poet whom most men would think capable of attracting many young women. Unfortunately for the unanointed, however, this is hardly the case.

To much of his chagrin, the beautiful and wealthy women of the European continent tumbled into Kingsley Amis' arms, and there wasn't really any reason for this other than Amis had somehow been anointed at birth by some Bene Gesserit wave of the hand, or perhaps a tapping on the head of a good witch's wand, that permitted the most attractive women in the world to express themselves sexually with Amis and many lesser-known poets like him—but not with Larkin. Somehow Amis' good friend was excluded and left out, like a baby thrown out with the bathwater, because no matter how hard Larkin tried, no matter how many stunts he pulled, all Larkin could hear were the crickets chirping from his lonely position on earth to infinite and empty space above when he propositioned women. And in the next house over it was Kingsley Amis who orchestrated the orgies that Larkin was never invited to.

Of course, we members of the literary world often credit Larkin's unanointed status with the grinds and frustrations that often produced his great art. But while Amis was also a good poet, we can easily say that because of his anointed status, he must have also been a much happier poet and infinitely more satisfied with his life's calling as though no other line of work would befit a man so privileged in this regard. It should also be noted here that there have been very few poets before Amis who have ever been credited with attracting the sheer number of wanna-be poets to the profession than he. They looked to imitate—not his poetry necessarily—but certainly his satisfying sex life.

And yet the curse of living the unanointed life also extends to women, believe it or not. One would think that the anointed theory only extends to men, but this is entirely untrue if we consider what some women have had to endure when they fall under the terrible curse. Many men may falsely assume that it is women who control the curse and that it is their doing that pushes the unanointed to the sidelines as they clear the way for only the most beautiful women to jump into bed with only a few anointed men. But this is not so.

Let's take a look at Christine Chubbuck, a Sarasota, Florida television news reporter who shot herself in the back of the head while giving a live news broadcast on-air from the anchor's seat one morning. This was back in the summer of 1974, and the on-air suicide rocked the nation and came to be known as one of the grisliest moments in all of television history. Many have blamed Chubbuck's suicide on her clinical depression and her inability to feel secure in her social interactions with her peers, and this is odd, because on paper at least, Christine Chubbuck was a successful reporter who had contributed to her profession in many ways but also to her society by helping the less fortunate at certain times in her life. But to the unanointed, the tired explanation of being clinically depressed and shy in social situations is really just window-dressing the problem.

From what we know of her life, the driving force behind her depression was her inability to find men who would ask her out. Because she was unanointed, she was constantly overlooked by potential mates. The men just weren't responding to her. They ignored her for reasons we still do not know or can't reasonably understand. The only possible reason is that she was unanointed by the same wand that had tapped the other women instead of her. And what's more, Chubbuck lost one of her ovaries due to a medical condition shortly before her suicide. She only had a month or two before she would be unable to have children at all. So now we're talking about being an unanointed female with time pressure involved, and this can tear any man or woman to shreds, as it did Christine Chubbuck.

Because, really, there was nothing really that wrong with her. She was well-liked and well-respected in her field of television journalism, was fairly good-looking, had a good, loving family, and also did good works and deeds. But she was also unanointed, and when it comes down to the bare bones of it, being unanointed can mark the difference between wanting to live and wanting to die. For some, like Christine Chubbuck, having an unanointed status is simply too much to bear, and so on that fate-ridden day in July of 1974, she simply gave up the fight. It's obvious to me now that being unanointed can have very serious life-or-death consequences that go along with its curse.

Interestingly enough, I had been somewhat obsessed by my status as an unanointed bachelor, given this information that had gradually come to light, when a local Albany friend of mine—a male friend, by the way, in keeping with the unanointed male tradition—asked me one morning if I'd like to go with him and a group of his friends to the Saratoga Race Track for an afternoon of horses, sunshine, food, and booze. What's more, my good friend said that our group would include a few women from the Saratoga area. Naturally, I jumped at the chance to attend, as there was nothing I wouldn't do to become anointed, and perhaps this outing would dispel the self-conscious ruminations I had been having on the matter and perhaps debunk the myth of my own unanointedness. Maybe I was just being silly about the whole thing, because if I met a woman at the race track, which was something that my friend said could very well happen, then I would no longer be unanointed, and it would have all been in my head to begin with.

I traveled to Saratoga by car with my friend driving, and together we sped into a sun-drenched afternoon towards Saratoga, which is about a forty minute drive north of Albany. When we arrived, we were both amazed at how crowded it was. Everyone was dressed in the most splendid colors. The men wore pricey polo-knit shirts, and the women wore flowery sundresses with wide-brimmed hats in keeping with the traditional fashions of the horse races. The place was not unlike an amusement park where a parade of thoroughbreds were led by their trainers through the colorful crowd . They were walked to the starting gate at the edge of the track.

These horses were probably the most splendid creatures I had ever seen before—their coats slick, shiny, and chocolate-colored. Their muscles flexed beneath their skins as they walked majestically along the winding trail that showcased how incredibly strong, and in many ways, how incredibly aesthetically-pleasing they were to behold. Their thick, sinewy bodies were almost feminine in their beauty but also as strong and well-built as any high-powered engine. For a man sentenced to an existence of lower-class bachelorhood, I certainly felt regal while watching this pageantry of horses. Their sun-kissed female fans hanging over the sides of the trail's railings adored these creatures as though they were infinitely more attractive than the boyfriends they were with.

And after a while of being near the women and the horses, I felt as though my unanointed status was slowly but surely melting away and being replaced by the confidence that came with the tap of the mystical wand upon the crown of my head, as I felt myself moving headlong into anointedness that afternoon. I could feel powerful forces at work tugging me towards that grail, and now all I needed to do was to meet these women that my friend had bragged about on the car ride over. I was ready to accept my new status in life and was glad to be done with the old.

My good friend led me towards the edge of a crowded pavilion that was covered by a wide awning that shaded us from the sunlight and permitted a cool breeze to circulate within. And next to a fully-stocked cash bar and a row of standing tables a small group of jubilant faces greeted us. There were two guys wearing aviator sunglasses, khaki pants, and buck Oxford shoes, and they were surrounded by four very pretty women in sundresses. I couldn't believe our luck, because as I calculated how this arrangement would work, there was a young and attractive blonde woman who would obviously be paired with me for the afternoon.

Finally morning had broken. All the clouds that had obstructed my eventual rise into the celestial realms had cleared, because this woman was the perfect match for me after years of going without. And when I was properly introduced, we immediately talked about the amazing day at the races we were all having and how pleasing it was to be there. Her eyes lit up while talking with me, as though for the first time during my long, arduous dry spell a woman actually wanted to have something to do with me. She wanted the particulars of my life, because as we talked, she slowly let me in as though she no longer needed her defenses and had no pretense for turning me away as she did the many unanointed men who had tried before me. And because it felt so uncharacteristic of my prior interactions with women, I sensed also that there had to be something terribly ominous about the way she reacted to me, because I could sense that something was just not right about the whole scenario. There just had to be something on the horizon that would surely eclipse the heavenly sunlight that bathed the day.

And this eclipse came as a slight feeling at first that grew stronger and more powerful, because the people at the edge of the bar started to stir a little bit, and soon people were saying 'excuse me' to some hidden force that moved through them. I couldn't see what all the commotion was about, but as the crowd parted I could feel the clouds suffocating the sunshine and bringing into our company a young middle-aged man in an electric wheelchair. He rolled through the dense crowd that parted for him and like a marauder he parked right at the side of the young woman I had been talking to all this time.

His wheelchair was controlled by a small on-board computer that came attached to it. He steered the wheelchair with a small joystick on its armrest. It was an amazing piece of equipment that was at the cutting edge of technological advancement. And he rolled right into our conversation.

After taking a long, sober look at this man, I realized that some terrible injury had befallen him, but as a courtesy I did not inquire how he came to be so disfigured. I assumed that he was in an automobile accident. And the girl who was once mine introduced him as her husband. She then excused herself to get another drink from the bar but not without a quick smile and quick wink that was meant for my eyes only. And through this simple gesture, I was sexually aroused right where I stood. It was a wink and a smile that begged me to take her away from her husband, to free her from her responsibilities as a caregiver, to break the chain that binded her to a man confined to a home where she had to feed him, clothe him, and bathe him every day for the rest of her life. Because even though this man in the wheelchair had suffered greatly from whatever accident he had, this same man, through some turn of luck, was still an anointed man despite all that had happened to him. He was anointed before his terrible accident, and he was still anointed now. No matter what shape or form he now took, he would always have his beautiful young wife by his side. And she begged me to set her free from him and the contraption that he rolled around in.

What action I took after that fateful day is not as important as what I had learned about the difference between those who are sentenced all of their lives to remain painfully unanointed and those who are somehow moved from this hell to the hallowed ground of anointedness. It's the same difference that divides the rich from the poor, the haves from the have-nots, the slave-owner from the slave, and the angels from the demons. Because I had a decision to make at the racetrack that afternoon. I understood the significance of the divine test I had been presented with. I understood the measures that many men before me must have taken to become anointed creatures after years of playing the misfit, the pariah, and the social outcast. And although it was no easy choice, I can say with every degree of confidence that the anointed and unanointed must both suffer equally in the terribleness of life.

THE CLOTH

Against the glow of a calm fire the young boy and his father ate their cooked lamb quietly within the dark confines of their hovel high on the Meccan hillside. They had just finished their evening prayers and were both equally famished from a day of trading trinkets in the city bazaar for whatever they could get for them. Every so often a cold wind swept through the home and fanned the fire they enjoyed, its warm light dancing and casting misshapen shadows across the dirt floor of the room. While picking at his lamb meat, the young boy gazed into the fire as he had done so many times before, wondering which parts of the kindling the flames would excite next. His father broke him out of this trance by warning him that he shouldn't gaze for so long into mysteries that he couldn't for the life of him understand at such a young age. The son heeded his father's advice that evening and finished whatever meat remained at the center of the thali. When the father finished the rest of the lamb, he boiled a tin kettle of strong black coffee, and both of them sat in silence for a time, sipping on the dark, bitter brew.

"Tomorrow," said the father, "I will not accompany you to the bazaar. You are quickly becoming a young man, and you will have to go by yourself."

An awkward warmth seeped into the heart of the boy, as going to the bazaar alone would only result in being bested by the other, more experienced traders. These traders would undoubtedly be much more aggressive and predatory in their tactics than he could ever be. His eyes widened and searched his father for any excuse he could give for not sending him into the fray alone, but the old man offered none, and so it was decided that evening that he would venture from the hillside into the heart of the Meccan capital and hope that he brought home at least some of his self-respect. The father, sensing that his son was frightened by this decision, finished what remained of his charred coffee and rummaged through his burlap sack of goods that warmed by the fire.

He pulled out a small package from the sack. It was wrapped in waxy brown paper and stitched up tight by strong thread. His father peeled off the packaging to reveal a soft turquoise cloth that had been neatly folded within. He passed it to the boy who was instantly charmed and fascinated by its beauty, its edges embroidered in geometric shapes of gold and the center of the cloth stitched in the patterns of the most careful Arabic calligraphy that read, "there is no God but the One." The cloth smelled of aged saffron, and a chalky dust layered its weave. Even though it was made from cotton, it felt like the finest of silks and was too fragile to hold for very long. The father returned it to the hollow of the wrapping and handed the package to him.

"I know we don't talk about it much," said the father, "but when your mother wandered the streets of the city, both hungry and cold from the desert winds, she found me in the bazaar and implored me to serve as your guardian, as she didn't have any food to feed you. You were too young to remember, as you were just a small baby then, and when your mother gave you to me, I wrapped you in this very same cloth that I'm giving you now. I've kept the cloth from you, because I thought that when you became of age, you could sell it and start a new life for yourself."

The boy gazed at it with wide, bewildered eyes. He felt comforted and secure holding it, as though it were the only security he had left, now that his father had ordered him into the bazaar.

"The indulgences we sell aren't getting us very far, you and I. No one is buying them, and when we do sell them, we are getting half of what we originally paid for them. The meat tonight was the last of our rations. There is no more, and our supplies are running low. You will have to fetch a high price for the cloth. Otherwise, you'll go hungry, which is why I'm suggesting to you that we separate for a time."

The boy never realized it would come to this. For most of his life he had been following his father through the few bazaars in and around the twin cities of Mecca and Medina. Trading was a skill he never possessed, and he had always assumed his father would carry him until he himself grew old and tired. He never expected their time together to end so soon. He somehow expected his father to nurture and care for him without the realities of hunger getting in the way. They always did without, and it was fine for a time, but apparently things had to change.

He didn't want to weep in front of him, as he thought his father would respect him less for doing so. Traders, after all, had to be very keen and wary of such emotions. It was a disadvantage to have them. One becomes vulnerable that way. He suppressed his tears as well as any show of emotion. He was helped by the charisma of the fire, its flames licking what remained of the few desert branches it fed from. A sweet, mellow smoke filled the small hovel, the fire devouring the wood with a slow and steady exactitude that seemed to harness a greater, more divine force. Even after spreading his blankets down for sleep, the boy continued to watch the glowing crimson embers of the fire burn, until the flames themselves were overcome by the darkness of the hovel. He fell asleep quickly thereafter, his father snoring lightly beside him.

On the next morning, his father bid him farewell by placing his hand upon his head and muttering a short prayer. He did his best to hide his tears then, and while he couldn't understand what the prayer meant, he assumed that it would somehow protect him from whatever turbulence and anxiety the action in the bazaar would bring.

"You should not sell it for anything less than ten rials," said his father of the cloth. "You have to be firm and insist on that price. Otherwise, you will have been cheated. Do you understand?"

The boy repeated his instructions until his father was satisfied. When he opened the door of the hovel, a brilliant, white sunshine flooded his vision, and an intense heat seeped into the pores of his skin. At first the sunlight blinded him, but after wrapping his head in white cloth, he adjusted to the climate and made his way down a rock-strewn trail that led into the center of the city. He tread silently on the jagged rubble and debris that littered the trail, and when others from neighboring villages joined him after a good hour of methodical walking, he made sure to look tough and remain both silent and cautious. He kept his eyes peeled to the ground and tucked the package securely into the twine that kept his garments in place. And while no one talked to him directly, he certainly was aware of the calculating whispers of those on the road who commented on his poor dress and child-like appearance.

"He will certainly be taken advantage of," he heard one of these voices say.

As the trail grew more crowded, these voices all seemed to be whispering the same in unison. Even the most remote of their palaver somehow related directly to him, and as the trail gave way to a paved road at the base of the hillside, the dry desert dirt that swirled in the wind had also swept away whatever fragments of confidence he had started the day with. Yet he kept silent and strong with his eyes fixed forward and the package at his waist snug and secure against his body.

The paved road quickly transformed into a small village with a kebab stand and a general store. One story shacks, both sagging and sullen, soon succumbed to marble mosques, outdoor restaurants, and two-story buildings that were sturdy and white-washed, their lacquered wooden shutters protecting its inhabitants from the blare of intense sunlight and road-dust that burned in the air. The road pinched into a narrow lane where a car or two buzzed through the procession like strange insects. These lanes were soon joined by other roadways and side streets that fed into the dazzling network of the metropolis. The mosques, filled to the hilt with believers keeling below tall, white domes, were both high and august, and the ongoing din of conversation that seemed to engage every pedestrian cleared the air of the same guarded silence that stalked him on the hillside. The odor of cooking meat and mild incense made him hungry and a little tired, but he knew he had to continue towards the bazaar and save these luxuries for after he had fetched the highest price for the cloth.

As he approached the bazaar, he discerned its canopy of white canvas tents rippling in the hot breeze. He heard the rough din of the shouting matches between the toughest of traders and the most uncompromising of customers. The traffic on the roadway festooned into a carnival of color. Stalls on the both sides of the street sold hand-woven rugs from Iran, leather jackets and accessories from Pakistan, gold-threaded robes from North Africa, and Chinese textiles that were rolled onto heavy cardboard tubing and stood erect, like rainbows, behind colorful salespeople and their equally illustrious buyers who yelled out their best offers. Pushcart vendors sold skewered meats and kebabs, and buyers wore their best garments in what amounted to a parade of Arab fashion. Collapsible awnings that swung out from the storefronts hid the street from the sun, and as soon as the heat became too much, large, white tents shaded most of the haggling, negotiating, and sudden bursts of emotional reasoning that distinguished this volcanic oasis from other towns and villages outside of the city.

Usually the boy quietly followed his father down these crowded side streets, but now that he was alone, the bazaar had a much different feel to it. He sensed that beneath the bazaar's spectrum of colors, expensive imported products, and hoarse shouts of traders haggling over prices, there was an invisible darkness in which the real elements of hunger and desire lay buried beneath a cosmetic surface. He had always known of this predatory darkness, or at least he had sensed it on visits with his father, but it was his father who usually confronted it while the boy watched from a safe distance. His father had often hoped that he would be able to manage this darkness one day—to make trading more of a sport than the fulfillment of predatory hunger and zero-sum conflicts—but now that he was alone, he was rife with timidity and soon lost some of his father's skills. He could only stay tough and hope that no one cheated him or goaded him into selling the cloth below its set value.

From a distance he eyed the activities of one particular stall that lined the street. Apparently, the trader and his stubborn customer were arguing over the price of what seemed to be a thin silver bracelet that was clearly meant for a young woman's wrist. The heavy-set customer soon ended these negotiations when the trader refused to sell it to him at the price he wanted, and the boy thought it the perfect time to approach this frustrated customer with the cloth he carried. He moved in cautiously behind him and tugged on his trousers. The man then turned to face him, and the boy gasped at what he saw.

This was no ordinary man. He wore a blood-red turban, heavy gold earrings, and an embroidered vest that hid a tan-collared work shirt beneath it. His skin was thick, red, and robust, a handlebar moustache gracing his upper lip, and his teeth were like heavy white blocks in his mouth. A long, deep scar cut into one of his ruddy cheeks, and emblazoned on his arm was what appeared to be a military insignia of sorts. The boy also noticed braided gold epaulets on his shoulders, distinguishing him as some sort of authority in the city or a high government official. He looked perturbed by the intrusion, but before he could swat him away with his heavy, brick-like hands, the boy quickly tore through the stitching that held the package at his waist together and unfurled the brilliant turquoise cloth that had been with him all along.

The official, awestruck by the cloth's inescapable beauty, examined its fine thread and fingered the heavy gold embroidery at its edges and center. Apparently he had never seen such a cloth before and decided that it was a gift that rivaled the thin bracelet he tried to buy earlier. The official's hard, cold scowl suddenly transformed into a seductive smile, the white blocks of his teeth glowing like polished marble, his frustration waning, and a subtle twinkle in his eyes restoring whatever strategies had failed him earlier. He licked his lips and breathed in a heavy gust of hot, desert air, as though a dead beast had been brought back to life.

"How much do you want for this worthless thing?" asked the official.

"What price do you propose?" asked the boy.

"Why this is nothing but the handkerchief of a peasant. I've seen this a million times before. It can't be worth anything more than five rials."

The boy, however, knew a little better than that.

"This is a very special cloth that dates back many generations. It is a magic cloth and will bring comfort to whoever owns it. I'll be willing to sell it for ten rials, nothing less."

"Why you insolent little monkey," thundered the official, "do you know who I am? How dare you insult me with your offer. Ten rials for a filthy scrap of cloth? I can easily buy such filth elsewhere for far cheaper than that. But I tell you what— since I am an official of high distinction around these parts, you and I can make a deal that will give you even more benefit than the price of that silly little thing you have there.

"Do you see these honors on my chest? I am a man who is well-respected by the powers that control this unwieldy city, and if you sold that thing to me for, let's say, seven rials, why I'd connect you with some of the most powerful people in the kingdom.

"Imagine yourself working your way up through the chain of civic command, only to prosper with the knowledge and skill that comes with shrewd politics and honorable governance. This entire city is controlled and maintained by some of the wealthiest men in the world. Not only will you intimately know the powerful statesmen who enforce our daily laws and customs, but you will have a chance to harness the power your downtrodden peasantry has sought after for so long. Imagine inspecting a line of troops or attending banquets with world-renowned dignitaries from all over the world, or having the satisfaction of crushing a rebellion with the wave of your hand.

"I'm offering you a chance at the reigns of power, my friend—an opportunity, if you will, to be a part of the political class that rules all of Arabia. Wherever you go, you'd be treated with the highest respect. People will respect you, fear you, and love you for the power you wield. The food will always be plentiful and your peasant masses will revere you as their long-lost messiah. Can you imagine the power of that? Can you imagine what a man you'd be? For seven rials you can have all of that. Just lower your price, and this city will open up to you."

By this time visions of grandeur had broken the seals of his imagination. The boy could think of no other life better than that of a man who had the power to control and maintain the vast complexities of the city. The offer struck a deep chord within him, as heavy silver thalis, thick with moist and tender meats, simmered in the juices of his mind. He could also see himself in regal dress, talking politics with the Sultan himself, or trading jokes with the commanders of vast armies, all of this under the high dome of a luxurious palace he calls home. He even imagined himself exercising his fierce power over the migrants who whispered things about him on the trail that morning, and how he would somehow force them to their knees in worship of the power he had achieved. They would never whisper bad things about him again.

All of this came into clear focus, and just before he gave his consent to the official, who stood there smiling and twirling the ends of his moustache, a bright blade of sunlight broke through the open sides of the tent and illuminated the gold embroidery stitched into the cloth. The refracting light snapped him out of his vague imaginings, and he quickly recalled his father's instructions. He tore himself away from these superb visions of power and summoned the same rigor and toughness that he carried down the hillside with him.

"Ten rials only," said the boy finally. "Nothing more."

The smile of the towering official above him soon tightened, and his angry, threatening scowl returned. His cheeks filled with scorching hot blood, and the twinkle in his eyes shot back a sharp darkness that would have immediately cut him to bits had he not stepped a few paces back from him.

"Why you dirty little rodent, do you know what the penalties are for conning a city official? Why I'll throw you in prison for the time you've wasted me. Come here, you filthy rat—"

The official tried to grab hold of the boy, but since he was a few paces away from him already, his heavy hands could only grab his shirt, which immediately tore as the boy stumbled back and ran into the thickest part of the bazaar. His small frame served him well as he weaved among the torsos of wandering pedestrians, the official behind him yelling vulgarities in the middle of the road and stomping his feet in heated madness. The boy then fled the bazaar and finally found rest on the outskirts of the marketplace, his heart beating beyond his chest and his panic and alarm at almost being thrown in prison subsiding into a calm but weary fatigue.

After his panic subsided, he was left with nothing but utter disappointment for ruining an otherwise glorious future. Luckily he still had the cloth, as he thought he had lost it during his escape. By this time, though, the cloth had lost its smoothness and was wrinkled and manhandled in his fist. He unfurled the cloth and tried to smooth the threads back into shape. It was just then that a slim man in a white, seer-sucker suit and wide-brimmed safari hat emerged from the chaos of the tents and smiled at him graciously.

"Hey, boy, what have you got there?" asked the man.

A renewed confidence lifted the boy from the doldrums. He displayed the full beauty of the turquoise cloth for this man who grazed his manicured fingertips against its fine cotton fibers and translated the Arabic calligraphy at its center with a small, leather-bound book he had been carrying.

"Hmmm, there is no God but the One.' Very interesting indeed," mumbled the man while translating the calligraphy.

His broken Arabic accent pegged him instantly as a traveler from a land far away. The boy had rarely seen such a suit of such high quality on anyone in the bazaar before, and his pale while skin, pink lips, and azure eyes suggested a noble upbringing and a class membership rarely seen in these humble parts of the city. He also had wavy blonde hair, which is something he had never seen on anyone before. The boy took a liking to his suave and courteous manners as well as his peculiar speech, which made his Arabic sound more romantic and complex. His language was fluid and less guttural, as though a date tree was lodged in his throat. The musky odor of his cologne also added to this portrait of a middle-aged tycoon who would never chase after him like the brutish government official had. There was something awkwardly civilized about his overall demeanor, and his first confrontation with this new brand of civility calmed his anxieties and allowed him to feature the cloth more boldly against his body.

"Yes, I see, that's quite a cloth you have there. How much are willing to part with it?"

"Ten rials only," the boy sputtered.

The traveler poked at his chin and thought about the offer in a relaxed pose reserved, it seemed, for wealthy men. He swept his hand through his sun-bleached scalp and ruminated on the offer for what seemed like several minutes. The boy thought he had finally made the sale and imagined himself immediately rushing to the nearest kebab stand, a ten-rial bill in his fist, chewing on thick slices of sweetness cut from large logs of lamb-meat warming against electric burners. His mouth watered, and his empty stomach growled in pain from imagining the meat smothered in yogurt and then eaten with a warm, buttery flat bread. But just when he thought he'd eat again, the traveler stumbled upon an idea that made his eyes widen with excitement.

"I tell you what," said the traveler, plucking an ivory-colored business card from his wallet, "I work for an import/export firm in London. It's one of the largest trading firms in the world. We have offices in twenty countries, from Europe and the Americas, all the way to India and into the jungles of Asia. Our stock has been rated one of the best by the wealthiest investment houses in all of Great Britain."

He also pulled from his wallet what appeared to be an ornamented paper that had the same gritty texture of a rial note he once held.

"Do you see this?" asked the traveler, waving the paper in front of him. "This is a one-pound note, and it is worth at least ten times the value of the cloth you have there. Ten times! Can you believe it? If you sell me the cloth for no more than eight rials, I will get your papers from the British embassy nearby, and you can leave this desert wasteland and come work for me. I can show you how to profit from goods like these by buying them extraordinarily cheap and selling them to well-to-do clients who will buy this same trash in bulk for very high prices. In other words, what are common items for peasants here in the kingdom are all exotic luxury items for the upper class in the civilized West, and if you work for me, I guarantee that you will make a small fortune in your first few years. By implementing my tried-and-tested techniques, you will retire a very wealthy man.

"I mean, just imagine leaving this squalor behind and traveling the world, staying in five-star resorts instead, and returning from your travels to a city mansion in South Ken, eating as much chicken curry as you bloody-well please. You can then invest your small fortune wisely, and when you're old enough, have children of your own and send them to the elitist of schools on the continent. They then go on to become doctors, lawyers, or businessmen after finishing university.

"You can have a family is what I'm saying, and a prosperous one at that. You'd avoid the cycles of poverty that are crippling your race of people and gain your freedom from all of this slavery such a poverty imposes on you, but only if you agree to sell the cloth to me at eight rials, nothing more. Just think of it—eight measly rials, and you can change your stars—alter your destiny is what I'm trying to tell you. You'd never be hungry or left wanting again!"

The traveler handed him the one-pound note, and the boy rubbed its coarse texture between his thumb and forefinger. He gazed at the crowned head of the woman on the face of it and was enraptured by the small watermarks that proudly displayed a royal crest or seal of sorts from the faraway country the man had traveled from. The single line of gold thread stitched into the note was probably worth more than the value of the cloth alone, as its radiance easily dwarfed the cloth that he was now willing to part with. Visions of dressing up in fancy suits clouded what little of his trading acumen remained. He imagined having piles and piles of these one-pound notes, and he would buy what he truly wanted—a ticket out of Arabia on an ocean-liner. He had seen pictures of these vast, floating cities pasted to crumbling city walls, and who really needed this poverty, he asked. Why his mansion in South Ken would rival the most exquisite palaces of the Arab princes, and there was much more to follow, if only he dumped this cloth and followed the traveler to the life of his dreams.

Suddenly a muezzin from high atop the minarets of one of the local mosques called the believers to prayer, and even though his voice was smooth and enchanting, the muezzin's song broke him from his visions. He soon remembered how much money he needed to get for the cloth, and to his own amazement and horror, he sputtered out again, "ten rials only," and stood firm and resolute on this final offer.

The traveler quickly snatched the one-pound note from his fingertips and returned both the note and the business card to his wallet.

"I just can't understand you people," said the traveler, shaking his head and talking to himself in his own foreign tongue. "I'm giving you the opportunity of a lifetime, and you deny that for some cheap and ugly cloth? It makes me wonder sometimes why the poor usually stay where they are in life. It's not like we don't offer them opportunity, because we offer it to them every day. It's just that they're either too lazy to work for it or too stupid to know when they see it. And then they complain that the government is not taking care of them. I mean, who do you think bought those clothes on your back anyway? It's people like me who are taxed to the hilt so that you can afford to lie around all day and live off of our charity. And meanwhile blackies of your kind come over by the boat-loads and expect to live side-by-side with us and marry into our families by doing nothing but begging and stealing and sleeping all day in those gypsy caravans that serve as your only contribution to our society. Savages, the lot of you. You can't even learn how to read and write, and then we open our borders up all over Europe. God, maybe Hitler's right."

The boy, of course, couldn't understand a word he said, but by the look on his face, the traveler was clearly angry with him. Luckily, he didn't threaten him like the official had, and he sighed in relief as the traveler finished his rant and headed towards another part of the bazaar. Nevertheless, the boy still experienced a deep sadness over the loss, as he could have made a good and prosperous life for himself in a much different part of the world. Life didn't have to be so difficult, he thought, as the muezzin's chants ended and the believers along the walls of the over-crowded mosque bended at their knees and offered prayers. He longed to take full part in these rituals too, but alas, he didn't know how to read and so never learned what the holy book said about, what seemed to be, a very punishing existence. Yet these punishments didn't last for very long, as a sweet, perfumed incense wafted through to the perimeter of the bazaar from a black tent that stood far apart from the traders' stalls.

He knew from earlier travels with his father that he should avoid this one particular tent. Actually, his father had forbidden him from going near it, but he never gave a clear reason as to why. In fact, the incense happened to be so seductive that it carried him to the tent's opening that flapped open in the breeze every so often. An alluring ghazal played on a small transistor radio from within, and he also heard several young women giggling playfully. He remembered that this was where stressed-out traders came to "unwind" after their hectic working hours.

He thought himself too young to enter, but his genuine curiosity for what had been forbidden, along with the mélange of the powerful incense, seductive ghazals, and girlish laughter pushed him through the opening with his turquoise cloth flung conspicuously over his shoulder. He looked like an emissary from another province of the kingdom or an important diplomat for one of the crowned princes. When he stepped inside, however, he couldn't believe what he saw.

His cautious footfalls tiptoed on soft Persian rugs that cooled his blistered feet. A gust of cold air from within the tent subdued the heat from outside. From every corner of the room large, plush pillows were assembled like heavenly beds upon fluffy clouds. A couple of tired traders lounged on these oversized pillows and smoked from large, heavy hookah pipes that stood like statues next to them. Their bloodshot eyes, billowing clouds of smoke, and slow movements showed that they were clearly under the influence of some strange medicine that seemed to carry them into faraway worlds. But what astonished the boy the most was the dozen or so dancing women in the middle of the room wearing next to nothing at all. They had nothing on by jeweled lingerie, their faces veiled by transparent pink chiffon. He tried to hide within one of the folds of the tent, as watching the display was a bit too much for his surging hormones, but before he could leave safely, the women heard his footsteps, and suddenly all eyes were upon him, as he was caught in the spotlight of their feminine gaze. After a moment or two of silent bewilderment, the girls broke into the same girlish laughter he had heard outside.

The boy blushed crimson red and hurried to find the exit. The madam of the establishment, however, floated near from the other side of the room and blocked his attempt to flee.

"Well, well, well, what do we have here? A young boy snooping in my parlor?"

Her stubby, jeweled hands held him by the shoulders, and she grinned mischievously, as though wanting something from him.

"Tsk, tsk, tsk—a very naughty boy," she announced. "What shall we do with him, girls?"

A bunch of them giggled again, and one of them cheered, "let's give him a bath!"

Another said, "let's see him dance, front and center!"

And a third said, "let's give him a rubdown. The poor thing looks like he's tired and lost."

Another round of giggling followed these deliberations.

One of the hoary traders in the corner took a long toke from his hookah pipe and cynically declared, "If only I were young again."

It all seemed a little too fantastic for the boy, who was both excited and also very afraid. He didn't know where these interjections would lead and feared that he would never return to his father again, as the old madam sells him into the services of North African tribesmen or some other terrible fate that only this giggling gang of gypsies could devise.

A large wart on the madam's cheek, as well as her jagged, ash-stained teeth, pigeon-holed her as the brains behind this particular operation. He would have much rather fallen into the laps of the soft warm bodies dancing happily in the center of the room than be held by the collar by the brutish madam. To his benefit, the girls begged that he be allowed to stay for a while. The madam, however, had other intentions. The boy followed her eyes to where the turquoise cloth hung from his shoulder. The madam stared into the depth of its color, and while rubbing the soft, fragile thread, her grin turned into a warm smile. She unhooked her hand from the back of his neck and bid him a fond welcome.

"Why don't you stay with us a while," she said, leading him to the women who now danced to the music uninhibitedly. She clapped her hands sharply and said, "Sasha, come here at once."

From the middle of their writhing circle emerged a woman whose long black hair flowed to her waist and whose silky fair skin had been slicked with fragrant oils. She wore a light make-up that accentuated her natural beauty and a wet lip-gloss that moistened her full, ruby-red lips. She glittered as she walked, and the pink transparent veil was the only scrap of clothing covering her voluptuousness. Naturally, the boy couldn't pull his eyes away from her abundant chest, jeweled navel, and long, meandering legs that seemed more wholesome to him than the thick butter-cream his father fed him as a child. He was immediately overwhelmed by this, the most beautiful woman in the room, her hazel eyes begging him to come closer and rescue her from all of this insanity.

"Not so fast," said the madam, her pudgy hands holding him in place. "First, you must give me something for her. How much would you give to spend the evening with my best girl?"

"I don't have any money," answered the boy, as the rest of the girls gasped in dismay.

"No money, eh? Well, maybe we can come to some other arrangement."

"I'd like that very much, madam," said the boy.

After all, he had the love of his life right there before him, and he promised himself that he would run away with her far beyond the kingdom's borders. They could finally live in peace, and even though they didn't have any money, he would find a way to take care of her and honor, respect, and obey her wishes for the rest of his days.

The woman in front of him smiled coyly. She too seemed to be enamored of him too, and he quickly turned to the cloth that hung from his shoulder. He recalled his father's instructions but would have rather given the worthless scrap of cloth away for a one-time shot at escaping the oppression of the city with the girl of his dreams by his side. In the city he would always be disadvantaged and lame, oppressed and sickly, dirty and impoverished. This woman would wash away these titles of despair and keep him fulfilled and happy in their mutual love. His eyes connected with hers, and they both knew it was right and just and wholesome and divine that they should belong to each other for the rest of their lives. But then a blast of warm desert wind blew through the tent's opening, taking the turquoise cloth that sat on his shoulder with it. The cloth unfurled in the gust of wind, and all of the women gasped at its aquamarine beauty floating in the air. It settled gracefully on the carpeted floor between the woman and the boy. The woman he had fallen for lost her focus and gazed in amazement at this wondrous cloth. It then seemed to absorb all of her attentions, and as soon as she looked away, the boy regained his composure and grabbed the cloth from the floor. His confidence and toughness returned, and he said in a forceful tone, "ten rials only, madam."

The madam yanked him by the collar and shoved him out the tent's opening.

"Get out, you little thief, and don't come here again, or I swear, by God, I'll have your throat cut wide open! No one insults my best girl that way! No one!"

The boy found himself on the outside of the tent accosted and maimed by the murderous light, his body supine on the jagged rubble that scraped his backside. He searched for the cloth and found it crumpled and dirty beneath his back. A sharp pain struck his body, and for a while he just lay there in the dirt, his eyes squinting into the blinding white sky. He picked himself up slowly, and just before retreating to the hills, he caught a glimpse of the woman who had captured his heart. She had since crumbled to her knees in the center of the tent, her hands covering her face and her Ledaen body shaking with sad and broken tears.

Soon the sun began to set beneath the tops of the burnt mountains, and shadows slowly crept out from under the sharp rocks and scattered pieces of brittle wood that pockmarked his slow climb to his father's hovel. Along the road other traders walked gloomily among debris that signaled the end of the metropolis and the beginning of a hilly wasteland that stretched for thousands of miles in all directions. These were the people who had failed, who lost money, who got the short end of the stick. The boy had walked this trail at this particular time of day countless times before, usually with his father leading the way. This time of day had been reserved for the beggars, the downtrodden, the indigent, the woebegone, and the unrighteous. These were the freaks, the lepers, and the deformed walking in loose procession to their squalid shacks on the hillside. This somber march of humped backs, hacking coughs, and blistered feet soon thinned out as the sun's power lost its edge to the twilight. The darkness enshrouded his mood, which vacillated from burning anger to frigid depression, and now he had to face his father who would probably shut him out of the same hovel he grew up in.

He fought the urge to lash out at the immortal God who had stolen his bountiful future from him, but he quieted the beast stirring within him and understood that the light would never extinguish from the stars hanging above him. He thought that perhaps, one day, he could carve out a simple life for himself in the mountains—a poor, nomadic life, yes—but an existence nonetheless. He had little idea what he'd do, but at least this simple idea seemed possible. His thoughts then returned to his father who would ultimately be disappointed with the son he had raised. Both his father's natural skills and hard work built the humble abode on the hill, and although it was only a meager hovel, filled with failures and disappointments in every corner, it still remained a proud tribute to a poor man's labor. Yet he knew himself an adopted son, a bastard of the bazaar, and while he carefully studied every nuance of negotiation, he soon realized from somewhere deep within him that he would never be as successful as his father was. His father, and his forefathers before him, carried such talents through their line—talents, he suddenly discovered, that he never had. He again stifled his urge to cry, and when he finally entered the hovel in the darkness, a small fire suppressed his tears and gradually warmed his bones.

His father was bowing his head in prayer in the corner of the hovel when he arrived. His father stopped what he was doing and quickly attended to him. The boy could no longer contain his emotions, and, trader or not, he had no choice but to let his tears loose before the man he admired most. The old man dropped to his knees and embraced his son more strongly than ever before. The boy spilled warm tears on his shoulders, and he too couldn't help but weep.

"You have come back to me," said the father, "But why?"

The boy loosened his fingers, and the turquoise cloth he had clutched so tightly fell to the ground. Even though it was caked in dirt, its thread still held together, as though it were some sort of small miracle.

"My son, there is something I must tell you. There is no reason to cry."

"But I couldn't sell the cloth," cried the boy. "I tried, and I tried, but I couldn't sell it."

The old man held him close and wiped away his tears with the edges of the fabric.

"When I was a young boy," he said, "my father gave me this same cloth, and your great-grandfather before him. From somewhere within the origins of our family line this cloth has been handed down through the generations. My ancestors were very skilled and experienced traders. They were great at what they did, but you see, not one of them was ever able to sell this cloth. We all had to make it through the same torment, and now that this day has come, I know in my heart that you are truly my own son. I know now that you were born to me, and I shall never leave you again, I swear it.

"So come, dry your tears and gather your things. Tomorrow morning we shall leave this place of sadness and head into the desert, towards a land where we can live in peace and prosper like our ancestors once did. We will leave the cursed place, and I swear, I will never leave you again."

THE END.

THE CUBE

In my son's playroom, which is littered with plastic toys of every shape, size, and color—everything from old train sets to action figures both big and small, to plastic swords, toy guns, and die-cast metal cars that have ceased to roll on the thick threads of the shag carpet that warms his feet—I one day noticed a small, almost innocuous object that sat on his baby-blue night stand. I slipped the object into the side pocket of my work trousers, and within a day or two I brought it out secretly for my own obscure pleasure. And while I'm usually not in the habit of stealing my son's toys from him, this colorful cube reminded me of a time when anything was possible, and when my once-capable skills and faculties could tackle any problem that came my way.

The cube itself is not that spectacular or remarkable to look at. I had the larger version of it in my possession before my father passed away some twenty years ago. I remember playing with it during his wake. I often excuse my former self for this, as I was merely a boy who didn't know any better at the time, but I distinctly remember sneaking into the coatroom of the funeral parlor and peeling off all of the stickers on the cube if only to paste them back on again until all sides were equally uniform. I then showed the completed puzzle to all of the adults, who were by this time kneeling at my father's casket and mouthing their quiet lamentations. They finally understood that I was indeed much smarter than they had originally thought. In fact, my reputation grew from a dumb, slightly awkward kid to a boy who would one day lift our family out of poverty by using an acumen I never possessed.

The cube's popularity back then swept the nation, and it quickly infiltrated the homes of many a teenager. I saw television shows where young wiz-kids my age solved the puzzle in just a few seconds, each of its eight sides balanced and resolute with the same colors, and this was done without removing any of the square, solid-colored adhesives that made it so interesting to solve. After a year of its release, the cube took on another dimension, as its creators added an extra, fourth side, if only to complicate my plans. I suppose people ultimately grew tired of the thing and abandoned it for some other activity. It still remains, however, an icon of the age. There wasn't a kid on my block who didn't want one, and after a year or two, there wasn't a kid on my block who didn't already have one.

After the funeral, I gave it away to one of my starry-eyed cousins after showing him the completed puzzle. He agreed that I was the smartest kid in town, and even though I was nothing but a charlatan, I soon believed the lie I had built for myself and paraded my genius in front of my widowed mother. She soon took me to the bank and funded an account for my higher learning. I was finally a good investment, she would often say, and to this day she still questions whether or not I was honest with her. When I visit her at the home, she still eyes me suspiciously, knowing somewhere behind the pale of her stark blue eyes that I had gotten the better of her. She poured all of my father's insurance money into that college fund and then waited for something spectacular to happen. After a semester or two of heavy drinking and pot-smoking, I was tossed out of college and happened to stumble upon my future wife at the campus watering hole where I had been soaking most of my misery and misfortune.

Finding the cube in my boy's room marked my triumphant return to the reputation I once held, and I had no choice but to take it back from him. I should also say here, in my defense, that my son has never showed the slightest interest in the cube. It is dwarfed by the other large-scale toys that command his attentions. The version I took from him fits into my palm. It was more-or-less made as a small key chain, a memento, if you will, of the larger version that had at one time captivated the smartest of people.

I now keep it on my desk, and when my mind tends to wander from my work, I reach for it, twist and turn its many sides, and hope to create at least one solid side and then move on to the more perplexing task of making solid sides of the others. It finds its way into my pockets, my car, on the dashboard and in the glove compartment, in my briefcase, and sometimes in the laundry. The pied-colored shingles, almost like the flashing bulbs of a Las Vegas strip sign, force me into fiddling with it, until somehow I am jarred from its trance and return to what my real life demands of me. And since I've had it, I tend to think of everything around me as a function of the cube—the brick-face of my house, for instance, or a stray appointment that needs to be twisted into an empty slot in my schedule, so that the entire day is solid and complete. Sometimes I find the cube in my pocket and stroke its glossy sides or thumb the soft edges of its corners, much like a teenager doodles in a book or a nervous woman bites her fingernails. Often it will come to me in dreams, its patchwork of motley colors blinking and winking at me, forming patterns that suggest the presence of some higher, intelligent being who is trying to shape me into something superior.

I often wonder if I am playing with it, or if it is playing with me. I have an itching need to unscramble its colors in order to decode the language of the higher being hidden at its core. Only then may I exorcise it from my mind. Even my body requires me to keep a safe distance. Several weeks ago, when I found it staring at me from the bathroom sink, it held me hostage for what must have been several hours, thereby ruining an otherwise satisfying interlude of light reading and quiet contemplation. After a time, I couldn't fathom being away from it, as though it had become an extension of my fingers, the center of my palm, or a portable appendage that I sometimes played "catch" with. I'd sit for hours on the living room couch bringing order to the chaos of its sides.

Soon it joined me in bed where my wife once read her romance novels. She often glowered at the object that slowly meant more to me than she did. I'd focus solely on its eight-sided mystery, and often my heart leapt in the middle of the night when the perfect square fit into place. Either that or my heart sank when I went fishing for a single square in order to complete an entire side, thus ushering in even more chaos to a puzzle that I had turned and twisted into order using nothing less than my unbending will. When she wanted to make love, I turned away, limp and powerless, always wondering where I'd find the cube next.

She said she'd always remember the image of my haggard, unshaven face and corpulent body sagging underneath the bathrobe she gave me last Christmas. I sat in the living room on that cold day, my head crooked to my lap, this same cube absorbing all of the awkward love that had now ended our marriage.

"It's either the cube or me," she said as she towed my young son down the stairs to where her packed suitcases stood at the door. Her bags looked like a cubist monument of sorts, a tribute to the disintegration of our five years together. I knew, however, she would return, and I made sure to let her know that I was the one in charge of this family, not she, and whatever power-plays she had orchestrated were only the futile gestures of a woman who really couldn't live without me.

She hasn't been back since, and even though I am still frightened to find the cube where I least expect it, either popping out at me from the desk drawer or flashing ever so briefly in the brilliant white light that accompanies crackling thunder, I'm still struck by how I have yet to solve it.

THE HEART OF THE SERPENT

The Peregrine falcon who made his nest within a craggy cutbank high in the mountains circled the narrow of the valley between two rocky cliffs on a search for prey. His blue-grey, spotted plumage shone slick in the hot sun, the warm, dry air gracing his beak and broad moustache as he tried to put the twilight of his years in perspective. He was, after all, the oldest of the falcons. He was also the wisest and the worthiest of predators to have ever hunted the mountains. He led his cast judiciously in all matters of their survival, and he had become so august a falcon that during his lifespan he had come to rule the mountain lands while forging good relations with the ospreys and the bald eagles that dominated the lakes and wider rivers.

Because he was getting old now, he could no longer swoop and dive so swiftly as before. His eyesight had dimmed considerably, and at any moment he felt as though the falcon God would take him from the mountains and set him off flying into the after-life. He relied chiefly on his sons to do most of the hunting these days, and now that they were also maturing quite rapidly, the falcon would soon have to bequeath his territories to them and hope that they would live, rule, and survive in the mountains as confidently and admirably as he had done.

While circling the sky in the dry, intense heat, however, he couldn't deny that he harbored some guilt for being such a formidable predator and so ruthless during his reign. He accepted his nature, though, and now wondered how his own cast would fare without him, considering that the black, band-tailed pigeons that they loved to feast on were rapidly disappearing from the valleys and the streams where they hunted.

When his wings grew sore and tired, and when his eyesight started to blur, he returned to the nest within the cutbank and fed on some of the sweet pigeon meat that his sons had stored there for him. He awaited their arrival eagerly, because he wanted to make a few changes in the bird kingdom to ensure the continued survival of his sons and the betterment of the mountain food chain that had provided him with so much. His sons had arrived in due course, and they brought with them the delicacies of swallows, jays, flickers, and even a few rare songbirds in their talons as tribute to their father. They would feast only after he had spoken with them at a general meeting. The sons hoped their father would finally discuss the divisions of the territories and the allocation of air space after his life had expired.

A short while after the cast of falcons had assembled at the nest, and after their father had looked upon each of his sons and determined that they were now fit to rule in his place, he addressed one of his main concerns: that their cast had always favored preying on black, band-tailed pigeons instead of the white rock doves that seemed to grow in numbers year after year.

"This is an interesting time in our history," squawked the falcon to his sons. "We were lucky enough to have survived the great poisonous plague that lasted twenty years here in the mountains, and we are luckier still to have such a kingdom that has been regenerated over the years by the falcon God in the hopes that we could survive yet another generation. And soon all of these skies will be yours to rule!"

"Not without you, father!" squawked the sons in return. "May you have many more years!"

"Thank you," he continued, "but the Falcon God now circles the mountains above me, and I can feel his presence within my hollow bones with every day that passes. But my sons, it would be irresponsible of me to pass on to the after-life without ensuring your survival as well. So let me explain what I must do in order to protect you after I am taken. Let me explain how I will restore order in the valley over which we rule.

"The falcon God has blessed us with much prey over the years, but somehow we have been much too short-sighted, and perhaps a bit unwise, in feasting on mostly band-tailed pigeons. They are darker, more feral birds, and as is natural to their flocks, their meat is much tastier than their lighter-feathered cousins, the rock dove. But as a result of their delectable taste to our appetites, we will soon pay the price if we do not do something about the band-tailed population. But you see, my sons, many of us don't treasure rock dove meat enough. We admire their lighter feathers, but compared to their band-tailed cousins, their bodies are too boney and their meat less satisfying. So in order to restore balance, we must make some necessary changes to create a new breed of bird so that their meat comes more naturally to us than band-tailed meat alone.

"From now on, let me decree that for every flock of rock doves living in the valley that they should take in the youngest born from the flocks of band-tailed pigeons and nurture these birds as their own. That means that for every flock of white pigeons there should be one black pigeon within their flock. These youngest born of the band-tailed flocks will grow with the rest of their newly-appointed light-feathered flock with the aim of breeding a new kind of bird. And in this way we will create a new species of bird whose meat is as sweet as its ancestors and whose feathers are still as colorful so that we may hunt them more easily from our positions in the mountains. So, my sons, before I bequeath the mountains, the valleys, and the skies to you, you will implement my orders throughout the bird kingdom. And not until I am fully satisfied that the youngest of the dark pigeons have been successfully relocated and assimilated into white pigeon flocks will I bequeath all of my lands and my territories to you. Once I am satisfied that this has happened, you will then take your places as fitful rulers, but not a moment before.

"It is this that I decree, and my decree will be implemented without delay. If there is any delay or any problems that I see in your implementation, then all of you will be sentenced to the harrowing task of fighting for these territories amongst yourselves—which is something that I would hate to see happen, but something that I am willing to allow if my plan is not thrown into action immediately."

After the sons had heard their father's decree, they understood that they must carry out his plan without delay. They did not wait to carry it out. As soon as the meeting adjourned, the cast of falcons darted from their ancestral nest and swooped down to their respective territories in the valley below them. They swooped into the agricultural lands and canopy-covered hillsides squawking their loud decree as they swooped by, their squawking so fierce and frightening that both band-tailed and rock dove flocks darted this way and that in fear of their very lives. The falcon's sons even brought a few band-tailed pigeons back to their nests in the process, thinking that a good hunt in combination with the implementation of the decree would reinforce their father's will over the pigeon population. A climate of intense fear enveloped these flocks of low-flying birds from that point onward, and with it came immense sorrow, as the band-tailed families would be losing their youngest born to rock dove families. Similarly, the rock dove families would now have to accept the youngest born of their feral cousins into the sanctity of their stable homes. The falcons never gave them an explanation as to why they had ordered this, only that they should start the relocation immediately or else face dire repercussions. All pigeons feared for their lives should they try to avoid the order. There was no telling what it would lead to.

***

Nestled in the narrow of the valley, a small mountain village with a factory and a few small farms had been built adjacent to a sinewy river whose waters froze to ice during the winter but was now thriving with birds of every feather during the summer. While there were many birds that stayed close to the river, the pigeons mostly stayed close to the village itself. They took up their nests in empty barns, building rooftops, and abandoned warehouses. Plenty of pigeons, both rock dove and band-tailed, used the same village to forage for food, but the two types of bird traveled in different flocks entirely. They never really mingled that often, as the rock doves were considered snobs of the highest order, while the band-tailed pigeons were seen as fierce and unruly. Both pigeons kept to their own territories. So when they heard the falcon's call from on high, they were petrified, especially those pigeons who lived on the small farms, because the falcons and the hawks often liked to hunt there. Quite naturally they were scared, but they had no choice but to accept the order.

At one such farm just a few miles from the center of the village, an adult band-tailed pigeon readied her only son—just a young squab at this point—for a flying lesson. They would practice in the loft of the empty barn in which they both lived. She had had her son as a young single hen not very long ago, and she swore that she would nurture him and protect him fiercely. She had to forage for food all day by herself, considering how her husband, a good-natured cock, had fallen victim to a hawk that hunted the fields. They were very much in love. She never saw her husband again.

After his disappearance, she decided that the best she could do was to forage limitedly so that she could look after her squab, but in return she would teach him how to fly through the lessons she gave at their nest. Unfortunately, she wouldn't get the chance to teach her squab very much, considering the orders that came shrieking in from above. Her immediate reaction to the order was to escape with her son, to simply fly away and take their chances. And yet she knew if the hawks or the falcons caught up with them, they would both be killed. Her squab, a very cute and sensitive pigeon, couldn't understand the falcon's orders just yet, so he asked his mother, "what does it mean, Mama?"

At first the mother didn't know what to say. She simply surrounded her squab with her wings and brought him into her pillowy breast. Tears spilled from her eyes. She must have held him there for several minutes not wanting to let go of him, but she knew they had to comply with the order no matter how destructive it was. The falcons promised that this would be better for the band-tailed community anyway, and yet she did not want to let go of her only squab. Someday, she imagined, her squab would return to her as a grown cock.

"What's wrong, Mama?" he mumbled, his head nuzzled against her soft breast.

"Darling," she said, "you're going away."

"Where are we going, Mama? Are we going on holiday?"

"No, darling. We are not going on holiday, but you are leaving today. Somebody else will teach you how to fly from now on."

"Where am I going, Mama?"

"You're going to live with some rock doves for the time being."

"Rock doves? What are rock doves?"

She found it difficult to elaborate further. She only hoped that her squab would return to her eventually, perhaps as a beautiful and brave cock, but this time more worldly and knowledgeable, and dare she think, more capable of evading the hawks and the falcons than his father. When the sun began its decent behind the brown ridges of the mountains, when shadows encroached upon the village and its surrounding farms, the mother hen took her squab by the beak and flew with him to an abandoned building near the center of the village to where a rock dove family lived. Despite her tears and her anguish, she bravely flew against the valley winds and arrived at the abandoned building. There she found the nest of the rock dove flock she had heard about. Their nest was empty, and she simply dropped her squab there by releasing him from her beak. She then flew back to the barn where she lived.

Seeing that night was quickly falling and that he hadn't learned how to fly yet, the young squab couldn't pursue his mother. He simply fell asleep soundly in the empty nest after tearfully witnessing his mother's wings grow smaller and more distant in the sunset. He slept so soundly that he didn't stir at all when the rock doves returned from their foraging expedition just before sundown.

The young squab awoke the next morning to the chirps and cries of the rock doves with whom he now shared the nest. And when he got up to move, the flock fell dead silent and eyed

230

him suspiciously. They didn't say a word to him. They only looked upon him with the kind of condescension and disdain that rock doves usually reserved for their band-tailed cousins. The abandoned squab could only look up at them slyly, not knowing what to say or what to do. He could only remain quiet and silent so as not to disturb their normal routines. Yet he hungered for a berry or a nut or even a worm to usher in the morning. As of yet the rock dove hen hadn't returned.

He fought their stares by pretending to fall asleep again— this until the hen of the nest finally flew in from a broken window above them. Her large white wings flapped as she balanced herself on the rim of the nest. With the greatest speed, the other rock doves gathered below her, and she regurgitated whatever food she had ingested into their mouths. It's what the squab's mother normally did for him, so in imitation of this routine, he took a place in the column of rock doves as well. But with a solid whack, the rock dove hen batted him away from the other rock doves when his turn came and said, "no food until you are finished with your flying lessons, you rat-winged squab."

The other rock doves simply laughed at the trouble he got into, but generally they were more interested in the food they received. Once breakfast had been served, the rock doves assembled in a row below their mother to receive the next flying lesson.

"You better come listen to this if you expect to eat tonight," squawked the hen.

The band-tailed squab followed her orders and lined up once again with the other rock doves.

"Gather around me nice and close," said the hen, "because today we will review the elements of flying."

The squab was a bit apprehensive about this, because he had never received the hen's first lesson. Also, he found it terribly hard to concentrate, since being taught with rock doves proved to be too unique an experience to pay attention to the lesson too closely. Instead, he could only stare at his surroundings and also stare at the brightness of their feathers, as he was instantly fascinated with them. This fascination came quite naturally to him. They were, after all, beautiful creatures. Their snow-white rumps and blue-grey necks enticed him into staring at one of the female rock doves more and more, until she too diverted her attentions from her mother hen and returned his stare.

The hen noticed their connection just a few moments later, and when she did, she flapped her mighty wings in his direction and batted the young squab to the other side of the nest. He barreled over in pain, and suddenly the entire lesson has been disrupted with the laughter of all of the young rock doves. The formidable body of the mother hen now towered over his small, black body.

"You better pay attention and stop looking at my children— especially her. She is not for you. If you're not ready to fly this afternoon, you don't eat. It's that simple. So you'd better decide whether or not you're really fit to be here, because I, for one, don't want you here to begin with, and you are certainly not going to touch my daughter. You can rejoin the lesson after you've thought it over."

The young squab looked upon the others confusedly as the lesson started up again. They all seemed to be understanding the lesson, but for him it was like another language altogether. It was nothing like what his mother had taught him. The rock dove hen furnished diagrams and charts with strange equations on them. Words like 'velocity,' 'wind drag,' and 'aerodynamic' flew way over his head. She said that they should all fly correctly or not fly at all.

Well, he thought, he had just rather rejoin the lecture and fly as correctly and gracefully they did. But he still couldn't pay attention to any of it. He spaced out at times. His curiosities were more geared towards making sense of the environment he now found himself in, especially remaining close to the rock doves whose feathers he found extraordinarily beautiful. He would have to show some cocky guts to fly like they did, thereby advancing him to a cock while still remaining the youngest and most vulnerable of the squabs there.

When the time finally came to fly, they all lined up in front of an opening near the nest. The opening in the abandoned building overlooked a small field covered with switch grass. One by one the rock doves flew from the opening's perch, and they did so quickly and effortlessly. The band-tailed squab was the last to go.

"I don't think I'm ready yet!" said the squab on the perch.

"You do want to eat, don't you?" squawked the hen.

"Yes, madam, but I don't think I'm ready yet!"

"Get out or I'll throw you out. And don't talk back. Now get out!"

The squab shut his eyes and remembered the few things his mother had taught him. With all the courage he could muster, he leapt from the perch and flapped his wings.

For a few moments he could feel himself flying above the field, and so he opened his eyes to judge his position above the switch grass. His small wings, however, started to flap too erratically, and suddenly they felt too fatigued and heavy for him to catch up the rest of the rock doves who were far ahead. No matter how hard he flapped, he descended steadily. He gave up completely when his wings had completely lost all of their strength in mid-air. At the middle of the field, he plummeted down to the ground among the sharp stalks of switch grass. He was knocked unconscious.

***

When the young squab awoke, he was surrounded by the strangest ring of shadow. He could see the sun hovering above him and also a patch of blue sky, but other than this he stayed cool in the shade of the wall. His head leaned against a cold, slick surface. He got to his feet eventually but couldn't hop over such a high, scaly wall. His foot was injured from the fall, and it prevented him from beating his wings and flying away. Suddenly, the wall gradually slipped away, as he now found himself face-to-face with a giant rattlesnake who had caught him in the switch grass and had coiled around him.

"Well, well, well," lisped the rattlesnake, his forked tongue probing the squab's dusty feathers. "It seems that I have you all to myself, but before I devour you whole, I just wanted to know, what kind of bird are you? I've never seen a black bird like yourself around these parts. You must be quite a delicacy indeed," as his long tongue licked his lips.

"What's your name?" asked the band-tailed squab.

"What's my name?" lisped the snake. "No one has ever asked me that before. Is that all you want to say?"

"What else should I say?"

"Why, I don't know, but for someone who's about to become my next meal—and a delicious meal at that—you are certainly the calmest bird I have ever encountered. Shouldn't you at least try to escape, or squawk in fear, or even tremble a little bit? Most of the white birds do so right away."

"I have no need to escape when I'm going nowhere anyway."

"How unusual," lisped the snake. "I've never come across someone like you. Don't you even want to try to fly away? I'll even give you a head start."

"I don't know how to fly, okay," sobbed the squab, "and I don't want to be forced to fly anymore. My mama didn't get a chance to teach me, and the other birds won't teach me either, and now my leg is hurt, and I don't know what to do."

The squab now sobbed uncontrollably into his wing and supported his body by leaning against the snake's slick skin. He wept for quite some time, and it left the snake confused and mystified by the display of emotion

"Excuse me, Mr. Bird," said the snake, "but don't you find me the least bit frightening? Don't I scare you?"

"No, not really."

The snake turned his head away for a moment and then returned with his fangs hanging out of his open jaws.

"How about now?"

The squab examined him even more closely and said, "no. There's no change on this end."

The snake turned his head away a second time and returned with what he thought was the most frightening face he could muster. His fangs dripped with venom, and they were ready to bite. He even hissed loudly enough to capture the attentions of the finches in the bushes surrounding the field. They darted away in apprehension when they heard it.

Upon final inspection, the squab said finally, "actually you are quite a handsome snake—very handsome features and nice white fangs."

"Handsome? Did you just say that I was handsome?"

"Yes, Mr. Snake."

"Not in the least bit scary or frightening?"

"No, Mr. Snake. I'm afraid not."

"Well then, how would I look scarier to the other birds is what I want to know."

The squab thought about this for a few moments and said, "well, the scariest moment of my life was when my mama dropped me off here. I hope she comes back some day."

"Your mother, eh?" lisped the snake. "You want to know what happened when our mother scared us one day? Why, we sunk our fangs deep into her and tore her to shreds. She never bothered us again."

"You did that to your own mother? Don't you feel bad about it?"

"Of course not. She was a ruthless old reptile, cold-blooded to the core. She deserved what she got."

"You mean, you didn't love your mother at all?"

"Love my mother? What is this 'love' that you speak of?"

"I tell you what, Mr. Snake. I'll explain it to you, but we have to repair my foot. My foot hurts too much right now."

"The best thing to do is to walk it off," said the snake. "I've seen my other prey try to do it. Here, let me see your foot."

The snake nudged his slick forehead against the squab's foot. He also probed it with his tongue.

"I don't think it's broken at all. Just try to walk it off is all."

"Okay. And as I walk, you can slide along with me, and I'll explain what I know, because I think I can help you, Mr. Snake."

They headed in the direction of the abandoned building, talking things over as they went.

"You see," said the squab, "there is a lot of pent up anger and frustration in you right now. I can sense your feelings of inadequacy at this very moment, and for you to move on with your life, you really have to come to terms with your mother's death. Did she not, after all, give you life and nurture you until you could hiss, slither, and crawl all on your own?"

"Kind of, but I don't think 'nurture' is a fair word to use here. She almost ate us once."

"And how did that make you feel?"

As their conversation moved from point to point, certainly the snake had urges to eat the squab, especially when the squab kept on insisting that the snake's family was not a bunch of ruthless and cold evil-doers, but in fact were quite revered in other parts of the world—this from a story his mother had told him once. But after discussing the matter for some time and after trying restore the snake's self-image, the squab actually found the weakness of the snake's heart—where it hid and where it bled beneath his thick, resolute scales. The squab concluded that the snake did indeed have a heart and not just a blood-thirsty mind.

"You are a marvelous creature, Mr. Snake. You are handsome and bold, but see, everything is in your head right now. It's your heart that really matters. Do you know what I mean? You think way too much, and when our feelings become trapped in our minds, our minds are clever enough to cloud them out in favor of more self-destructive behavior aimed primarily at destroying those feelings, because the mind finds these feelings too uncomfortable to bear. You should focus instead on your heart. Move from the mind to where your heart lies deep within you. Every creature has one, as that is our nature too. If it's all stuck in your head, then quite naturally the love that you need and the love that you could give others is twisted inside-out. Your mind cannot fathom love, but your heart can, and when that power is discovered, it's a power like none other.

"So when you return to your rhumba tonight, show them your heart, Mr. Snake. And if they don't show you theirs, then they're just not worth being around, and you should leave them. Your heart has to develop and become what it should be in order for you to be a more capable snake."

"And your mother taught you all of this?"

"It was one of her first lessons, but I'm on my own now. I have to make my own way. I can't fly very well, but I know that I have more heart than brains, and this is how I've survived so far, even when no one wants me around."

"It looks like your foot is better. I would invite you back to our nest, but we'd just end up eating you. I hope you can understand."

"Of course, I do."

"Where will you go from here?"

"I'm going to try to find my Mama. There's nothing else I can do. The rock doves hate me living with them, and it's better if I just left."

"That's okay, because I'll make sure to eat one of them for you."

"Now remember, Mr. Snake," said the squab taking flight, "this time you must live successfully. It's the heart that wins—not the mind."

The squab then flew off into the distance. His flying was both erratic and wobbly at first, but he could tell that he slowly got the hang of it. The squab's small, frail body soon disappeared behind the abandoned building. Perhaps it was the last time he'd get to meet such a bird. In the meantime, the snake continued to crawl on its belly through the switch grass, but this time he recognized how truly hungry he was. But he remembered what the squab had said—that he should nourish his heart first and the mind second. The squab confirmed that he indeed had a heart beneath the armor of his scales.

He returned to his rhumba's nest completely famished. It was an underground lair with a hole in the ground that served as its entrance. He slipped through this hole, and within the dimly-lit cavern he found his two brothers and his old father feasting on the field mice they had brought home that night. They immediately noticed that their brother had arrived with empty fangs to which the father of the rhumba said, "I hope you plan to go back out there."

The snake, now famished beyond belief at witnessing his rhumba feast on the mice, said, "I thought we could all share our meal for a change."

"What's gotten into you," hissed the father. "We don't share our meals here. Go on back out, or you'll stay hungry all night."

One of the brothers said, "you heard him. You won't get a lick of our food."

"But my brothers, I insist. If we are to survive, we have to share our food when one of us goes hungry. That's the only way, and it's the right thing to do."

At this point the two brothers stopped what they were doing. They stood squarely in front of their meals in defensive positions.

"Something's quite wrong with your thinking, brother. You heard what the old reptile said. No sharing."

Fairly soon, the snake felt something move within his chest. It sent waves of emotion through his slippery body, and a newfound resilience and energy had found him. Even the father of the nest sensed this energy emanating from him. The two brothers immediately moved in to attack him, but with one swift move the snake sank his fangs deep into the body of the first brother that attacked. He whipped his body to the side of the nest where it writhed and hissed wounded in the dirt. And then the second brother attacked. He was a bit older and much meaner than the first. The snake had enough cold-blooded emotion flowing through his veins, however, that he defeated his older brother without getting bitten in return. The two brothers now lay in the dirt coiling around each other and hissing in pain. They struggled to survive the snake's poisonous venom, but after a few moments, they lay dead against the wall of the nest.

Only his old father remained. He had been watching this battle unfold from a cautious distance, as he alone protected the stores of mice and birds behind him.

"I always knew you were the one," lisped the old father. "I always knew you were the strongest and the most venomous of snakes ever to grace this lair. I knew it right from the beginning. And I loved how you slayed your brothers. Yes, you have been my prodigy for a long time. I will see to it that I treat you well from now on."

The snake, confused by his father's tactics, couldn't decide whether it was his heart egging him on or his mind that was being seduced by his father's trickery. Whatever the case was, his cold blood coursed through his veins and rose to the surface of his very being. Finally, with all that had taken place, he could feel his heart pumping rushes of blood through his scaly body.

The father sensed that he would kill him after all, but said, "spare my life, my son, and I'll show you more field routes that you could ever have imagined possible. I know where all the mice in this field make their homes. I know where the birds sleep at night. You would be the most well-fed snake this side of the valley, and I can show you all this. But you need my help. You need my directions and my instructions on how to capture the sweetest of meats. You can't do it without me."

"Is this how you thought of us before you ordered us to kill our own mother? You promised us the same things back then. Did you actually think that you could leave this earth with everything? Is that what you thought?"

The father stayed quiet and rose to a defensive position in front of his treasure chest of dead mice and birds.

"You need me," he hissed. "You are nothing without me. You will not survive without me, so don't do anything you'll regret."

The snake again felt the beating of his heart and the sheer magnitude of his emotions. With a swift blow he sank his fangs deep into his father's skull, and when the fangs were well rooted in his brain, he pushed and drained all the remaining venom that he had left. Within moments, the father collapsed to the dirt floor from where he stood, as dead as the rest of them.

***

The snake's heartbeat slowed after this. He returned to normal and feasted on all of the mice and dead birds that he could possibly eat that night. He never remembered eating so well. But he understood that he had sacrificed his entire rhumba for the heart that now beat at his chest. He could hear it beating in his ears as he coiled up for sleep that night. He even shed a few tears for the tragedy, because the trouble of his heart demanded nothing less than a tragedy.

THE LAST ONE

He remembered that it was soon to be his sixteenth birthday, and that as a present his parents would give him another DVD to add to the collection of them that had piled up in his closet. Most of them were like artifacts. They were films he had seen over and over again, as though each film was another variant of an earlier film from a forgotten era that had been pulled from a vault, only that the newer versions replaced older actors and actresses with newer ones, newer music perhaps, a newer symphony of sounds to accompany similar plot lines. And it seemed as though all the videos he had watched before had all converged into a stew of blended images where all of the stories depicted were universally the same. These stories had been told a million times over.

The books that lined his shelves were no different. Each character within literature looked the same to him, as this was the best he could imagine them. Each bit of dialogue had been culled, it seemed, from older books. His books seemed somewhat meaningless for a time, as the material within them no longer merited the same enthusiasm, as they all seemed to say the same things over and over again—just with new people in them—and every once in a while a new style had emerged that mostly influenced how these characters carried themselves.

The boy wasn't exactly bored with the films and books that cluttered his room. They were links to what he thought existed beyond his four walls. Considering that these videos and books did deliver new faces and new people, and considering that his parents gave him new equipment, represented in the many gadgets he had used to play the DVDs and copy them, he didn't exactly want these videos and books gone, simply because he wouldn't be able to see what happened outside of his room otherwise.

Above all, though, he did take a certain pride in how he had arranged his room. The carpet that covered it was fire-engine red, and the sofa that he sat on while watching the television was navy blue. Posters of his favorite movie stars and music bands had been tacked to the walls, and although he had known their names when he had asked his parents for their pictures and their posters, he realized just then that these people also looked quite similar despite how differently they were marketed. These were the same faces—but exhibiting different types of people. Yet he liked how the posters on his walls, the bright red carpet, and the blue of the sofa excited the room with the same bright and organized color that could be found in the Mondrian paintings he liked so much. In fact, he had bookmarked these paintings in one of the heavy Art History books that now propped up his feet as he sat on the sofa. A combination of the posters, the colorful furnishings, and also the loud book and DVD covers that cluttered the room created a kaleidoscopic nest that at times had delivered its own form of entertainment and excitement when there was seemingly none to be had.

Even the pajamas he lounged in were colorful, and since all of the inanimate objects in his room were carefully organized into balanced squares and rectangles, all leveled and lined together properly, the chaos of spectral color was really no threat to the order that these objects exuded. The only companions that lived with him were those that flashed on his wide-screen, liquid crystal television set. His television took up the entire length of wall in front of him. The remote control in his hand made his room an automated tribute to anything he wanted to see, hear, or contemplate whenever such inclinations found him in need.

Lately, however, he had grown a bit irritated by how the others on the television screen weren't always as walled-in as he was. He witnessed how these beautiful stars on the television were magically beamed to exotic locations and also participated in activities that he wasn't allowed to participate in. The program he currently viewed featured a couple of scantily-clad women on a wild and exotic vacation. Their bodies were slender and tanned, and they giggled wherever they went. In this particular episode, they stayed in a five-star resort villa overlooking a breathtaking view of the ocean, and during their journey they drank cocktails with miniature bamboo umbrellas sticking out of their glasses and danced the night away with others who were also scantily-clad and unbearably happy.

He had seen these types of programs many times over and was at the age where he questioned why he couldn't do the same things that these men and women did on the dance floor, their bodies pressed together in ways that kept him watching. But most of all, the allure of the locations they frequented caused him the most envy. The program followed the two women as they toured the castles of Germania, museums in Gaul, the jungles along the Ganges, and the monasteries of Asia Minor. Their day trips were usually followed by a visit to an exclusive club that was both dark and colorful, where male bodies pressed against theirs in what at first seemed like a ridiculous ritual, but a ritual that continued to arouse him, and so he still kept watching it.

Sometimes, though, he could think of nothing more than to throw the remote control at the television screen. Of course, he never really got around to doing that. It was more a feeling or a thought among other rebellious ideas and thoughts that had never manifested in any action on his part, because, oddly enough, as soon as such a rebelliousness entered his mind, the doorbell to his room rang.

Safe it to say that his mood had taken another turn for the worse while watching the latest episode of the girls on vacation, and when it did, the doorbell, which was more of a steady, irritating beep that led to the door to his room sliding open horizontally, revealed the woman who had taken care of him for all of his sixteen years and had attended to his every need while living in the room. He couldn't think of anything else to call her but his mother, although lately he sensed that there was something more distant about her, as though what was once a more nurturing and steadfast love for him had gelled into a more adult relationship that was more severe than how she had loved him as a younger boy. He missed her more childhood love at times, such as the way she used to sing him the same lullaby before he fell asleep. But such displays of maternal affection on her part had ended several years ago, even though she hadn't aged one bit. And when the door slid open with a quiet, hydraulic swoosh, the same woman stood there—her eyes the same sparkling blue and her figure a perfect hourglass, her hair bleached with the same streaks of blonde that shone in exactly the same places.

She walked straight in and stood before him. The door shut behind her, and as he sat on the sofa and tried to avoid her, as she had blocked his full view of the television.

"What's wrong, Adam?" she asked. "Having another bad day?"

"Why are you so concerned about it," said Adam, a little unnerved that she had arrived just when his frustration with the television program had hit its peak.

"You're obviously down about something," she said. "Maybe it would help if we talked about it."

"We've already talked about it. We talk about it every day. It's the same talk we had yesterday and the day before. It has no end."

"What's troubling you, sweetie?"

"You asked me the same thing yesterday, and I told you."

"But you're still upset about it, is that it?"

"Yes, mother, I'm still upset about it. I don't want to stay here any longer."

She smiled knowingly and said, "I know it must be hard for you, but we're all doing the best we can under the circumstances. Everything you need is right here. You'll never need anything else."

"How can you be so sure?"

"Well, what else might you need?"

"I want to go outside," he said.

His mother paused for a moment and then took a seat on the sofa next to him.

"We talked about this, Adam."

"And we keep on talking about it," he said.

"Why are you so fascinated about going outside? Why are you so adamant about it?"

"Because I want to experience things, like these people do on the television."

"But Adam, the reason why we brought you the television and all of the books and DVDs was so that you can experience the same things that those people experience without ever having to leave your room. You're quite lucky in that regard. You should be grateful for the room that you have. Not many people get the opportunity to travel to these wonderful places without having to move an inch."

"I want to feel these things. I want to meet these women. Don't you understand? I want to meet her," as he pointed to the woman he liked the most on the vacation show. "I don't just want to watch her, and I don't just want to see her travel. I want to travel to the same places they do. I want to be there with them."

"This is silly," said his mother. "You can't go outside. You have to deal with that fact."

"I know, but at the same time I have to go outside."

"Even though it would kill you? Darling, please be reasonable. You are just too sick to go outside. It will kill you if you take a single step outside this room."

"But I feel fine, I tell you. I feel just fine, and I want to go out."

"I'm sorry, honey," she said, "but we just can't take that risk."

"I'm sick of it in here. At least let me change rooms."

"But Darling, we've given you everything you've ever needed right here in this room. What difference would it make if you switched rooms?"

"At least a room with a view of the outside," he said. "At least a view where I can see people. You can at least allow me that."

"I'm sorry, but it's just too risky. I know you're a growing boy, but you have to live within your means. You have to live with what gifts God has given you."

"Well, it's not enough."

"Please, don't be so adamant. You've always been such a stubborn and determined boy."

"Obviously it runs in the family. Listen, I just want to go places for a change. You owe me that."

"Let me see what I can do about it, okay?"

"You said that the last time."

"For now, you can't leave this room—not now, not ever. You have to get used to it. Otherwise it will be the end of you, and I certainly don't want to see that happen."

"Neither do I, I guess."

He turned off the television set when his mother left the room. He thought she had acted strangely, more like one of those therapists he listened to on the sound system—always consoling him and identifying with his pain but unable to relieve it. She acted as though his fascination with escaping the room and going outside was worthy of being relieved and not the pain of being closed in.

Instead of watching more television, though, he cracked open a book. The book, however, failed to interest him since the narrative resembled that which he saw routinely on the television. And while he tried to imagine the woman who was now the main character in the novel he read, his imagining was such that he could only picture the woman who had been on vacation, the same woman who had danced on the television show that he had just watched. She inhabited his imagination, as she was also the same main character in the book that he read. And perhaps some of the scenery and the clothing they wore had been depicted by the novelist a bit differently from the television program, but the outcome of the chapter he read was basically the same. It was the same old television program but only in book form, as though there were really no difference between the books he read and the programs and DVDs he watched.

He didn't quite know what to do about this dilemma, but he reacted to it by slamming the book shut and trying another book that had different subject matter entirely. And yet the same two girls touring the beaches of Cabo St. Lucas returned once again, as his inability to imagine any other people inhabiting the narrative he read frustrated him all the more. He had little choice but to dim the lights and sprawl his body out on the sofa until sleep overtook him. He realized that there was nothing so unique anymore about the books and programs he absorbed. He simply dreamt of one day leaving his windowless room, although even within the dream he couldn't imagine anything that loomed beyond the hydraulic door that kept him shut in tightly.

He awoke some time later to an alarm that brought him to consciousness. The alarm had come from the small kitchenette area. His tray of food had arrived through the food processor for his evening dinner. He was hungry, although he didn't feel much like eating. He walked to the kitchenette and out of the service door came a tray of piping hot goop in a bowl. He never knew what the goop was made of, but whatever it was, it stood the test of time as being the meal he had been served three times a day for what seemed like many, many years. While the goop tasted good in many respects, he had to admit that he was a little bored with it. But there was no choice but to accept it. He figured he was like a rat who has accepted that the same wedge of cheese will always be his reward. The meal itself and its redundancy, however, wasn't the source of his problem just yet. He still wanted to go outside but was prohibited from doing so.

He took his bowl of goop and ate it with a spoon in front of the television set. Another episode of the program with the women appeared, only this time they were on Safari in Africana with a couple of white male studs who served as their guides. All of the various animals were shown, such as zebras, elephants, giraffes, and a couple of lions, even oversized ants from which the male guides humorously protected the girls. But interestingly enough, when the two girls returned to civilization and back to their hotel where they immediately visited the hotel's dance club, Adam suddenly noticed how the two women now talked to a young blonde-haired boy at the bar—a new character who had suddenly made his inaugural appearance on the show. That boy, for some odd reason, looked exactly like Adam. He had the same shaggy blonde hair, the same height and build, the same blue eyes, the same voice and pattern of speech. It amazed him to see an exact replica of himself dancing with the two women, and the replica of himself certainly seemed to enjoy himself in their company.

And with newfound delight Adam watched the program for several hours straight as this new replica of himself was now traveling with the women to different locales. The replica drank as the ladies did and danced seductively as the other men in the clubs did. It calmed and soothed him to see himself doing all of these things on the television screen, and this quieted him for several days.

He noticed that other actors just like him had also been introduced on other programs, and this brought Adam a lot of joy and satisfaction that he could now finally identify with what he watched. The new replica became the new star in each program he watched. Adam was finally represented, and even a few of the books that had been sent through the delivery chute featured a main character who was just like him and who harbored the same frustrations as he did. But the main characters always dealt with these frustrations by being grateful, and the new characters never escaped but instead found contentment in the lives that they had already. Such programming kept him absorbed for several weeks straight.

It wasn't until the travel show had progressed to the point where they showed his look-alike kissing one of the girls, the girl that Adam liked, that he sensed something was wrong about the things he was now watching and reading. His replica had toured the lunar-like craters of the volcanoes in the Canary Islands and followed this up by having cocktails with the girls in their hotel room overlooking a breezy beach at evening. The replica of himself went up to the girl, who happened to be in a bikini, and kissed her squarely on the lips. The two of them fell into an extended kiss where their tongues and mouths were locked together and their hands wandered all over each other's bodies. And after the scene had ended, Adam was ready to throw the remote at the television again, as his angst and rebelliousness had suddenly returned. He believed that this time he wouldn't fail at hurling the heavy remote at the people on the screen, but then again the thought and the analysis of doing the deed delayed the actual deed from being done, as though his mind had to go through all sorts of red tape and permissions in order to carry out the act. But by God he would do it this time, because somehow his replica had the real-life privilege of kissing the bikini-clad women without suffering as Adam had been suffering being confined to his room. He wondered why he couldn't do the same things as his replica did. The only option that remained now was to destroy the television set and the women who let this fake version of himself kiss and fondle them. It was downright unfair, he thought.

At the exact time when he thought that he just might throw the remote and see if he could get away with it, the doorbell's extended beep rang again. The door swooshed open. His mother, wearing a kind smile, walked in and sat next to him, hoping to diffuse whatever angered the troubled teenager.

His mother looked as radiant as ever, as she hadn't changed at all in the several weeks since he had seen her last. She had the same twinkle in her sea-blue eyes, and her hair fell in a wave to her shoulders. Her presence made him suddenly forget about why he had wanted to throw the remote in the first place. Her presence calmed him. There was no one but she with whom he could discuss his attitudinal problems and his developing cynicism about the pressures of being confined to a room.

"Adam, my darling, why are you in such a terrible mood?" she asked.

"Funny how you always visit me when I'm in a bad mood. I hope you're not too disappointed by it."

"Nonsense. Not in the least. It just so happens that I always come down here when you're in a bad mood. It's a mother's sense of knowing, you could say."

"Well, mom, I am in a bad mood," he confessed. "I'm not sure why."

"Maybe you've been watching too much television. Maybe you're even reading too much. Is everything alright?"

"Yes, everything's fine. It's just that—well, you wouldn't understand."

"Try me," she said. "Have you been eating properly?"

"It's not the food."

"Then what can it be?"

"It's just that I really want to go outside, and I know that I can't. And this feeling of wanting to go out just hit me a few hours ago, and I really can't stand being in here for much longer, especially when there's so much fun to be had."

"But aren't you having fun already?"

"I was, but there's something missing in all of this. I mean, I really do relate to the guy on the travel show, but there's something missing."

"Like what? Isn't the television show everything you've always wanted? I've been watching the show too, and it's wonderful how a boy just like you is having so much fun. Isn't that a good thing?"

"Yes, mother, it is, but there's something that's missing."

"First of all, you should always be grateful for the things you have, not what you don't have. God has already given you everything you need, and I'd certainly thank my lucky stars that you can now see yourself doing all of that traveling and having so much fun with your friends. It must feel wonderful. You're a very fortunate and lucky boy."

"But that's the thing. I mean, it's me who's having fun, but it's not really me. That guy is me, but he isn't really me."

"That doesn't make any sense," she said. "How can someone be you and not be you?"

"I'm not the one on the television doing all of those things. I'm still stuck in my room."

"But that's nonsense, Adam. It is clearly you who are having all that fun. Didn't you just go to Amsterdam? And then a week before you visited the Great Pyramids of Egypt? That was you who went, not anyone else. I saw it myself."

"Mother," he said angrily, "I haven't been anywhere. I've been here, and all the while I've been watching myself do all of these things, but I was not the one doing them. Can't you understand that?"

"I see," she said resignedly. "You want to be inside the television yourself doing all of those things with your friends. I can see your point."

"No, you still don't see my point. My point is that you're going to have to let me outside, so that I can actually experience these things for myself instead of being locked up in here."

"Oh, I wouldn't say that you're locked up in here."

"Yes, I can safely say that I am locked up in here, because I myself have never experienced these things but can only relate to another version of myself doing these things on the television. I don't do anything but watch him doing the things that I would really like to do. I actually don't do anything—not a damn thing!"

"I never knew you felt this way about yourself," she said. "Haven't we provided you with everything you need? If you ask me, you're being a little too ungrateful."

"I'm being ungrateful? Mom, you have to let me outside. That's the only way I'll have any gratitude at all for what you've given me."

"I'm sorry, but I just can't do that. You're too sick to step one foot out of this room. I thought I had made myself clear the last time we discussed it."

"I just can't live this way anymore. I don't care if I die out there, but you're going to have to let me out—not next month, not tomorrow, but right now! I don't care if I die!"

"Just calm down, sweetheart, okay? I know you're frustrated, but I can't allow you to do it. I care so much about you."

"Damnit, let me out!" he yelled, grabbing her by the shoulders and pushing her away from him.

His mother fell back on the sofa, her eyes wide in bewilderment and shock at the way her son was behaving. Adam then ran towards the door, which was shut tight, but he searched frantically for something to open it—any switch or button or even a blunt object in the room to cleave the door open. He spotted the chair by his reading table, and he was about to throw it full force at the door, but just as he clutched it, the door swooshed open, revealing a handsome, middle-aged man with a square jaw who towered above him.

The man wore what seemed to be a uniform of some kind. It was a tan khaki uniform with shining gold medals pinned to his chest, a gold clip that held his tie in place, and on his head he wore a tan officer's cap. When Adam judged that the man was too much too strong and tall to pass, he let go of the chair and fell to his knees in anguish. He let out a cry, but as the hot tears that blurred his vision cleared, he knew the man in the doorway was his father, a man he hadn't seen for several years. Ironically, the last time he had seen the likes of him was when, as a younger boy, he had erupted at his mother in quite the same way, threatening to kill her if she didn't change the meal of goop he was regularly being served. And now his father, a handsome and resolute man, appeared before him and smiled a little. He offered him his hand and hoisted Adam up off the floor.

"Hello, son," said his father. "It's good to see you after all this time."

Adam embraced his father. Strangely enough his appearance hadn't changed one bit. His hair was the same yellowish color, and his skin hadn't aged. He actually seemed taller and more muscular than before.

"God, I'm lucky I got here when I did," said his father. "Adam, you really should behave yourself when you're with your mother. Maybe I've been absent for far too long."

"Yes you have," said his mother who joined them near the doorway.

They all hugged each other, as they hadn't been together in quite some time. And since kisses and hugs were exchanged, Adam forgot about his need to escape the room. Instead, the three of them sat on the sofa, and the father told them of his adventures fighting the Mesopotamians who were ligving a thousand miles away. He had returned from the war untouched and unscathed, and he carefully explained the medals he won for his bravery in battle.

Adam had almost forgotten all about his father, but he suddenly remembered how he held him in his arms as a younger boy and said that he would some day return. Apparently the military had discharged him suddenly—at the exact time Adam wanted to leave the room, as this is how it has always been. But Adam drew a great deal of comfort from the sight of him and how certain patterns and cycles that typified his return were still very much embedded within the confined life that he led. The three of them drowned themselves in their own familial mirth from that point forward, and his father continued to explain how the President had honored him for his bravery on the vast wastelands of Mesopotamia where he fought the enemy and how the war was almost won because of his heroism. Just a few years longer and they would have captured the land, making the world safer for all human kind.

Yet after his father informed them of the coming victory overseas, the conversation soon returned to Adam's rebellious behavior. His father apologized for being absent for so long.

"You mean you're here to stay, father?" asked Adam.

"Well, they've moved me back to the mainland, yes, so I'll be around much more. This I can promise you."

"Oh what a relief," sighed his mother.

"But Dad, now that you're back, maybe you can let me go outside. Mother here won't allow it."

His father looked a bit concerned by the question, and he then asked his wife to leave them alone for a few moments to discuss their son's radical idea.

"You two, I'm sure, have a lot to talk about," said his mother. "Honey, it's so good to finally have you home."

"Thanks, hon. I'll be up in a little bit."

The father and son discussed the details of the war in Mesopotamia first, and while Adam didn't have too many questions about what had happened over in that part of the world, since he was more concerned with the women he saw on the screen and the fun they were having, his father still went on about how he was captured by the enemy and was tortured for some time in a cave in the desert. His father even thought that he was going to die at one point.

Adam looked up at him in awe, not necessarily because of his heroism in battle or the tortures he endured in Mesopotamia but mainly because his father's body had been perfectly preserved. Because even though he had endured such hardships being a prisoner of war, he didn't have a single scratch on him. In fact, his father looked no different from when Adam had seen him several years ago.

"So what I'm saying, son, is that you have to be grateful and thankful for what you have today. I know you want to go out. I know sometimes it's not so easy being in your room all the time, but son, your mother and I have gone through many, many sacrifices to keep you safe and sound. So you shouldn't get so upset with her. It's the circumstances that are upsetting you. Be grateful is what I'm saying."

"I am grateful," said Adam. "It's just that I don't feel connected to anything anymore, as though everything that happens happens only on the outside. Not in here."

"But you have everything that you could possibly want in here. Is there something that's missing?"

"I guess I'm feeling kind of lonely. There's no one to talk to besides Mom."

"Oh, now I see," he smiled. "I can't believe we didn't see this coming."

"What?"

"Maybe we should have you meet someone. Maybe you need a companion. I mean, after all, you're sixteen now, going on seventeen. No wonder you're getting so angry, son. You're a growing young man, and maybe we've overlooked a few things."

"Like what?"

"Just leave it to me," said his father with a wink. "Now for a few weeks I have to be away. I'll be in the nation's capitol to receive an award—"

"Another award? But you just got here."

"Yeah. They just don't seem to want to stop giving me those awards. Y'know how it is—'an example for my country' and all. So I'll be away for a little while, but in the meantime sit tight, okay? Remember to have gratitude, and you should thank the dear Lord that you have food and shelter, all the entertainment that you need, and two loving parents who support you. Always remember that we love you and that God works in mysterious ways to help you. Don't forsake the gifts that you have already been given."

His father hugged him then, and his warm embrace comforted him. His father then donned his officer's cap and walked gallantly through the swooshing door, leaving Adam to wonder when he would return. But what was important now was that he no longer felt the same urges to go outside. Being with his father had reminded him to be thankful and grateful. In fact, he was grateful to be indoors where he was safe from the enemy and the terrible things in life, like war and bloodshed. He should at least be thankful for that.

He turned on the television, since there was nothing much to do after his father left. He continued watching the drama that unfolded between the actor who looked exactly like him and the two women who traveled the world with him. Apparently, all three of these scantily-clad party-goers had fallen in love with one another, and so the new drama concerned whom the boy would pick out of the two girls to spend the rest of his life with, as he was clearly in love with both women. And after it had been resolved that the actor would delay such a decision and, for now, take both women as his girlfriends, the party on an exotic resort island in Europa continued. There were even bigger dance parties, more kissing, hugging, and giggling—everything a sixteen year-old boy could ever want. These fantasies manifested themselves on the television screen like odd witchcraft. He watched the program for several days straight, and he decided, finally, that if he were to change his own life, he would have to marry the woman he had originally liked, the same woman that the actor on the screen fooled around with. And together they would live in his room happily-ever-after.

His mother entered the room again, even though his mood was quite content with the new twists the drama on the television took. The programming had grown even more R-rated since she had visited last. The girls were now sunning themselves topless on the beaches of St. Tropez, and this had aroused him to the point where he had thanked his lucky stars that he had listened to his parents and had overcome the angst of wanting to leave the room. But now that his mother had arrived, he tried to shoo her away and to block her view of the topless women sunning themselves on the television for fear of embarrassment.

"I'm a little busy right now," said Adam.

"I know you're busy, darling, but I have a surprise for you. Can you lower the television a bit?"

"Do we have to do this now? I'm in the middle of something here."

"It will only take a minute, sweetheart. Turn off the television for a sec."

He turned the equipment off and sat with his mother at his usual spot on the sofa. He couldn't understand how or why, for this one time, his mother had decided to show up, as he preferred watching the television privately without any interruptions.

"I have a surprise for you," she said, her eyes gazing at him brightly.

"A surprise? For me?"

"Yes. You've been so good lately that I brought someone here to see you."

"Here? You mean someone actually came here? But I thought I couldn't have any visitors—that I might kill them or something."

"We've made an exception, and we've done a full medical workup to ensure that she is no threat to you medically and that you are no threat to her."

"You mean she's a woman?"

"Yes."

And then she entered the room, the same girl whom he had been watching on the television screen, the same girl he wanted to live happily-ever-after with. And she looked stunningly beautiful in her short skirt and her ripped t-shirt that exposed her midriff and soft, supple shoulders. Her hair fell to her abundant chest in fiery blonde ringlets, and her eyes were as warm as the tropical ocean she had swam in in St. Tropez. Adam had never seen a sight so beautiful. She graced his room like a goddess or any angel from heaven would, and he thought for a second how there really must be a God, as God had just answered his most secret of prayers.

The same woman he had just seen on television sat right next to him. His mother smiled and winked at him before leaving.

"Hi there," she smiled.

"Hi," said Adam a bit nervously. "I was just watching you on television."

"Yeah," she said. "I hear you're a big fan of the show. So I thought I'd visit you."

"Wow," he said. "All the way from St. Tropez?"

"I just got in last night."

"How long are you staying with us?"

"Well, the show is on hiatus for a while. I thought I'd stay here with you."

"You mean here? In this room?"

"Yeah. If that's okay with you?"

"Of course it's okay—as long as you don't get sick or anything from being here."

"I've been given full medical clearance to stay with you for as long as you want me to—that is, if you want me to stay with you."

"Sure, I'd really like that. In that case, let me take your bags. I can make up the sofa."

"Why do you need to make up the sofa?" she asked.

"Because you need to sleep somewhere, don't you?"

"I was wondering, if you don't mind, if I could use your bed."

"Oh, I'm sorry. How rude of me. Of course. I'll take the sofa, then. How terribly rude of me."

"I didn't mean it that way."

"Oh? Then how did you mean it?" asked Adam nervously.

"Well, I get really scared and lonely at night," she said, "and I thought, well, if you agree to it, that we'd just sleep in your bed from now on."

"That should be fine," he stuttered. "You mean together, right? I'm not misinterpreting you or anything?"

"No."

"Then that should be fine. We'll be sleeping in the same bed. That makes sense—I mean why make up two beds if we don't have to, right? But before we have dinner, because I think it'll be arriving soon, I should really know your name."

"Evelyn."

"That's a very beautiful name, Evelyn. It's good to finally meet you."

"You too," she said. "I've waited such a long time to meet you."

When the goop had arrived via the food processor, Adam wondered why Evelyn didn't want to eat anything. They had spent the half-hour or so before dinner watching themselves on television, as the actor on the screen now rid himself of one of the girls and stuck with the actress who looked exactly like Evelyn. The two actors on the screen then went on a romantic holiday in Jamaica. Once there, the two simply closed themselves in a bungalow that overlooked the Jamaican shoreline. When the woman actor on the screen hung a 'Do Not Disturb' sign on the doorknob of their room, Adam, watching this from the sofa, realized that the current season of the show had finally ended, judging by the teasing trailer that came on afterwards. There now wasn't much left to watch except the next season's opener, which was a week or two away. Both the boy actor, who looked like himself, and the girl actor, who looked exactly like Evelyn, were expected to be married, and so without much regret, Adam shut down the television equipment and the high-fidelity sound system and simply sat on the sofa next to Evelyn as he ate the hot goop.

He tried to offer some to Evelyn, but she simply said she wasn't hungry and that maybe she should change into something more comfortable, seeing that sleep was the next activity on their list. Adam didn't put up any argument, and when the lights were dimmed and the empty bowl from his dinner had been returned to the processing unit, Evelyn asked him to get undressed. She didn't take such a reserved and shy approach any longer. Adam laid on the bed, and wiggled his clothes off underneath the comforter. She then removed all of her clothes and stood before him nude in the dim light. Her skin glistened, and he looked upon her with the fierce fascination of someone who had fallen instantly in love with what he had wanted all along. She smiled knowingly, no longer exuding the same laughing and ebullient demeanor that she did on the television program. Rather, she stood there in the nude as a more serious work of art would, allowing Adam to absorb every inch of her soft skin with his eyes. After he had finished his examination of all of her features, he knew that she was the same woman whom he had seen on the television all season long and that he had never beheld such beauty before.

She sat on the bed next to him and ran her fingers along the length of his exposed arms and chest. She then slipped her hand beneath the comforter and found the place where Adam had been expressing his love most, and before he even knew what was happening to him, she bent down to him and locked his lips in a kiss so passionate that it released his heart from his pent-up longings for the girl. Her lips were soft, moist, and whole, and he kissed them with an energy he never thought he possessed. She then slid under the covers, and from there he entered her heart with the slow protrusion of ecstasy that transported him to the same exotic locales that the television show had featured, only that he was simply in his own bed and in his own room being comforted by the woman of his dreams, her body entwined in his and her flesh warm and perspiring, muscles that he had never used before suddenly aflame, his body gyrating into hers. With a whispered moan, he released all that he had within her quivering, febrile body as though nothing in the world mattered any more but the ecstasy of his release into her.

His strength slackened then. He fell on top of her exhausted and dizzy, and while still within her, he simply fell asleep in her arms, hoping never to be released again from the bliss of living within her warm, parasidal enclaves ever again.

He must have remained in bed with Evelyn for several days, both of them nude under the covers and doing the same thing until he exhausted every inch of himself. Yet still he wanted more and more of her, as though each time they made love, he sought to move closer and closer to her heart for fear that her love may have only been a passing fancy. But there was little evidence she was going anywhere. Between her moans, coo's, and soft giggles, her invitation remained open to him, as she opened herself up to his slightest whim. Adam couldn't have been happier or more satisfied. There was really no reason to watch the television programs any more or read any of the dead authors that lined his bookshelves. He had found exactly what he had searched for, and he simply looked into her eyes as he climbed on top of her again. He whispered, "I think I'm in love with you."

She smiled at this and said, "I think I'm in love with you too."

When they did decide to get out of bed, Adam went to the sofa again and turned on the television. The travel show he had watched prior to Evelyn's arrival now featured both actors on their Honeymoon in Bali. Evelyn didn't watch too much of it. Instead she straightened up the place and served him more of the goop that arrived through the food processor.

"You'll need it," she said after placing the steaming hot goop before him.

Soon everything in the room was as neat and tidy as a pin— the bed was made perfectly, and the furniture was realigned with the posters on the walls. They donned their day-clothes, and their night clothes were folded neatly and put away. And together Adam and Evelyn watched themselves on the television screen as they traveled by yacht to yet another exotic island where the fruit fell directly from the trees and naked children played in the sand, the clear blue waters rushing over their merged bodies as though he had seen it all before but had merely forgotten that such a happiness was possible and now actually existed.

After a few days, however, a few things started to change. When he decided to question Evelyn one night about how the both of them came into being as children did who ran on the sand, Evelyn simply avoided his questions about the origins of life. She also avoided the more specific questions about why her parents weren't around and other such curiosities. She responded to his questions by kissing him all over again and leading him into bed where they continued their same routines. Adam had to admit that when she moved in to kiss him, he had grown a little frustrated by her obvious attempts to evade his questions. She always seemed to move in for a kiss when he questioned her about the origins of her own life and her family. These answers would have normally been plain and matter-of-fact, but she never answered them. After some more time had passed, he simply asked her these questions more directly, and yet she wouldn't really answer them but resorted to her careful evasion of them. Evasion seemed to dominate her entire language. She answered him vaguely without any specificity whatsoever, or what was more the case—she turned same questions onto him where he was then forced to state the facts and events of his life without knowing anything about hers. And after successfully avoiding his interrogations night after night, she would kiss him once again, just as before, and make love under the sheets of their bed. It was almost as though Adam had been talking to and questioning himself all this time. In a strange indirect way, he also felt at times that he was merely making love to himself as well, since her personality thinned to the point where she was simply a body without a personality that supplied a context or a history of her life.

This interesting dilemma stumped him for a few weeks more, as his routine of questioning her and then their love-making became a matter of routine. Slowly, however, he started to become less fascinated with her. He couldn't describe it really, but one afternoon, after the latest episode of their television show had ended, he simply said, "why won't you answer any of my questions?"

"C'mon dear," she pouted again, "don't get so angry."

"I'm not angry. It's just that I can't get a straight answer from you. I don't know where you're from, who your parents are, how you got here. I don't even know who the hell you are for Chrissakes!"

"Oh, sweetie, I'm the woman you see on the television every day. Look at all the wonderful things we've been doing together."

He sensed that if he pressed the issue any further, then his mother may just have to make another one of her surprise visits to their looming den of despair, and he certainly didn't want to see his mother or even his father, especially not now, as Evelyn moved in again for one of her signature kisses. Soon they were in bed all over again, and although he never grew tired of sleeping with Evelyn, this time around he was thoroughly frustrated with her, and in bed he was rougher with her than he had previously been.

What was so strange about the severity of his love-making and the rapid, spit-fire energy that he employed to express his ever-deepening dissatisfaction with her this time around was that she still moaned softly and giggled as he pounced on her in the darkness, as though Evelyn couldn't differentiate the times when he loved her with the whole of his heart and the point that they had reached now—his body pounding into her and riding her so roughly that he thought his legs would fall off. The flat of his palm slapped her backside as thought he were trying to break some kind of wild animal. And Evelyn's response to his severity was simply the same—a flat and steady line that didn't waiver, diverge, or fluctuate. It was a flatness more typical of an inflatable toy.

"That was great, dear," said Evelyn quaintly as she rolled over onto her side of the bed and hoisted the covers on top of her body.

Adam had little choice but to fall asleep, but when he awoke, he found that he had hogged all of the covers, leaving Evelyn's back exposed to him in the dim light of the room. He admitted once again that her body was a thing of intense beauty, but quite suddenly he noticed an interesting imperfection. His eyes wandered to the part of her body that he had slapped and spanked with all of his might. There he found a thread of skin that had ripped away during their love-making. This thread of skin was not unlike wrapping material that had been torn slightly open to reveal something hiding beneath it. The loose thread exposed a white, polished surface underneath it.

Adam recalled how once he had pricked himself with a knife at an early age. His mother soon got rid of all of the sharp objects in the room, but he remembered how warm, red liquid spilled from his finger. He gawked at surprise at Evelyn's torn patch of skin, as there wasn't a single drop of blood that flowed out of the tear, just a loose flap of skin revealing—what was it? Plastic?

He knew that he should make immediate attempts to calm his mind. Otherwise his mother would pay them both a visit. So he remained calm and collected in his bed while burying whatever anxieties he felt. He even tugged at the flap of skin a bit more, and as soon as he did so, Evelyn sprang to life. She turned over to face him and asked, "what's wrong, honey? Can't sleep?"

He could only act his way out the situation. He simply rolled away from her and feigned sleep. Interestingly enough, Evelyn then got up and went to the bathroom, the flap of skin waving like a price tag from her backside. And when she returned after a few minutes, her nude backside no longer displayed the imperfection. The tear in her skin had been repaired somehow, her skin as smooth and supple as the first time she had stood naked before him.

He knew then that something was wrong, but he waited until morning instead of erupting into any sort of emotion. He continued to feign sleep until he could compose a more logical and intellectually-based plan, now that he discovered that Evelyn might not be a human being at all.

He slept with a cautious eye open for the time being. He waited patiently until the lights brightened and another bowl of piping hot goop had been served. Evelyn brought it to him. She walked to the kitchen barefoot and with a nightgown on. She also seemed a little bored now that both of them had gone without the television for several hours. Adam simply sat on the blue sofa as she served him the goop. He placed his hand just slightly over the bowl, testing its heat. As soon as Evelyn smiled and sat down next to him, he firmly gripped the bowl and threw the piping hot goop all over her bare arms and shoulders.

Evelyn, however, didn't shriek or scream in pain. She simply sat there quietly as the goop burned her thin layer of soft skin, revealing a hard shell of plastic underneath it.

In a few moments, his mother, whom he hadn't seen for close to two months, entered the room just as he expected. He quickly leapt to his feet and made straight for the open door, shoving his mother aside in the process. Once on the other side of it he could see nothing but a long, dull corridor that had no end. From there he ran with all of his might down the corridor, but as soon as he took his first few steps, red sirens that were attached to the edges of the ceiling spun and cried, the corridor now bathed in red swirling light and a siren so loud that it hurt his ears.

He ran in a mad sprint, wondering where the corridor would lead. It seemed like it was several miles long, only that as he ran through it, the air grew increasingly colder such that he could see the fumes of his own hot breath. By the time the sirens stopped, his feet were numb and paining, his muscles stretched to their very last. As he tired, he also heard running footsteps behind him. They grew louder as he ran, as whatever followed him through the corridor had been closing in on him. He took a quick look behind his shoulder, and within the dizzying bath of flashing red light his father in his officer's uniform, his teeth clenched, pursued him like a dog in pursuit of his prey. His father missed him when he first tried to grab him, and up ahead Adam noticed the cracks of a brighter light that emanated beyond a hydraulic door that marked the end of the corridor. But Adam barely had enough energy to reach the door, as his father's strong hand pulled him from behind and dragged him down to the cold concrete floor.

"Father, stop! I beg of you, stop!"

His father wrestled him to the floor and wrapped him up much like a thick python would. Adam's head was locked in the vise of his gargantuan arms, until he could do nothing else but pass out just inches away from the door that would have otherwise set him free and perhaps deliver him to the outside world.

Before waking, he heard a faint voice that was both tender and stern to his ears, and then the snapping of fingers that brought him to full consciousness. An older man stood above him smiled kindly to him. He had never seen this man before. His hair was white and thinned along his scalp, his face gaunt and clean-shaven. He wore a black robe. Adam was startled by the look of his eyes, which were a peculiar kind of blue. He knew these eyes to be synthetic or artificial eyes. They weren't human eyes. And while the man looked like a perfectly composed gentleman, Adam could tell that he was made of the same plastic parts that had lined the interior of his parent's bodies—and also Evelyn's body, which he vaguely missed.

"Hello, Adam," said the old man.

Adam looked around him and discovered that he was in a bed, his sore body covered by white linens. Along the perimeter of the room were men who looked exactly like his father. They worked at computer terminals, typing things into them and studying the bright colors of the monitors. His bed was the only thing that seemed remotely cozy and familiar within this sea of electronics, as though his body under all of the soft linen didn't fit in well with the seriousness of purpose these duplicates of his father had.

"How are you feeling?" asked the old man, his peculiar eyes observing him.

"A little sore, I guess," stuttered Adam as he moved upright on the bed.

"You've had quite a day," smiled the old man wryly.

"Where am I?"

"That's a very interesting question—a question that may take a lot of time to answer."

"Can't anyone give me a straight answer around here? I've never found the people here—or whatever you are—so vague before."

"It's our charm," said the old man, "and sometimes we have to be as vague and as delicate as possible. But to answer your question more directly, I first need to know if you'd like the longer version of the story or the shorter one?"

"Please, for once in my life, I ask that you state things plainly. No more beating-around-the-bush. I think I deserve a good explanation, because right now I'm freaked out as hell."

"Since you must know, you are currently in a complex that's approximately ten miles below the surface of the Earth."

"You can't be serious."

"Oh, I'm being quite serious. You are now far removed from the surface of the Earth, and we are the ones who have been taking care of your every need for all these years."

Adam absorbed the full shock of this admission, because somewhere he knew all along that things were never quite what they seemed to be. He realized that his life spent in his room was not real at all but an ersatz life that had been constructed to hide reality from him.

"So who am I, then?"

"Well, you're definitely a human being, I'm afraid. If that's what you mean."

"Then who are all of you?"

"That's a more difficult question, but since you want me to be direct with you, we are all androids—every one of us."

"Androids? You mean like robots?"

"Yes. That's what they used to call us, but we prefer 'androids,'" smiled the old man. "Unfortunately, you are a very special person to have been brought down here."

"What do you mean?"

"You see, at your birth, when you were just an infant, actually—and this is to make a much longer story shorter— there was a great war among the many fragmented parts of your world."

"What kind of war?"

"A war where it seems that every human being on the planet had perished—or so we think at this time."

"Every single human being? How can that be?"

"You see, several clairvoyants who had been in your government, just before the bombs were dropped and the missiles launched, had prepared for self-assured destruction with such—how do we call it?—with such accuracy, I should say, that they had quickly assembled androids in case such a war devastated the planet, which it did."

"My God. There's no more Earth left?"

"Not exactly. There is still the Earth above us, but it is not habitable earth or sustainable earth. A human being can no longer survive on it."

"It was a nuclear war, then?"

"Think of a nuclear war but five times its size. That's how bad it was. And yet we were programmed, after the first missiles had touched down, to scour every patch of devastated earth and search for any sign of human life in the hopes that humanity would continue."

"And you found me."

"Yes. We found you buried beneath five tons of rubble, as our sensors detected that there was some life left where we found you. So as we were programmed to do, we brought you down here—to save your life."

"I had no idea. But why should I believe you? You've lied to me about everything else so far. My entire life is a lie."

"Yes, and I believe we had to lie, given that we wanted you to develop fully as a human being, and also given the severity of our present circumstances."

"But you could have just told me. You didn't have to lie to me. You didn't have to build a fake life for me."

"I know you're upset, but you see, when the clairvoyants programmed us, they insisted that we try to create the same environment that human beings had been accustomed to in order to preserve the same biological development and evolutionary trend of humanity that had existed just prior to the widespread annihilation of your kind. In other words, as our probes looked for any signs of human life on the surface, our creators saw to it that we also try to recreate the same life that was tragically, well—disconnected—as a result of the war. So you see, you are the last human being, and you have been educated and instilled with the same aptitudes, traits, and culture as the human beings who lived directly before you."

"You mean I'm the only one left? Oh, God, no."

"You are the Last One. But we are still searching for other signs of life, if there are any to be found. We have been programmed to recreate your species and repopulate the surface above once conditions improve."

"You mean there's no other human being at all? This can't be. This just can't be."

"Our search continues. We have but a few sturdy probes that are now canvassing the surface of the earth, hopefully to find a suitable female to be used as your mate."

"Oh, no."

"I'm sorry, Adam, but the only thing we can do is wait for these probes to find another compatible life source. Hopefully it's a woman, but as of yet, no one has been found."

"And there's nothing that can be done?"

"I'm afraid not. We did, of course, think of creating 'another you,' but we didn't think that would help our situation any. Actually, we were very close to creating a duplicate copy of yourself using a graft of your skin. We even thought of using your kidneys to create another life from you. Even your rib."

"My rib?"

"Yes, but as of yet the technology doesn't exist to make a copy of a fertile woman, and so rather than recreate you, we've been waiting until a woman is found on the surface. We are now steadily at work collecting data from our probes, which is what you see us doing here. As of yet, we haven't found any signs of life, I'm afraid. I'm sorry."

"So what happens to me now?"

"I'm afraid there's nothing else you can do but wait. Of course you won't have to stay in your room any longer, and I suppose the television programs and the electromagnetic monitoring of your thoughts and your moods won't be necessary either—unless, of course, you enjoy the television programs and the companionship that Evelyn provides. But I can understand if you'd like to discontinue the services of our domestic androids, unless you should still need them for self-maintenance purposes."

"I guess I won't be needing them anymore, no. But I'd still like to live with Evelyn if I may."

"Of course. We'll supply you with a new unit with whom you can make your home. We can configure her appearance any way you like, although we are not fully equipped to furnish her with a more dynamic personality, which we know is something that you especially need."

"That's okay. Just another version of Evelyn should be fine. But see, here's the thing—I still want to see what it's like on the Earth's surface. Maybe there's something that I can make out of our situation that you haven't seen yet. Maybe you've overlooked something."

"I'm afraid that's just not possible. After the annihilation of all life on the planet, the atmosphere has steadily grown more corrosive and poisonous for any human life to handle. The Earth right now is much like it's sister planet, Venus. Only our probes are able to withstand the harsh environment in their search for life, but you, as the Last One, would die instantly if you were exposed to the open air of the planet. I'm afraid I can't let you out."

"There must at least be a way I can see the Earth. Through a window or something?"

"Actually, this is possible, as we do have an observatory that has a view of the planet's surface."

"Can I at least do that?"

"I would advise against it," said the old android. "I think it's better that you avoid it so that we may prevent any psychological strain that your view of a devastated Earth may cause, even under the protection of the observatory."

"I think it's important that I see it. In fact, I should see it right away. I have to know what awaits me if a woman is found alive."

"If you wish. But I must warn you that what you'll see may cause you much strain. You must realize that the world is something that you've not seen before. It is not what you've always imagined it to be. It is completely and irreversibly different and forever altered because of the devastation. May I suggest that I give you a strong sedative before we go to the observatory."

"I'll take one, sure."

"You must realize that all you've ever known and all that we have shown you thus far have only been the most beautiful and exotic places on the planet that used to exist, and that we've shown all of this to you through digital images that catered to your specific wants and desires. So before you view the planet's surface, you must understand that such places no longer exis and that the terrain of the Earth has been dramatically altered. That is why I advise you to take the sedative—to lessen the effects of your impending grief."

"How bad can it be? I've lived in a room for all of my life. Any change is welcome."

The android smiled at this comment. Adam sensed that there was much more the old man wanted to tell him, as he now had the rest of his life to learn what had happened.

"You see, the clairvoyants never expected to find any life at all, which is why they didn't provide any female eggs or any embryos for us to work with. In fact, we are at the point in our research where we are asking if such an annihilation had taken place before at some point in human history."

"You mean, there may have been the same kind of war prior to the one we just had?"

"Precisely. But what we can't understand, really, is how we found you. Our programmers, the clairvoyants, actually predicted that there would no life left at all. They didn't expect anyone to outlive the war. Somehow you were the exception, and that's when we knew that we had to repopulate the species as soon as possible, as we were programmed to do just that. Yet the probability that we would find you was approximately six billion to one. The clairvoyants, in the common parlance at the time, would have called this 'a miracle.'"

"What are embryos?"

"I beg your pardon, Adam, but we'll save all of that for a later time."

The old android led him down another corridor after Adam was fully dressed and ready to see the Earth. The corridor led away from the main computer room and ended at a massive elevator that led up to the Earth's surface. The old android pulled out a cylindrical device and quickly pressed it to Adam's neck.

"Ouch! Hey, what was that for?"

"My apologies, but this device has just delivered a sedative to your blood stream. By the time we reach the observatory, you'll feel more relaxed."

They then entered the large elevator and took their seats on a couple of cushioned chairs. The android buckled him in.

"It will take approximately nine minutes and fifteen seconds to reach the observatory."

"What if we don't find a woman?" asked Adam suddenly, as his body slackened and lost its gravity.

"Then we'll simply recreate you, and another human replica of yourself will have to wait another lifetime until we finally find a compatible mate. And over these successive life spans our technology will have improved. We also have robotic scavengers out there now who are searching for raw materials and special metals from old technologies that we hope to find that were spared the destruction. There's still a lot of material on the surface that we can use to make better versions of ourselves and perhaps a living and breathing mate to accompany your successor. We may soon be able to journey beyond the Earth's atmosphere one day and broaden our search to include the other planets in the Solar System. Of course our progress is slow, and it may require us to duplicate you until such technologies exist."

"I'm feeling a bit woozy," said Adam. "I'm feeling a little light-headed. God, what's in this stuff?"

"Just be patient. We should be arriving momentarily."

When the elevator jets below them had brought them safely to halt below a wide metal dome, the old android turned a switch that split the top of the dome open. Like an eyelid, the metal sheathing of the dome opened and revealed an insulated, transparent layer of glass. The sky was slowly revealed.

But there was no sky to be seen exactly—at least not as Adam had imagined it. There was only a light grayish spot that shone through thick, dense clouds. As the dome opened more fully, the android told Adam to brace himself for what he was about to see. The metal that slid open revealed the Earth as it now was—a place that he had somehow known before, as though he had seen it in his dreams, its charred surface memorized by the blood that suddenly rushed through him. And once exposed to the view, he could do nothing but scream and cry so fiercely at the sight of it that it silenced the dulcet sounds that had always nurtured him through the childhood he spent in his room. His scream was so violent and monstrous that only the heavens above could address them now, and the heavens did so by making the view too traumatic for him to witness for very long. He soon fainted in his seat, his senses too jarred and confused to remain conscious.

THE MAYOR OF OAK JUNCTION

There was something about incumbent Mayor Gerard Nickel's ability to look into the future and know at a very early age that he would one day be running things in the town of Oak Junction.

He sat at a window seat in the local coffee shop on a street named for the town's founder, Anthony Gilby, who in 1899 sold his vast acreages to hungry working class miners in return for a cast-iron statue of himself in the town park and also his nameplate on the only major dirt path to cut through the heart of a then-evolving village. Gerard Nickel often used Gilby's name in his speeches. The town had elected him to five terms as mayor, but he wouldn't be surprised if this young, up-and-coming star on the town council this year, this union leader at the plant, this Lester Showalter his name, defeated him when November rolled around.

Gerard now sipped at his coffee, and lately he had been taking it black. His older age and notoriety in the town afforded him the window seat so that he could admire the pleated bone-colored skirt of one of the housewives who ambled by, pushing her crying toddler in a stroller that seemed to swerve as it went. He once had a life like hers, he mused, as he found his coffee much too bitter and added another sugar to ease its ugliness. The bad thing about him and his coffee was that he never knew how many sugars to put in it, and the waitress always served it piping hot. He usually went back to Town Hall with a burnt tongue that nagged him until evening. At home, his wife sometimes gave him an oral analgesic to soothe the burn, but the leathery burn never went away. He'd been drinking a lot of hot coffee lately, ever since his numbers in the latest Gazette poll took a nosedive.

It was a sunny day out, and there were plenty of people milling about the town. It was just around lunch hour, and the diner was as busy as usual when his campaign manager, a round, heavy-set man named Burt Burly, hurried into the place with the aim relaying some interesting news. Burt always had an ever-present trickle of sweat running down the side of his face, especially during the summer months. It was no surprise to Gerard that Burt's sweat often bled through the oversized tarps he wore for shirts. They could never make a suit that fit Burt's large, pear shape, and the Mayor laughed to himself at how ridiculous he looked.

"Gerry, we've got some interesting news," said Burt as he barely fit into the seat across from him.

"Not while I'm drinking my coffee," said Gerard.

"This can't wait."

"Oh, yes it can. Don't you know how I win elections by now?"

"I know, I know. With patience."

"That's right. With patience. Patience is probably my only friend when election time rolls around. And drinking my coffee is an example of my patience. I've just about said hello to every man, woman, and child in this whole goddamned restaurant, and do you know how I did it, Burt?"

"Let me guess. With patience?"

"That's right. One of my many virtues. I wasn't born yesterday."

"But this is important."

"Talk about something else, will ya? This coffee is too good."

"Please, Gerry. I've got other work to do."

"Like what?"

"Like making sure Showalter doesn't bury us in the next opinion poll. It's too close to call this time, Gerry. We haven't seen anything like this before."

"You don't think I can do it this time, is that it?"

"Oh, I think you can do it, but it's tricky this time around. Lester Showalter isn't exactly talking too nicely about you these days. He's got the folks at the plant all riled up about improving working conditions and giving pregnant single-mothers sick leave and a lot of other stuff he's promised them."

"Is that so? Well then let's hit him with the Commie line. That usually works."

"The Cold War ended about fifteen years ago, Gerry. There's no more communism."

"Very well then. Tell our fellas at the Gazette that he's been cheating on his wife."

"That won't work either. He's got us nailed, not only with the guys over at the plant but with this—"

Burt pulled out a business-sized envelope. He had been carrying it in his breast pocket and fished it out as though he had been rehearsing the maneuver all day. In it were glossy photographs that had been mailed to the Mayor's attention.

"Take a look at these," Burt said, as if the trumpets of the apocalypse were about to sound.

Gerard looked at each photograph carefully. He was neither shocked nor bewildered. He calmly perused the photographs as though he were waiting for an elevator and was bored as hell with the music.

"And?" asked Gerry finally.

"And?!" asked Burt, massaging his knuckles.

"Listen, Burt, you worry too much. You make mountains out of molehills. These pictures don't mean anything. You know it, and I know it."

"But it shows you and that whore Lisa Snodgrass kissing, among other things. Don't you think that's something to worry about?"

"Not really, no."

"Okay, Gerry, tell me where I'm wrong here, because I'd really like to know."

"It's a simple problem that can be corrected. Who sent them to you?"

"How the hell should I know? It came in a blank envelope."

Burt slid the envelope over to him. Gerard looked at the pictures curiously. He slid his thin fingers over the middle of them. The envelope was postmarked a day earlier, so it must have come from within town. He then held the envelope up to his nose, closed his eyes, and inhaled deeply.

"Gerry, what are you doing?"

He opened his eyes with the envelope still under his nose and said:

"Leave this matter to me."

"Y'know, if the Showalter camp finds out about this, we're through. We've come a long way, Gerry. I hope you know what you're doing."

"Insult my intelligence one more time, Burt, and I'm gonna take a hammer to your balls, you got that?"

"Sorry," said Burt, "it's just that we have a lot riding on this one."

"You worry too much."

"My job is to worry too much. That's why you hired me, remember?"

"Well, stop it. This is no big deal."

"My kids are in college, Gerry. I can't afford to lose this one."

"You remember a long time ago, in my second term, when that smelly-old chemical plant had their little spill over by the river, and half the town came down with the flu? You remember that?"

"Sure I do."

"Well, you worried then, and you're worrying now. We won that year, Burt, and no one really gave a rat's ass who got sick or who died. Accidents happen. That's why I'm the fucking mayor of this town. I know how to clean things up. I know how to make people pay for their fuck-ups, and this is no exception. 'A Nickel is better than a Penny,' remember the slogan that year? That was the year my idiot nephew got arrested for drinking too much, getting behind the wheel of his Dad's Buick, and slugging one of our patrolmen. You remember that? And what happened after that?"

"We won by a landslide."

"Hey, now you're coming around. These photos are the least of our problems. I already know where they're coming from, and no, my family will never find out about this, because like a snake in the grass I bite into the problem, Burt, and leave my enemies brain dead. Does that make sense to you?"

"I take it you'll take care of this one?" said Burt nervously.

"Damn right I'll take care of it. Don't I always?"

"Well, there was this one year you got caught buying a Carribean vacation with DPW funds, remember that?"

Gerard cracked a smile at this, and so did Burt.

"I'll take care of it," said the Mayor. "Go home and rest up. We've got a meeting with the spics over on Seneca tomorrow. See to it they have the coffee and doughnuts ready this year, and I want it hot. I want to be in and out of there in a half-hour."

"Right."

"And Burt?"

"Yeah, boss?"

"Lose some fucking weight for Chrissakes."

The rest of the day was much too humid for it to stay sunny, and the weatherman called for thundershowers all afternoon. Gerard didn't think in advance enough to bring an umbrella, and instead he sat in the coffee shop alone while thumbing through the photographs of him and Lisa Snodgrass lip-locking outside a local watering hole a few blocks from Town Hall. He inhaled the envelope a second time and was certain it was the same perfume Lisa had worn the night that the photographs were taken—a kind of rosy, chemical-laden scent that had soured his tongue when he had licked her neck. His wife didn't know a thing, and instead of getting angry over the photographs, he calmly tucked them into his breast pocket and finished up his coffee as the rain came pouring out of the sky, dousing the passersby on the sidewalks. They were all potential voters, he thought. Every last one of them.

He dropped a five dollar bill on the counter and left the diner without saying goodbye to the owner, who also happened to be one of his most loyal supporters. He had a date with Lisa Snodgrass that evening anyway, and he wanted to be on time for a change. He went home instead of the office and changed out of his wet, government clothes. He burned the photographs in the fireplace and emerged from the fairer side of town with urges to make love to his mistress hard until sunup, maybe even spank her a few times for what she did. Regardless, he told his driver to wait outside her house until he was done. It had been their clandestine routine for about a year straight, and he'd be damned if a little thing like blackmail lost him his sixth term. This time he remembered to bring his umbrella from home and stood out in the rain ringing her doorbell.

No one answered at first, but her car was in the driveway, so she was either sleeping or washing her hair. She lived on the second floor of a mother-daughter walk-up along a suburban street that led into the more economically challenged areas. Lisa Snodgrass was one of those women who stayed in Oak Junction instead of hightailing it east to New York, which was about an hour's train ride away. Gerard met her at a fundraiser one night, and ever since that moment he couldn't think about anyone else. He had the nerve to ask her to see him after she complained a good while about property taxes one evening.

After the fifth ring of the doorbell, Lisa came barreling down the stairs. Her eyes had the pinkish glazed look of a woman who had become so bored with doing nothing in particular that she had fallen asleep while watching a reality courtroom television drama earlier that afternoon. She always wanted to be on television, and she certainly had the looks for that sort of thing. But she never left Oak Junction, and Gerard had no idea why. Her parents even moved down to Florida to get away, but she remained, and ever since she graduated from the high school, she must have fucked every police officer and public official from Oak Junction to Wilkes-Barre, earning just enough to purchase the house she lived in the hard way while renting the bottom floor out to a couple of kids from the local community college. Of course, she was half Gerry's age, but for him it really didn't matter. He would never leave his wife for her, and Lisa accepted that.

"Gerry, my God, you shouldn't be out in this rain," she said after letting him in.

He barely made it up the stairs his legs were so tired. The curves of her lithe body gave him enough motivation to climb the stairs, and he noticed too that she had colored her hair blonde, her roots showing her natural brunette. It was something drastic enough to give him all the evidence he needed to know that she was the one who sent the photographs to his office. Maybe she was planning to leave Oak Junction after all with the money his campaign fund would undoubtedly provide her. But all he wanted from her just then was another evening in her bed, and he didn't feel like buttering her up as he usually did. He remembered he was there to teach her a hard lesson about money and politics.

"Get me drink," he said upon entering her living room.

"What'll it be?" she smiled.

"Scotch on the rocks with a splash of water."

"My, my. What's the special occasion?"

"Oh, nothing. I just need a drink right now."

She handed him a glass of the stuff, which she pulled off the top shelf of her kitchen cabinet. As she reached for it, she exposed herself at the waist. His lower region tingled for a moment, as he sighed at what a good-looking woman she was. Lisa divorced her husband several years ago, and their only kid died young of Leukemia at ten years old.

"How's things downtown?" she asked.

He took a long of sip of the scotch and then moved in close and put his arms around her.

"Forget downtown. I've been smelling you all day."

"Oh you have?" she smiled mischievously. "And what were you smelling?"

He kissed her slowly, and she kissed him back. They kissed all the way to her bedroom, the sheets soon tangled over their bodies and her clothes from the day before strewn all over her faux-Persian carpet like some childlike collage. Her house was always sloppy when he visited, and he still couldn't figure out what she did with her time. She changed hobbies and interests like winds that changed direction, and it was hard to say what hobby or interest captured her attention this week. It didn't matter anyway. By the time he peeled off his clothes on the Lay-Z-Boy next to her bed, they were fucking as though it was the last time they'd ever have the chance.

Lisa Snodgrass was in the middle of moaning below him when Gerard reached over her and fished his gun out from the side pocket of his jacket. He waited until she came, and right when her lips formed a glossy crimson 'O' below him, he covered her face with the nearest pillow and fired two muffled shots into it.

Her writhing body shook nervously and then fell warm and flaccid on the bed. He didn't want to see her face at all. He left the bleeding pillow on top of her blood-soaked face and calmly slipped out of her. He quickly put his clothes back on and stuck the revolver at the small of his back. He locked the door from the inside and immediately returned to the diner for his favorite dinner of meatloaf and mashed potatoes with mushroom gravy.

When his belly was full, he ordered coffee, served black and piping hot as usual. He was still trying to get the sugars right when Burt Burly huffed and puffed his way through the doors. Burly saw him eating there and squeezed into the seat across from him.

"I talked to some of the management people over at the plant. They say Showalter is organizing some kind of protest strike. The union's backing him. His numbers are expected to go way up."

"You worry too much, Burt. Did anyone ever tell you that?"

"Yeah. You tell me that every day."

"Well, I took care of the problem with the photographs."

THE PARTY

She didn't think it such a terrible idea to attend the gathering at Paul's that evening, considering that the money supporting her fatherless children came directly from him. Paul never asked for sex or anything like that, but lately he had been acting a bit strangely towards her by insisting she do things she normally wouldn't do. Just last month, in fact, he convinced her to walk in the gardens adjacent to the capital building with some of the male friends he introduced her to, and then, when their exaggerated descriptions of faraway lands, distant adventures, and military conquests made her yawn in the urbane affectation reserved only for the horniest of them, she would lead them back to their apartments and sacrifice her body to their ever-expanding egos until the hot morning dawn made it too uncomfortable for her to get a good night's sleep. And then, like an abandoned animal, she would walk back to her place amidst the muted stares and offhand insults of the Republic's poorest citizens who hawked their wares in the desperate city streets.

In fact, she was invited to the party by Theresa, Paul's wife. She hadn't seen Paul in over a week or so, and suspected that he had turned gay since their last encounter, or at least he was so uninterested in her sexually nowadays that the only real reason for sharing her with his friends was to grease his own steady social climb. Paul had always been an opportunist this way, and there was no telling when he would smile at her the way he did when they first met several years ago. But Theresa always cheered her up, and she would accompany her to the party even if Paul was too busy to escort her on his own. Who else but Theresa would have given her so much comfort after so many years of sorrow?

She looked herself over in the mirror and figured that she didn't look bad for a widow with four children, and maybe she even looked good enough to make love to a man without Paul ordering her to do so. Either way, the kids had to eat, and Theresa, fanning herself in the cabriolet downstairs, couldn't be kept waiting just because her children didn't want her to leave. Perhaps Theresa would stick it to Paul on her behalf.

A woman only had so much energy during the hot, midsummer months, and she missed the simple act of going out on a casual date with a guy who didn't demand sex. She did, after all, count on the likes of Paul and Theresa for her very survival, and she knew it too risky to question them about anything they ordered her to do. Question them, and she would again wind up in the streets with the very delinquents who had caused all of her misery in the first place. She'd rather do the party circuit than be a slave to loud rebels waving flags, beating their drums, dressing like fairies, and smelling like sewer rats. Such was the nature of political soirees—there was always a rebellion brewing just outside their closed doors, and it really didn't matter who served whom, because even the wealthy had to serve somebody. Her circle of friends just happened to look better doing it.

She kissed her children goodnight and handed them off to the nanny. She rode off with Theresa in the mosquito-laden heat, laughing and gossiping the entire way there. The warmth of the evening wetted the facades of the beige stone walls they passed, and Paul's apartment was already crowded by the time they arrived.

Tobacco smoke from long brass pipes and the acrid, fungal scent of spoiled red wine filled the spaces between fastidious men and cultured ladies chit-chatting and munching on hors d'oerves. She and Theresa sat on vintage maroon lounge chairs apart from the action, hoping not to be noticed, as they were having way too much fun ridiculing those who put on their best airs for a party that would ultimately sink into debauchery.

While searching for even more people to poke fun at, Theresa pointed over to the far end of the room where a short, quiet young man with thinning hair and a threadbare officer's uniform stared right back at them. He was alone and gazed at them with the kind of intense longing that suggested he didn't really know how to approach a member of the opposite sex, let alone dress himself appropriately for a social event.

"How ugly," said Theresa, whispering into her ear. "If only Paul's friends washed their clothes every once in a while."

She wasn't the type who easily went along with another woman's cruelty, but she laughed at Theresa's remark if only to get along better and make the evening more enjoyable for them both.

The man staring at them was indeed very short, and he was also a slob who didn't seem to belong in the company of the other nobles gathered there. He also looked a bit child-like, as though he were a toy doll that a girl wouldn't mind sticking her pin-needles into. He certainly wasn't handsome in any way, and yet she soon discovered, when the soft candlelight hit him right, that his sharp, blue-green eyes exuded a sadness she couldn't quite define but vaguely identified with. The man must have known they were laughing at him, because his peculiar, sad stare then slipped into an anger so pronounced that she was afraid this dwarfish creature would rush over and scold them both for their blatant disrespect. But he awkwardly stood still and accepted their mockery as though he gained some sort of strength by it, or at least he was able to access a deeper rage that silently motivated him to withstand such mockery. He was defiant in a way. Even if he were to take a bath and put on better clothes, he still wouldn't be worth it. Although she had learned very early on not to assume such crass things about men, this guy was the very definition of something she should avoid, not just because of his looks, but because he also seemed to have a latent talent for greater sensitivity and, therefore, would know nothing about how to command a woman. He would be unable to please her when it really mattered.

It was just then that Paul sauntered up next to her and kissed her soft hand. Paul looked as handsome and dashing as ever, his bronzed skin and pearly-white smile contrasting sharply with the stumpy officer who by now had floated along the edges of the room and out of sight, nibbling on a wedge of goose-liver as he went.

"Who was that?" asked Theresa.

"What do you think of him?" asked Paul.

"Why he's absolutely horrid," said Theresa.

"And you, Josephine? How about a dance with him?"

"You wouldn't dare," said Theresa angrily, rising to Josephine's defense.

Josephine only needed to see the slow grin growing at the corners of Paul's mouth to know that she would eventually have to take to bed the only man in Paris she would have otherwise avoided. After swallowing the rest of her wine, Josephine rose from her seat and searched through the crowd for the man who would one day make her the Empress of all of France.

THE RACE

On a dry June afternoon, the two brothers, both in their high school sweats, stood side by side facing a flat and empty field ahead of them. The field itself, burnt in places from the latest drought, stretched on for about an acre or so and ended at a natural boundary of tall oaks rising up like an ivy-covered wall. A crowd of onlookers had already gathered in a semi-circle behind them, as throughout the week most of the townsfolk had been placing bets on which brother would outdo the other. The race between them was the talk of their small, peculiar town and had been dubbed by many as the town's most anticipated event, even surpassing the extreme fighting tour that had rolled in a couple of years ago. It was no wonder, then, that as even more obsolete cars streamed into the small parking lot at the foot of the field, the crowd gathering behind them had multiplied and swelled with anticipation (and also a bit of abandon) until there was no longer any room for the two brothers to move. The two of them stared down a long strip of yellow grass that ended at the dark wall of forest beyond. The townsfolk filled in the empty spaces on either side of them, some clapping, and some jeering.

The Mayor of the town even showed. He was a round, heavy-set man with ruddy pink cheeks and a bulbous nose that would have resembled a clown's had he worn the right costume. His teeth were tobacco-stained, and his smile,

293

eclipsed by the expansive shadow of the forest, looked more like a jaded grin than a wholesome attempt at placating the unruliness surrounding the two brothers. Members of the town council and the business development committee, having just adjourned their weekly meeting at Town Hall, were also in attendance. They were like trolls against the big-bellied outline of the mayor and wore stern business suits to match their stern faces. It wasn't even an election year.

Soon the brothers' parents, sporting dark blue overalls and trucker's caps, were rushed through the thick of the townsfolk until they too stood near their children on the starting line. They couldn't have been prouder, as they had raised their two sons right and worked particularly hard at making sure they ate three square meals a day and spanking them, no less, when they didn't behave. They taught their children that hard work and duty to one's family and community preceded the bountiful gifts of food, water, and shelter, and that the two of them should honor such a bounty by doing well and excelling in all aspects of their lives, which the brothers certainly took to heart.

A couple of photographers from the town's weekly newspaper, just released from their encampment at a downtown saloon, captured the moment by taking pictures of the proud parents smiling and holding their thumbs' up in the background as the brothers stared at the foreboding wall of tall oak trees and judged the distance they would have to travel.

The principal of the local high school brought his family, and a few of the teachers in chalk-dusted tweed jackets brought along their rambunctious students, and it seemed that nothing would stop this race from being the most memorable event in the town's history. Some of the locals from the nearby slaughterhouses even made large banners that were painted red with the brothers' names on them, and the Girl Scout troupe set up tables around the edges and sold blood-red steak, cold coffee, and lukewarm beer in Styrofoam cups to a crowd that gladly doled out their pocket change for a taste of the good life. The din had grown so complete that the two brothers were pulled out of their deep concentration of the acre or so they had to run and actually had the nerve to look at each other for a moment or two before the Mayor, having pressed enough palms to exhaust his guttural laughter, quieted everyone down by whistling through his tobacco-stained teeth and waving his pudgy arms.

"Welcome, welcome one and all!" said the Mayor, settling the crowd, "and before we begin, I'd just like to thank these two wonderful brothers for thrilling us with their competitive spirit. We've all been waiting a long time for this, and by God, I should say that this is the largest turnout we've ever had!"

The townsfolk applauded, and even the small toddlers on top of their parents' shoulders shrieked with glee.

"Never before in this town's history has a competition meant so much. It shows us that our town is certainly one of the best places to live in this great land and that no matter what, our town means business, and we will compete with anyone, anywhere, anytime for our way of life, because the battle lines have been drawn, my friends. Make no mistake about it that there are some people out there who just don't appreciate the way we do things around here, and those who don't just aren't welcome here, no sir. These two brothers are the finest specimens this town has ever produced, and if you don't like 'em, well, you can just get the hell out then!"

Again the crowd cheered. A few even poured beer over themselves, and the children again shrieked and screamed with delight.

The two brothers looked each other over carefully after the mayor had finished with his introduction. They were indeed the best specimens the town had ever produced. Ever since high school, they had always competed for what they considered to be rightfully theirs.

Take sports, for example. In their ninth grade year, both of them tried out for the quarterback's slot on the Junior Varsity team. They ran three miles every day after practice on the rocky terrain that led from the foot of their farm out on Route 6 to the edge of Elks Pond and then back again, only they did so separately and without discussing it afterwards at the dinner table, where they ate in silence with their parents after the sun ducked below the cornstalks. In the basement of their farmhouse they lifted weights into the deep reaches of the night, and soon their chests barreled and their biceps bulged as hard as the land they plowed every morning before school. And yet they hardly spoke a word to each other, and the group of friends that followed them around the small high school were suddenly separated into two camps, each rooting for a different brother, until the entire school seemed divided between the two.

The head coach at the time tried to stop them from taking football so seriously, but by then it was too late. Both brothers had poked the same competitive vein for three straight months. The coach, however, gave the position to another player, if only to spite the town and the family that had encouraged such fierce competition between the two brothers. It was no surprise, then, that soon after the season was over, the townsfolk fired the coach whom they saw as a threat to the way of life the mayor had alluded to in his speech. "A communist," they labeled the coach and simply ran him and his commie wife out of town one afternoon after he sat down and lectured the two boys on sportsmanship on the gridiron.

The very next season began with a similar competition for starting pitcher of the baseball team, and luckily there was enough room for two starters on the mound that year and not just one. Seats in the town's small stadium, at one time noticeably vacant, were suddenly filled, and a ballpark whose wooden infrastructure had been pockmarked and crumbling from decay and age now had a new scoreboard and a couple of new dugouts to separate the players from the rest of their unruly fans. The townsfolk came to the park in record numbers to see the two brothers throw fastballs and curveballs until their arms turned to jelly. They both blew out their arms on the last game of the season, against their arch-rivals from the next town over.

The brothers always knew they would both go far despite their rubbery arms, but on the ball field that warm evening, they hid a quiet knowledge at their guts that the town would never let them leave, even if they wanted out someday. They indeed belonged to something sacred that neither of them could explain, as though their futures had been mapped out beforehand. It seemed they meant more to the town than what anybody had told them directly, and instead of going to college after their senior year in high school, they stuck around to take care of the farm if only to take it over from their aging parents one day. That was when the drought came along and laid their spring harvest to waste. In fact, it laid every farm's harvest to waste within a hundred-mile radius.

When a new girl named Sally Evermore moved into town a month after they had graduated from high school, the two brothers were at it again. Sally moved in from the big city up north and brought with her tall tales of the fast lane and bright neon lights and drinking liquor at all hours with the many friends she had left behind. Most of her peers believed these tall tales of hers only because her beauty outshone whatever stories she concocted. Her long flaxen hair, blonde and luxurious, separated her from most of the other dark-haired girls in the town, and she had crystal blue eyes that a young man could swim in if the light hit them right. The two brothers fell hard for her just as equally, and being that they were the two most popular boys at the high school that year, there was little question that one of the two brothers would make a good wife out of her. But which one?

The competition for her hand became yet another spectacle for the town to revel in, and gossip abounded as to which brother would win her heart. The boys took turns taking her out on dates to the local coffee shop in the center of town or even to the movies at the small cinema further down Route 6. They often split the time with their father's old Buick, and rumor had it that they dressed so sharply for each of their respective dates that one would think the two boys were from the big city themselves and not from such a small and quiet town. Of course the two brothers never talked to each other during this chilly period in their relationship. Whether they competed or not, it was an odd day if anyone saw them speaking to each other at all.

It wasn't until a few months later that Sally Evermore's belly started to show, and with it a new scandal broke. The brothers denied they had ever gotten that far with the Evermore girl, and after they denied it, the search was on for Sally Evermore herself who had mysteriously disappeared from her home in the middle of the night. The talk amongst the townsfolk quickly turned to ridicule and slander, and the reputations of both Sally and her family were hurt beyond rescue. For a young girl her age it was apparently too difficult to take. A few days after she was pronounced missing, her pregnant body washed up along the banks of Elks Pond, and after the local sheriff pulled her water-logged body out of the algae-covered murkiness, he quietly alerted the Mayor of the town, who in turn didn't tell anybody anything.

The two brothers kept quiet the entire time and denied accusations that they had a hand in Sally Evermore's death. The Mayor let the issue go after a thorough investigation. The poor girl had indeed committed suicide, a town meeting had concluded, and to protect the town's reputation, the Mayor thought it best not to reveal who the father was to the newspaper monkeys gulping down their whiskeys at the local saloon. Most of the town agreed with the Mayor, albeit tacitly, and they buried Sally Evermore quietly at the town's only cemetery, about two miles from the brothers' farm.

Of course, that never stopped the townsfolk from feeding the incredible rumor mill that soon drenched them in a torrent of suspicion wherever they went. No one really disputed the fact that the issue of Sally Evermore had been put to rest all-too-quickly. The town's hard-won reputation with the other adjacent towns, as well as the stability of most of the local businesses, still thrived and continued as opposed to the suffering they would have endured had the scandal dragged on. To this day some still say that when the midnight wind whips over the surface of Elks Pond, they can hear poor Sally Evermore's plaintive cries for help penetrating the loose planks of timber that were used to build the ancient farmhouses along Route 6. Although Sally Evermore was indeed a dead issue, the townsfolk never completely forgot about how the two boys might have been involved. But rather than sentencing them to a life of ridicule and suspicion, the Evermore incident only deepened the mystery surrounding their popularity. It also heightened the pitch of the town's excitement for the race itself. They were, after all, the perfect specimens for a race such as this, and whatever secrets they kept to themselves would all hang out after the Mayor shot his pistol into the air to start them off.

The two brothers tried to keep their eyes off each other until the Mayor waved his pistol around, which was more than just a kid's cap gun. Beads of sweat trickled down their foreheads, and just before the race began, one could have sworn seeing a subtle overture by one of the brothers in a last-ditch effort to broker some kind of peace between them. But the crowd, especially, wanted none of that. Their cackles and jeers could be heard from miles around. The brothers had been trained well-enough, and after a few moments of thinking it over, both must have thought the idea of a peace between them a little silly, or at least something only the weak-minded fell prey to when they couldn't handle the pressures of winning. Both of them turned away from each other and returned to their old, stoic molds.

All became dead quiet before the Mayor fired his pistol into the air. The two brothers faced each other and then gripped each other with their bare hands before wrestling each other to the scorched earth. The crowd quickly swallowed them, shouting and taunting them to give it everything they had. From all the blood they spilled and all the bones they had broken that afternoon, only one of the brothers would come out of the race alive. Either way, no one really cared. The town would always find another pair next year.

TWO PAKISTANI MEN AT THE BAR

When his older brother walked through the doors in a suit and a wrinkled trench coat and squeezed his way between the pressing bodies on the dance floor, Mustu knew that he wouldn't be too happy to see him. His older brother's brown, pudgy face hung heavy with a five o'clock shadow that hinted at too much work for too little pay. Add to this a delayed and uncomfortable flight out of Newark, and Mustu could see that it wouldn't be a very pleasant visit.

Mustu, as usual, had found himself in an awkward city with awkward friends who were now as equally broke and drunk as he was. Shabbir took the bar stool next to him, as Mustu had been reserving it for him. His older brother looked like the family man he was meant to become. Shabbir had married a Pakistani woman and had a couple of bright brown Pakistani kids to match. He worked for the State back home as a Medicaid fraud investigator. He was the pride of the family ever since Mustu, the younger, had fallen into prodigality and spent his time and money at nightclubs and casinos in Las Vegas. He couldn't say what Shabbir had heard about him since he left home. He didn't know if he really knew his older brother at all anymore.

"Well, at least you're not dead yet," said Shabbir, ordering a beer.

"Why would I be dead? I'm a survivor," said Mustu, nursing his cocktail.

301

Shabbir looked at Mustu squarely and said, "judging from the telegram you sent, we all thought you'd wind up dead out here. You asked for too much this time. Dad won't have it anymore. You should let him retire in peace."

"Just a few thousand is all I asked for."

"Well, it was a few thousand too many. What the hell are you doing out here? You're not a kid anymore. You can't go around like some Middle Eastern playboy and spend all of Dad's money. We're not that rich. You should get a goddamned job is what you should do."

"Thanks for the advice, but go ahead and take a look around you. Just take a good look."

Shabbir rolled on his bar stool and faced the crowd. Most of them were young exquisite women in their college years wearing low-cut, skimpy dresses, their blonde skins exposed to the multi-hued lights of the dance floor.

"They're the beautiful people," said Mustu proudly.

"And? What does this have anything to do with getting a job?"

"I'm trying to marry one of these women, Shabbir. That's why I'm here—because I'm in love with blonde American women now."

Shabbir shook his head and laughed. "You mean to tell me that you've been chasing women down here to find one to marry?"

"You got it."

"At least you're in much better health by the looks of things. I'll give you that. You must have dropped fifty pounds since I last saw you."

"You wouldn't believe what I've had to go through though. Why do you think I haven't come home yet? I'm here to find my American bride."

"You haven't been home in ten years," said Shabbir. "Ten fucking years. If it were meant to work out with an American woman, it would have happened by now."

"But I'm almost there. I think I've finally unlocked the code."

"The code? What the hell are you talking about?"

"It's the code. Don't you see? I've almost cracked the code."

"You're not making any sense right now."

"I can explain. It's really very simple."

Shabbir ordered another beer, as he knew he needed one. Why his younger brother had to disgrace the family had been reduced to the logic of this one tidy explanation. He hoped his brother would finally make some sense.

"Please continue," said Shabbir, rolling his eyes.

"Okay. Remember when I was overweight?"

"How can anyone forget. You ate fast food, you smoked, and you drank too much. We all thought you'd have a heart attack. That or type two diabetes would have taken you."

"An American friend of mine told me that the reason why I wasn't getting any of the women to go out with me was because I was too overweight. I was too obese for them, in other words."

"And now you've lost all that weight."

"But it wasn't that simple. Do you know how hard I worked to lose this weight? Every day I had to avoid cookies and snacks and sweets and cakes, and then I had to go out walking, then exercising until my legs fell off. Do you know how painful and ludicrous these things are to Pakistanis?"

"I commend you, Mustu. You've done a good job in losing the weight."

"I'm as fit as a fiddle right now, but all of that sweat, labor, and starvation didn't crack the code. It was only the first part of the combination—and a lengthy process it was just to get through that initial stage. The next part involved losing my politics as well."

"What you mean?"

"You know, my need to save the world and rid it of poverty and disease?"

"Oh, yes. I remember," said Shabbir. "This was right after college. You were quite the left-winger. You wanted to be a martyr for the poor, and you hated that our father wanted to be rich. Who could forget that period?"

"I was a hardcore socialist back then. You remember?"

"I already said that it's hard to forget. What's your point?"

"Well, when I told my American friends that I wasn't getting any dates even with the weight loss, they knew exactly what the problem was."

"Finally—a clue!"

"It turned out that the women didn't like my politics. Actually, they couldn't stand what I stood for. They found my positions utopian and unrealistic, and they hated the fact that I wanted to overthrow the government and give equality and power back to the people. They truly hated it. They saw me as an annoyance is what they saw me as, especially when I brought it up on social occasions. And so, I had to change my views."

"I can only see this as a positive thing."

"It would have been positive if it didn't take such a huge toll on me. Imagine having to unlearn everything you've ever known? To test one's very core beliefs and turn them upside down? Or to find yourself in poverty only to start imagining nice pillared mansions in the suburbs? Don't you appreciate the challenges of this transformation?"

"What did you have to do to cross that bridge?"

"Lots of suffering, Shabbir. Lots and lots of suffering, until I found myself turning into that which I once loathed: a fascist."

"You a fascist? I find that hard to believe."

"No, I'm very serious. That's how badly I wanted to crack the code. So I surrendered my beliefs. Blotted them out, in fact. I uprooted them out of my mind. I even supported the war against my own people. Can you believe that? All of it to win the hand of the white woman."

"And let me guess. You didn't succeed."

"It was then that I started figuring a few things out about this fascism business. For one thing, I felt extraordinarily powerful wherever I went. It was really quite a change in attitude. It was down with the poor and up with the corporation. And the second thing is that even though I felt all-powerful and confined myself to mostly white Americans when socializing, there was still a certain quality about fascism that I couldn't shake."

"What sort of quality?"

"It's not easy to explain, but I'll try. You see when one is a fascist, one has to be heavily involved in the affairs of men. There has to be that special something—whether it's charisma or loyalty—that draws people into you and sets you free to lead them. You see, my charisma and charm worked on most men, but there was one significant problem."

"That would be the women."

"Precisely. I wasn't able to cross the divide between men and women. I just stayed on the male side of things until it started to become a bit, well, peculiar."

"How so?"

"Well, I had involved myself in the affairs of men so deeply that I started to have a liking for them."

"How so?"

"You know what I mean."

"No, I don't know what you mean."

"Do I have to spell it out for you?"

"No, you don't. I'm finding this a little hard to take right now."

"Because really, the way into a woman's heart, and what she really wants, is for people like me to serve her better by turning into homosexuals."

"Don't tell me you did something stupid. Why do I feel like smacking the shit out of you?"

"I'm still haven't done the deed, if that's what you're wondering, but with fascism it's quite hard not be gay eventually, which is why I found my salvation in Christianity, which was the next step in cracking the code."

"But our family is Muslim. You do realize that, don't you?"

"Yeah, but would you rather have a gay fascist quasi-Muslim dictator on your hands or a straight Christian gentleman?"

"Now I've heard it all. They should lock you up. You've betrayed your family, your race, and now your religion. And you almost betrayed your own sexuality."

"And yet I'm on the brink of cracking this code, and once I crack it I will have access to all of the white American women I could possibly want—just for me and only for me. I will never, ever have to sit through the humiliation of not having a beautiful American girlfriend ever again. She will love me, and I will love her—like it's written in the stars."

"So what's the last hurdle?"